Katy Carl's *As Earth Without Water* is a sharp and moving meditation on freedom, choice, and the creative life. "Art is from the soul," one of Carl's lost painters insists; this novel certainly reads like it is.

—**Christopher Beha**, Editor of *Harper's*, author of *What Happened to Sophie Wilder* and *The Index of Self-Destructive Acts*

Katy Carl gives us a vision of love that refuses to be caught up in consoling fantasy. Amidst the darkness of human sin and self-deception, Carl reveals the true complexity, depth, and promise of human longing. A powerful and stunning debut novel. Carl is an artist whose cleverness and skill is tied to a clear vision of reality, and I cannot wait to see what she does next.

—**Jennifer Frey**, host of the literary podcast Sacred and Profane Love

As Earth Without Water

· Katy Carl ·

Wiseblood Books

Wiseblood Books
P.O. Box 870
Menomonee Falls, WI 53052

Printed in the United States of America

Set in Baskerville Typesetting
Cover Design: SILK Studio

ISBN-13: 978-1-951319-93-9

Fiction / Literary

Wiseblood Books
Milwaukee, Wisconsin
www.wisebloodbooks.com

I stretched forth my hands to Thee:

my soul is as earth without water unto Thee.

—Psalm 142: 4-6

". . . [S]atiety had been succeeded in me by a thirst—akin to that with which a parched land burns—for a life which my soul, because it had never until now received one drop of it, would absorb all the more greedily, in long draughts, with a more perfect inhibition."

—Marcel Proust

"Everything has to become mud before it can become vision."

—Matthew Kirby, painter

I

July 2010

Halfway up the rise of a dark steel forest, arrayed against a gradient of blue—a staircase of ambition, the skyline of Chicago—this is where I found myself, the morning he found me: on the fifty-seventh floor, in the unforgivably blank offices of GryphoLux, Inc.

My office phone trilled. A window opposite mine threw a shard of reflected sun across my vision. A click, then a voice, a dactylic triplet: "Angele?" Dylan's voice. I strayed toward the window again, judged the distance to the street below: an abyss of dizziness I had learned to ignore. Now I forced myself to look down, to feel again, as if the glass were not there, the body's natural shock at seeing itself supported at such heights.

"Speaking."

"I've missed you." Not "How have you been?" or "It's been a long time," but "I've missed you."

"Not that much, apparently. When was the last time I heard your voice?"

"Doesn't matter, I'm here now. Come downstairs. I'm in the lobby."

"I thought you were in New York."

"Nah, I'm downstairs."

"Okay, but why?"

"In town for a show. Come down."

I lowered the handset into its smooth black cradle.

He couldn't have missed me: what a lie. Had I missed him? The question felt dangerous. After I moved out of his Williamsburg loft, I had been too exhausted by the demands of my own life to keep up with the pace of his: shut out of the workshop hours, no longer invited to the parties. I had told myself I hadn't minded: what a lie. No call to tell it again. I tucked my cell into my blazer pocket and shut my office door behind me.

The summer evening that had marked the end—*really, I should leave*; *yeah, you probably should*—I had slashed an art razor in a wide arc across the belly of one of my own canvases. The piece had been in progress for months, since the autumn before, when Dylan and I had visited The Cloisters together to make studies. Within eleven months he had made and sold his series from the visit; always a slower worker, I had decided in an instant that August night that my scene would never live up to the lost vision that lit and judged it. I had seen glory that day. I felt a need so desperate to translate it into form and color that it hurt my hands, my heart. But after repeated fierce passages of effort between catering shifts, I saw only mud on the gesso ground. Compressed into two dimensions, it languished, losing all brilliance, all substance. By contrast the blue heat from the picture windows of Dylan's studio, where I often worked then, seemed to mock me, to press on my face like a bully's palm. Only the heat felt real; the paint felt false.

My razor had bitten with such confidence into the stiffened fabric that the decision seemed to spring from the metal in my hand, not from the muscle that drove it or the mind that instructed it. As I grasped and pulled down, the blade snapped rows of taut crossed threads with a sound like a zipper. A flap of cut fabric dangled into the buckling aperture, heavy with layers of yellow umber: a wreck, irreparable.

The sound of tearing made Dylan flinch. He had stared at me in the stillness afterward as if it were my own skin, not merely my work, I had just torn.

"Don't," he said, "please."

"Don't what? Don't correct mistakes? It was a terrible canvas," I had said. "I can't earn enough to support myself here and still find time to do this work right. And if I can't do it right I won't do it anymore. I'll find a regular job. I'll learn how to be someone else. Until then, I'll do what I want. I'm an artist just as much as you are: I won't be anyone's dependent, and I won't be some sorry hobbyist."

I had kept control of my voice until the last "I won't." Then the razor flew into a corner, where it struck the baseboard and spun back in a loose arc, like a minute hand broken off a clock: the work my hand had done.

After I had left New York, as far as Beatrice had been able or willing to say, Dylan had shown neither signs of relief nor of sorrow. He had carried on just as before: painting all day, drinking and talking all night, barely ever sleeping unless with someone. What could have gone wrong for him? Something must have, or he would have stayed away from me.

Whatever he might claim to the contrary, his coming here now was likely no more than a flare-up of his old desire to see himself as I saw him, another move in Dylan's unwinnable game. In it I could never be more than a mirror. He needed to see his own light refracted on another face when this mood struck, or he could not see it at all. This game qualified as a thing that might have gone wrong, that did go wrong as often as it began. What other reason could he have to visit me—why else couldn't he have his show without waving his success and my failure in my face? The worst of him was that he meant no harm by any of it.

No matter. That scale of values, those rigged games belonged to another life now, no longer mine. Even the carpet's lanate mottled loops, crushed under the slick divided soles of my new shoes, served to assure me of this. If there was no real crisis for him—and I hoped there wasn't—thirty words and a handshake should close this door again. But if he thought he needed some favor, I'd determine whether

3

I wanted to help and, either way, tell him so. Set the boundary promptly without guilt, as Aunt Rachel, or Beatrice, might say.

As the elevator sped down to the lobby, all my good intentions dropped away. The back of the elevator car was plated with the kind of wavy copper, tacked in by rounded nail heads at regular intervals, in which you can see your reflection but your reflection distorted, warped as the metal is warped by the force that secures it against its inclination. Its muted gleam painted on my face a forged expression of confidence: only a work of artifice. My palms left damp marks on my skirt's hip seams.

The voice on the phone had stirred up, like moths from old fabric, weaknesses I thought had been washed away: worry, fear, desire, anger. And underneath, and worst of all, this abject, this irrepressible delight. Dylan called. He wanted to see me. This shamefully credulous yearning. This little tongue of fire, asking only to be fed.

Smother the flame—it could burn down the building. Better to think of what has become of me as a series of self-improvements, optimizations. The thing to do now, the only thing left for me to do at this point, was to sharpen. To be sharp. To cut a way through the world before it cut me instead. To cut through bullshit—such as *I've missed you.*

The elevator bell chimed; I stole one last glance at the bronzed, blurry image: black suit, pointed heels: no sign my heart raced like a bride's, a prisoner's.

The back of his head—its same dark, rattlesnake sleekness—rose above the low decorative wall that separated the lobby from the elevator bank. The wall obscured everything below the shoulders of his paper-white shirt, its open collar shrugged slightly back, careless, showing where the tapering arrow of stippled hair had grown back after being trimmed off and, below that, where it faded again into the clean line of his neck.

When I skirted the barrier, said his name, he turned to me that same face, those same haunted eyes, glass-green as clear water.

The quality of their attention, that made his regard so much better worth having than other forms of reward, undermined my sense of proportion.

He took both of my hands in both of his and kissed them, kissed my cheek: on his skin lingered a scent of pine resin and rosemary. My body raised a clamor of responses. *Shut up*, I told it: *not here, not him, not anymore, shut up, shut up*.

Jena from reception strode out of a back cubicle. The sight of us flustered her; she became all a blur of jade silk blouse, smooth flicking hair—"Ms. Solomon? A Mr. Fielding to see y—oh, I see he's seeing you right now."

All three of us forced laughs.

"Yes, thank you. We'll go up."

Jena nodded with professional restraint, but as soon as Dylan's back turned she threw me a knowing look, mouth puckered, as he and I turned again to the elevator.

In my office, Dylan at first ignored the chair to which I'd gestured in an attempt to contain him, to define him: visitor, not lover, not stranger. He stepped past my desk to stand at the window, commanding the view as if the entire lakeshore belonged to him.

"Tell me everything." He laughed, and the laugh reached his eyes: all the old gentleness, the seriousness, the unbearable hope. "Look at this. What a place. How are you, really? Sit, sit."

And he sat, now that that meant obeying his own request: at least he had picked up the minimum cue: take the visitor's seat.

"'Assistant Director of Artistic Vision,'" he read off my nameplate. "Fancy. So you're a 'creative' now."

"Creative," said that way by this man, connoted its opposite: compromised servant of corporate kitsch. *Ignore him*, called Aunt Rachel from the back of my brain, where it was her habit to tolerate no speck of yielding or self-doubt.

"We do visual design consulting for advertising campaigns. It keeps the lights on."

Dylan's raised eyebrows made a silent remark into which I read volumes, read the end of all our arguments: *okay, but this work doesn't deserve you: you gave up too soon.*

"So you missed me?" I shook my head, teasing. "You're not allowed to be lonely. Why visit me; why not call Beatrice? Even if she's too busy to pick up, she'll be there when you get home. She'll take you to the Roof Garden, and who needs more than that? Who was it who said that if you're tired of New York you're tired of life?"

We both smile—"That was London, anyway," he says—but the seriousness didn't leave his eyes. When I really looked at him I wished I could take it back.

"I'm on tour," he said. "And is it so strange that I wanted to say hello?" Chill and edge crept into his voice as he added, "Still. I am tired. Not tired of life, only tired."

He flicked his fingers as he spoke, the way he would when he wanted a cigarette but couldn't light one: as if his hand already held one, lit. As if flicking away imaginary ashes would produce their real source. As if his hands could work in the world the transformations they worked on the canvas.

"It really does sound like we need to have a drink," I said. "Could I text you after work? I leave around six most days. Where are you staying?"

Dylan nodded slowly. "We could do that, too," he allowed, not answering my question, "but then what I came to show you is worth at least your lunch hour, if you haven't taken it yet. It's still early."

It didn't feel early. Two meetings into the day, my team and I had already obscured plenty of origins and purposes. I felt ready for a break. But I didn't respond to Dylan right away, didn't even show I had heard him. Instead I leaned over my desk to the monitor, shook the mouse, checked my e-mail, tapped in a trivial one-line response to Dani: a criticism of a client's ill-advised choice of central motif. Fired it off, read it afterward, hated the sound, thought *Shit*, thought *that sounds bitchy*, thought *the cost of doing business, sharpness at all costs,* thought *even at the cost of making unnecessary enemies?*, thought *oh well, too late*. Thought *this is how we lose our way*.

"Yeah, let's go," I said then. "I'll skip lunch."

"Really? You're shivering. This building is cold as a meat packing plant. Wonder what they spend a year on that. Come on, let's get out of here."

He gripped my wrist gently.

"Hang on," I said.

I stepped out of the black stilettos, used my toes to fish up the spare flats that I kept under my desk, slid these on instead, and kicked the taller shoes away. As the pumps tipped over, top-heavy, I noticed Dylan noticing the gleaming pink of the inner leather lining, the distinctive lettering of the instep branding; heard a critique implicit in his smirk; felt, again, the weight, the resistance, of the judgment.

We descended again into the violent noon heat, out through the revolving door with a whoosh and down West Adams, moving fast in the direction of the lake. The horns of taxis, stuck in traffic, hooted fruitlessly as we joined the flow of pedestrians beside them. He strode so fast, taking so much ground in one lope, that I nearly had to run to stay beside him. All the same I kept pace—but without speech. No point in fighting, out here in a world already so hostile. No point in setting up defenses. No point in saying any of the things I kept thinking at him, so loudly that my head thumped and vibrated with them like the car speaker that blared deep bass rap as we passed:

Look at the way you're dressed; don't say a word to me about the damn shoes. If it comes to that, I notice neither of us is wearing paint-spattered, thrifted oxfords anymore. As if that were authenticity. As if authenticity were that easy. Don't stand there trying to make me feel like a sell-out when you know this is my second choice. I wanted what you have and couldn't attain it on my own: sure, that stings, but what do you expect me to do?

And even if I sold out, so what? It was never selfish of me anyway, not to be interested in getting ahead by doing what Beatrice said we had to, "rubbing elbows with the right people." Not to care who "the right people" are. When she said we could never make it as artists without "the old New York boys and girls club," was it selfish of me to think: I'll pass, thanks? For me art is the rendering of vision, not a question of who's in and who's out. Not interminable late nights full of shameless flattery, damn the cost of entry. Fine, you know, whatever, you're right: if it was selfish of me to leave you behind, to stop helping you in whatever obscure way you thought I was helpful, then yes, fine, guilty, I'm selfish. But then who taught me how to be selfish in the first place?

Although Dylan had tried hard to convince me otherwise, I now believed his attempt to persuade me to stay in New York was rooted in an ugly truth Beatrice had acknowledged to me, near the end. All Dylan had really wanted from us both, she'd said, was "the privilege of models without the setback of payment, the advantage of studio wives without the bother of marriage." Trying on that role, even as a form of play, had left me both too broke to keep up with the "right people" and too drained of energy to do good work of my own. But here in Chicago, by the time I had found a job that afforded me space and time and resources, the impulse to do the work had fled. So our interminable dispute—what does it mean to succeed as an artist; is success still real if no gatekeeper ever acknowledges it?—was a conversation I now only had anymore with myself.

We glided past polished lobbies seen through bronze-framed plate glass, more revolving doors awhirl like carnival rides, whorled plinths of silted marble aglint with mica, gilded address numerals as tall as my body. I didn't know where he was taking me; I didn't know him anymore. Yet I let myself be led. A wind off the lake whipped my hair, midsummer though it was.

We passed through an open breezeway of concrete rectangles, a brutalist cloister walk with no golden mean, in through glass doors and down a long corridor.

He looked around and swore then: "Shit, sorry, this was where we set up last year. This year we're down the street."

Down the street, and down. North, and then east, and then with a flood of adrenaline I knew where we were going. *Here?* Yes. The lamps arched across the bridge ahead, their bulbous lanterns glowing even in the daytime.

We followed the crosswalk, turned the corner. The garden in the courtyard. The Naiad in her niche. The verdigris-stained copper lions. *No.* But yes.

Past the lions, up the stairs—past urns spilling purple leaves, red canna flowers, thick vines, sunlight pulsing through the stems' green tangle—through the turnstile, into the membership corridor as Dylan swept a guest pass across the desk.

Not here, surely. Down slick floors under romanesque arches, lozenged ceilings, revelry of stonework, mineral carnival: surely not *here.*

But what should I expect to see? If the showpiece of a new exhibit, then one or more of those panoramic canvases he had begun to prepare when I left New York. These had been expansions of scenes he had first sketched out when we studied abroad with Signora in Rome: modern details foregrounded over ancient, timeless forms. I had seen in them, not for the first time but in a new way, what was meant by *the pageant of history.* Sidewalk performers, living statues, flower vendors, resting travelers, flocks of European teenagers, rose into brighter relief against architectural splendor, glorified by—I would say inimitable light if it were not precisely, maddeningly, his gift to be able to imitate the light: not in the floods of whites and yellows I had attempted, but in exquisitely careful development of color and value, not losing a single shadow cast by any object. Just before I left New York I saw the first finished canvas, understood what he was planning to do, and could not credit the idea—even as I could not stop hoping—that he might pull it off.

Though I would not now admit it to Dylan, I longed to find the series finished. I had seen what he was after: shifting balances of light and shadow, weddings of disparate details into wholeness: shouted, jubilant hymns to vision. Little heavens living on earth's largesse.

With a fervor I had thought was dead, how I now wanted to see the work done. How I wished I had time to start fresh.

Around a corner now, into a smaller gallery, lower ceilings, newer rooms; cloth banners heralding current exhibits; winking titles to nudge us, distract us. After the gasp, the glory, of the entryway, I resented the attention they demanded.

Then one of the banners commanded recognition. A spill of auburn curls, and under the russet landslide one arching temple: Beatrice's. These colors, these lines: I'd seen them. I had been there as they were being painted. Beatrice after Beatrice, row on row like crops in a field, marked a path down the dark hall toward an exhibit room. *But what did you expect to see?*

The back of the room lay cluttered with clamp lights, sheer drapes, pallets of unbuilt wall. Canvases leaned upright, stacked between boards meant to separate them: setup was still going on. But the front display was finished.

When I saw it my heart constricted, still, now, again, here, incorrigibly. *No*, I forbade it, *shut up*; *yes*, it ignored me, *look*.

"Look," he said.

I looked.

"Do you like it?"

I didn't.

"Say something."

I couldn't.

"It's mine."

I knew that. But it wasn't. It was his, and it wasn't his. It was me, and it wasn't me:

A young woman with long dark hair reclined in a room at dusk, nude, in profile against a blank duvet thrown over a chair. Her face rose outlined against a sunset window. Long blue shadows lingered along her cheek, her neck; beneath her breasts; under her left instep, her right ankle bone. Her limbs sank back into the drapery, only half visible.

The Florence skyline hovered outside the window, barely legible unless you stepped closer to the canvas. The gold was tightly held and bounded by the windowpane, but crescents of it traced her shoulders, her chest, her knees, her hands. Her long fingers lay immobile in her lap, curled around a book that languished there unregarded, gilded the same as her skin. Her eyes were directed at the skyline, at the light, of which the pupils held the smallest glint.

And there I stood, confronted with what I was, and the *what* erased the *who*, or obscured it beyond hope of recovery, which added up to the same.

"Why did you do this?"

He shrugged. "You let me sketch you. You had to know it was for a reason."

"I didn't mean why did you paint it. We've been over that." I felt too furious to say more.

"You mean why did I show it again."

"Yes. When I asked you not to."

"I wanted you to see it in place this time. With the rest of the exhibit. The way it deserves to be seen."

"That doesn't help. The piece doesn't belong here. It doesn't belong anywhere."

"It's under consideration by a very important dealer."

"I'm not sure I care."

"Be reasonable. If you had painted it yourself—?"

"What I painted wasn't—Dylan. Don't." I put my hand to my mouth and then dropped it again. "We don't have to go into all that right here. Now."

We stood there, under the judgment of my lost innocence, for several silent moments. We didn't speak, didn't touch, only looked.

"I mean, it's how I see you," he said, more softly. "You're glorious."

"Shut *up*." I hadn't quite planned to say this aloud—I had meant the words rather for my benefit than for his correction—so that when he complied I was sorry.

The whir of an electric handheld drill overtightening a screwhead was followed by a scream of cross-threaded metal being stripped out, a crackle of wood split along the grain, at the back of the room. One of the art handlers cursed with verve.

"I have to get back," I said.

"Now? Take a long lunch."

"Can't, sorry. Team meeting at one-thirty."

"Huh. Well, come back this evening if you can? There's a talkback. Think about it. Right now I should clearly go conduct a progress check."

He slipped past me, brushed my cheek with his lips, disappeared behind the unbuilt section of wall in the direction of the screaming drill. *Damn him*, I thought, then whispered it aloud:

"Damn him."

The curse word carried no intention in my mouth, in my mind: no more than a mental stagger, a dart of anger. I thought less of the first word than of the second, not so much of *damn* as of *him*. Next, in silent self-laceration, I reeled off a list of epithets for myself, names I would never name any other person. Wanting, hating myself for wanting, hating the wanting itself. And under it all the little fire, the pilot light. Hungry.

Ten minutes remained to spare before the long walk back down Michigan alone. I stalled then in front of his other paintings: ten minutes to recover, to hold off, hold my own, against *maximizing conversions* and *staying on-message*. The paintings rose above this. The paintings drew me in, compelled me forward, out of the moment that had just passed, and back, into the years when what had happened to me—*improvements, optimizations*—had not happened, was never going to happen.

Leaving aside the portrait, to which I could not and cannot reconcile myself, better judgment has forced me by now to admit it: These paintings are more than who Dylan is. They are the finest way in which he shows up in the world, better than his best self. No wonder he has so needed to make them. No wonder he has not been able to stop. That day I lost time in their presence. Memory closed over my head:

In the Piazza Navona the frost of rain and moonlight blurred the jangle of vendors' trinkets. Over a countryside checkered with ploughed fields, a thunderstorm pressed in to drench wheat fields plush as velvet. Pines and cypresses clamored up the hills to breathe air back into being. Spicy poppies in tall grass scattered a meadow path that passed between two silver rows of olive trees before winding down a valley to disappear.

Woven between and around growth and space, or displacing and shouldering them over, stood monoliths, mosaics, viaducts, statues, cobbled roads, tiled roofs, iron lanterns; church porches, arches, soaring domes; stone walls, crenellated walkways, facades, ruined colonnades. The whole weight of history lurked in their lines, signaling the necessity of self-defense, forbidding the weakness of pity. *It has always been like this,* his artifacts said, *like this and far more awful. Nothing is given you to work with; things are only thrown at you, to catch or to be struck down by. You must first destroy if you intend to build, and what you can build is blocked by what stands beyond your power to wipe out. Get used to inhospitable gray walls, get used to limitation, exclusion.* Only Dylan's wild things, his plants, clouds, skies, spoke in another voice. Only they whispered invitations.

I cannot now, could not then, believe that either side told the whole story. I could see what another viewer might not, the place where he gave himself away: just there, in a small canvas, a rendition of the Bernini Holy Spirit window flooded with sun, so bright it looked as if it would be hot to the touch. In it Dylan had made stained glass from paint, the pale and the umber yellow stroked outward to the corners, the points of the cadmium white dove's wings sharp as knife tips, the ivory black filigree built in on top to render the lead lines that fuse glass together. He had met the mark here: nature transfigured through artifice, so as to point beyond itself.

I could see him again then as I saw him in St. Peter's in the spring of our senior year of college, when we sat crammed so tightly into a row of overheated tourists that the outsides of our thighs pressed together. I looked at the amber light gilding, transfiguring, his face; I breathed the cedar scent on his clothes, the clean slight dust of graphite that cracked from the tips of pencils to smudge his fingers and mine before falling to the floor. In that moment of receiving together the light and shadow from the Bernini window, the portrait had never been made, might never have been. In that moment from his face, and there again in Chicago from the light and shadow of this canvas, I received, free and clear, the stillness I had been craving.

A moment of reprieve was all it was. On my way out of the gallery the old portrait loomed over me, its blues and golds indicting the colorlessness of my current life. At the same time its coyness, its pretended disclosure of secret things, revealed the mindless object I both feared I was and knew I was not: the unremovable disguise that was also my own skin. If only he had drawn the pose I had asked him to take, the curve of my cheek reduced to one more gold crescent, all other features turned to the back wall, hidden: then the work would have been, as he says, glorious.

It is my own face that ruined the piece: my expression, as of one who knew what was being done but who lacked the will to object. Even now I do not know whether to rejoice or grieve that I can never be this person again, never again have what she had, never do what she could have done instead.

On the way back to work, passing the same lobbies and store-fronts, I watched my own reflection in the pewter light that glanced off the plate glass, trying to catch any sign that might slip through to reveal the difference between myself and the woman in the portrait: between who she had become and the person who could have built something more, who could have known better, done better. I saw nothing.

II

November 2015

Behind the monastery guesthouse at night, beyond the flagstone path that borders the back garden, the novice monk crouches near the cypress hedge. I sit still lower, grateful for the shadow. We are side by side, unevenly supported on a low ragged rock wall that separates incense-scented evergreens from an empty flowerbed that, he says, in the spring will hold daylilies. Our hipbones, our hands, are chilled by the stone.

Nervously the novice's fingers flick and flick: a familiar gesture, dismissing imaginary ashes. He would be smoking now if cigarettes could be had here, if the smoke would not betray his location. It is late autumn in Kentucky, and leaf fires have been springing up all day like golden crocus in yards and gardens, but the residual smoke would not mask the smell of tobacco, if it could be had.

Under my hand, in my coat pocket, rests the last of a pack with a matchbook tucked inside. Would it be a sin to offer him a light?

We have been talking for more than half an hour now and, although I have listened with all patience to phrases like *the discernment of the spirits* and *following the path of prayer* that he evidently feels explain everything, I am no closer to understanding what he wants to say than when I found the note he left atop the guestroom desk. The frosts have barely started, but the novice monk is shivering. Around us the scent of hay and wet leaves rises from the fields.

"I always knew I couldn't get safely through the world alone, but I never realized before coming here that I didn't need a family so much as I needed a community," he is saying, not for the first time. "They've been amazing through all of this. It'd be terrible to leave now. I don't know what I'd do without them."

"You said you're not supposed to know I'm here. How did you find out?"

"Guesthouse check-in list on a clipboard. It's always left sitting around by the community message board where we get our chore assignments. I like to check who's come here; I take an interest. Like I said, secrets don't keep in the cloister."

"You didn't tell anyone about meeting me either."

"I told the prior and my director I was writing to you at your place in Chicago to invite you for a visit. I've been forthright. As far as that goes. Admittedly it might not go far enough."

"But this isn't usual?" I describe an arc like a bower over us, my index finger painting the air, taking in him in his habit and black fleece jacket, me in my jeans and aubergine peacoat, the cypresses, the wall, the cold night.

"Yeah, no, but I'm meant to be on retreat right now. To meet with you in the normal way this week, I would have had to ask permission, and I doubt I would have been given it. So our timing didn't really work out. That's my fault; I forgot to put all that in my letter. But I'm glad you're here. I needed to talk to you."

"Why do you need to be here? Why not go somewhere where your past won't matter, somewhere where you won't be judged?"

He hesitates before he answers: "The past always matters. The past leaves marks. I am more than the choices I made, but those choices are part of me now. Wherever I go, they'll follow me until I face what they've made of me. What I've done to others. To you, yeah, but not only to you. If I don't face that here, I'll have to do it somewhere else. And so I may as well try to stay in the place I've come to love. I may as well choose where I stand."

"But you've already chosen. Why this doubt now? Sure, you made mistakes when you were young—I don't even think you need to call them all mistakes. They're just called 'youth.' Was I a mistake? Don't answer that." I laugh a little too brightly. He smiles, but then he smudges his hand across his face. "Still, even so. What about forgiveness? Don't you believe in that now?"

"I am forgiven. For all of it. That's not the point."

His voice has come out too high at first, like a young teenager's. When he speaks he does not meet my eyes, does not look away from his hands, so finely articulated at the joints and tendons: elegant, capable. These fingers have stopped their unconscious dance and now lie on his knees simply shaking, cold or unsteady or both. I want to take them in mine, to warm them. I lean over as if to reach for them but he is holding himself so strangely still and so far from me that I fear the ways the gesture could go wayward, and so I stop.

"I am forgiven," he goes on. "It's not a question of that." He is not boasting; he lays claim to mercy as a flat, even regretful, statement of fact. Is my doubt showing on my face? He looks as if he wishes he did not have to say any of this.

"It's a question of trust. Trustworthiness."

Another whole person could fit on the wall between us. I lay my hands as flat as I can on the gritty stones, one on each side of me, feeling the need of solidity.

"Do you trust the people in charge here?" I ask him.

"More than I trust myself," he admits.

"But if you can't trust yourself, who can you trust?"

"Ha. The opposite's the case. It's been only too easy for me to trust almost anyone. A better question, one I'm learning to ask, is whether anyone else should trust me."

Never have I seen him in any such state. His shoulders slope downward, his profile angles away, toward the rim of the tree-clouded Appalachian valley in which his monastery now looms darkly: Our Lady of the Pines. The guesthouse is founded on a slope that rises slightly above it. From the garden, the path to the main house descends.

He cannot lift his eyes to meet mine. A strange anger rises into my throat.

"What are you telling me? Are you saying that you think—or are you saying the community here thinks—that you shouldn't stay? Won't you end up having even more trouble if you leave?"

"I *am* trouble. You should know." His tone, for all its play, carries an edge.

"Sorry. Devil's advocate."

"Be my advocate instead." He tries to smile, but his lips quarrel with another impulse.

"Help me understand, then. You said you were so happy here. You said you never wanted to leave. What went wrong?"

My head aches; my eyes blur; my hands numb themselves against the stone. I tuck them into my pockets again, feel the pack, the matchbook. Only one. No, it would be unkind.

"I'll do my best," he says. "I don't fully understand it all myself. But I know I would have even more questions if I were you."

"What should I be asking you that I'm not?"

Like a sick man flushed with a jolt of health, he manages to lift his face, now, but not toward me. He squints against the wind that scours the stars in a purplish sea of air. Turning toward me he still avoids my eyes, fixing his instead on the gray horizon, where light pollution from Louisville pours over the pines. Over us the waning moon has risen, gibbous. Its glow on the flat drape of the novice's habit obscures his form. His features in the eerie light are closed off, scrubbed of expression.

I try again. "Let's go back to how you first came here. From what I heard, you ghosted everyone. Even Beatrice—"

After I had left New York to start fresh in Chicago, Beatrice used to forward me the e-mail newsletter she wrote and circulated for him. For me, above the header line, she would add wry little personal updates full of dishiness the official version omitted. I had caught more of her than of him in these, and small wonder.

But early in 2011, not long after the new year, those notes had stopped coming. The last one had ended *Who the hell knows when I'll send you another one of these. You never respond anyway.* So I surmised I had only stopped hearing about Dylan because I had offended Beatrice with my silence. To have found out instead that the letters had halted because the Dylan I had known was gone, was calling himself Thomas Augustine, had thrown away everything that in his place I would have fought so hard to have kept, but not before becoming engaged to his publicist and then, just as quickly, breaking it off—

"I—it was wrong of us, of me, not to tell you," he says. "But you were so far away from it all, we really thought you had found your own way. That you might not even care. I felt that if I reached out, I'd be dragging you back into . . ." Into what? He doesn't pursue this line of thought past the trailhead at which it begins. "Anyway, after Beatrice announced it—I had asked her to keep it private a while, and she'd put a notice in the *Times*!—I—I couldn't—already the next day, I knew I couldn't live that way anymore. I had been knowing. The announcement pushed me into taking steps. I didn't come here right away at first. But it was the beginning."

"You—okay. And you never saw fit to—okay." Beatrice must have lost her mind to have asked him. Think of the life they would have had. More questions, unaskable, irksome, float to my lips, must be submerged: *Could you have been faithful to her as you never were to me? Would you even have tried?* Beatrice would, eventually, have minded his many other lovers. She wouldn't have let him make a fool of her—as I had.

"I could never have gotten married and stayed married, and I was wrong to be chasing after that. It isn't what I'm meant for in this world," he offers. As if this is any help.

"So let me make sure I understand: You broke the engagement, which, why did you let things go that far if that was how you felt about it? You told your friends in the city goodbye, the woman you—loved?—and you must have burned a lot of bridges too, all the best bridges, you have to admit, however good for art a quiet life might be. But you—but why a monastery? You weren't even *Catholic* then. Why not just some cabin in the mountains? Why not your old place in Florence? And why—alone—"

It is all coming out wrong, out of order. "And you didn't say anything about it. Until now. Until you wrote me that—what do you call that, what kind of letter was that? After five years?"

"Really, I'm sorry. There was no excuse for how I left things with you."

"Or with her."

The next thing he has to say comes out only after some labor. He presses his hands flat together, one to the other, with the fingertips lined up and angled toward the ground. Keeping, between them, some invisible remnant of feeling under control.

"If I could ever have gotten married and stayed married, I think now," he says, "it would have been to you."

I have to laugh. "Are you kidding me? We wouldn't have survived it. We are both such insufferable people."

"Not to each other we aren't."

There is some truth to this. I have to collect my thoughts, reorganize them. He goes on:

"Beatrice and I wouldn't have stayed together, I know that now; she was using me for status and image, just as much as I was using her. She's easy to pity, given sufficient distance. No, you know, it wasn't her fault. She'd been trained her whole life to think that way. She wasn't upset for herself when I left to come here, or so she said, but she told me I was letting down the Cause of Art and disappointing everyone we knew, and I thought: *Good.* But once I knew what I had to do, once I knew I had to come here, I was afraid I'd lose my courage if I didn't do it right away."

"How did you 'know'? What do you mean 'had to'?"

"I know this must feel abrupt. I'm glad you were able to make the trip."

"'Abrupt' isn't what I'd call waiting five years to tell me what was going on."

"I've missed you. What has life been like for you since I saw you in Chicago?"

He doesn't merely miss me. I scent some deeper reason for his behaving like this, calling me out here into the cold.

"Not much different until last week. I was let go from GryphoLux."

"Oh no. I'm so sorry. But why?"

"No good reason. The stupid economy."

Even this late—at night, in the year, in the history of the earth—a grasshopper perches on the wall. Between us its filigree wings pulse against its small body. Its chitinous legs scrabble. It hops in an ellipse atop the granite like a person looking for a lost possession.

"You'll land on your feet," he says. "And I hope this weekend gives you time to recharge. I'm glad you're here. Really glad. It's good to see your face. Hear your voice."

"But really, why did you ask me here? You said you wanted *me* to talk to your prior before you took your vows. What is it I'm supposed to say for you that you can't say for yourself? About us, back when, or . . . ? All that was so long ago. How does it matter now? Are you thinking of leaving to marry Beatrice after all?"

I had hoped this last would make him laugh, but now as it leaves my mouth I can hear that it will not land. It is no joke to him. His face in the moonlight is set like a statue's.

"You don't take this seriously," he says.

"No, I do," I say, standing up. "I need to go in now."

"No, no," he says, and I can see his younger hand grasp for mine, clasp it, but now, no, he sits unmoving. There is a thickness in the air, a ghostly density that repels touch. Whatever influence Dylan—no, Thomas Augustine—can exercise, it will have to come through his voice.

He says: "Stay. Please."

"What time is it, even." I feel dizzyingly drowsy, check my phone: 1:05 a.m. "I need to go to sleep."

"Just—if I could finish saying it."

"Why am I *here*."

"Please. Thirty minutes. I need to tell you what happened."

I flick the black screen, watch the numerals spin upward. "There. I'm setting a timer. When this rings, I'm going inside the guesthouse, and I'm going to sleep. Let's hope no one trips over us before that."

"The groundskeeper doesn't make a patrol. This isn't a prison."

"No, I know where the prison is." I point to my forehead, then to his. He flinches as if I have slapped him. All that is left of his hair is a strip about an inch wide, circling his skull. The crown has been shaved off entirely.

I soften my voice. "Sorry. You said I should meet you here. You said you needed to talk to someone who might understand. Okay. Whether or not I can understand, I'll try to. I'm here now. I'm listening."

As, at last, he begins to speak, my defenses fall, fade, dissolve into numb disbelief. The numbers on the timer spin their way toward zero, measuring our wasted time. I feel as if I have been sitting across from him, trying to understand how he sees the world, for as long as we have known each other. Yet what he has just told me defies understanding.

When the phone alarm chimes I cut it off, reset it, and keep listening. It is nearly three in the morning when silence finally falls.

At three-ten the chime rings again. I show him the clock on the screen and say:

"You have just enough time to sneak back. Don't get caught."

"Not me. I'm invincible now," he laughs.

The grasshopper leaps off the stone wall. The ghost that has lingered between us now floats up and hovers, follows him down into the shadow of the valley.

III

July 2010

Back at the gallery, Dylan's opening night, I claimed the same bench where we fought at lunchtime. The floods, white overheads in rows of metal cups cut at sharp angles, spilled so much light that looking too long even at the polished floor caused me to squint. The solid walls, like those of a black-box theatre, stood starkly athwart the gleaming marble.

The walls, the lights, swallowed the canvases in a way they hadn't in the daytime: too sharp a contrast, too harsh and imposing a setting for viewing Dylan's subtle, complex paintings. Professionals should have realized this. Maybe they did and still chose to supply what the onlookers wanted more: bright lights, the flourish, the sense of importance.

Broken Hallelujah: Dylan Fielding's Renaissance (Re)Vision, proclaimed the exhibit brochure. A trifold trimmed to the shape of a Romanesque arch between columns, the front panels opened like Ghiberti's bronze doors, down the middle, to reveal Dylan's artist's statement. I read his early drafts so many times—one or two of the phrases, I could swear, were mine—by now I could quote it to myself. To me the words called up the exact bridge in Florence—near a row of jeweler's shops where white jewels glinted on rose velvet—where he first swore, against all our shared training, all we thought we held in common (Beatrice shaking her head, my mouth shocked open, the wind off the Arno pushing strands of my hair over my incredulous lips): *Art is from the soul.*

Now he wrote it, now he added on: *I am following a golden thread of imagery, a sacred glow, a phenomenon that is its own manifestation, an undeniable attraction*: Dylan's unique brand of obscurantism. Once it wooed me, won me over. At this moment it no more than tested my patience.

A pair of university students, boys nineteen or twenty at most, stood in between my body on the bench and my image on the wall. One pushed his hands low in the back pockets of his brick-red skinny jeans. The other wore his grey pants so tightly I doubted the pockets could open. Both of them—plaid-shirted, long-fringed, not a scrawl of five o'clock shadow between them—appeared to have hands and feet too large for the rest of their bodies, heads a little too small.

Grey Pants had a notebook, a pencil, thick glasses, and a New Jersey accent; he said to Red: "Okay: assignment sheet says, here, we're supposed to look for five minutes and then write down what we see. Uhhhh."

Red snorted: "I see an easy explosion."

"Eff you," replied Grey equably, scrawling in his notebook.

"Take the stick out of your ass, dude," Red pressed on. He pulled a smartphone out of one back pocket, displayed the gallery preview site on his screen. With a reverse pinching motion that slipped along the plastic he inflated my portrait. He dragged the jpeg around, zoomed in on one nipple, waved the phone with its distorted blue and charcoal pixels at Grey's indifferent jaw. "Who wouldn't want to do her? Even alone?"

"Will you shut your face," Grey said, acidly, still writing. "Some of us have real work to do. Only let you follow me here 'cos I thought you'd be cool. I wouldn't be caught dead with you in Soho."

"So-*ho*," sang Red. "But you couldn't get in-*to* NY-*U*, could *you*."

"Well, you're too young to ride the Metro alone. But since we're here, why don't you kindly do the fucking task for class."

"Asshole," Red said, fell into a sulk, and began to type with his thumbs.

In the quiet that fell then, the small red dot in the bottom right corner of the painting loomed forward, a sale sticker that was not there earlier in the day: so I have a new owner. *Sold, for good and valuable consideration.* A desecration. Yes, that. For there is love or something like it in his brushstrokes. It has allowed him to capture something here that had no place in commerce: though the pose is a whisper shy of prudish he has caught not mere nudity but nakedness, vulnerability, a moment meant to have been private. A gift. The painting is the proof that it meant something to him: he saw it, he loved it, it changed him: I changed him: but not enough.

But so for years now, or decades, until there is a reason for another sale, my body will hover at the end of some dimly lit corridor under a special recessed lamp, or over some stranger's bed. And for this I am expected, I suppose, to be grateful. This is a *success.* And why can't I just say *yes,* why let my qualms make it something less?

The bench had no back, so I tucked my knees under the skirt of my brown silk wrap, spun away from the boorish kids. The gallerist's evaluation sprawled and swooned on the brochure's verso: *With an honesty to ordinary human sight that transcends the merely photographic to encompass a surrealism that hints at absurdity, Fielding problematizes the canon even as he explores it with an almost quaint respect. . . . Questions of the day literally fuel his reinterpretations, as in his* Found Analogy, *which displays bewildering technical mastery in the reproduction, with oil paint, of the distinctive film of iridescence caused when water is tainted with petroleum, superimposed over Greco-Roman ruins. . . . In idioms that are consciously borrowed and inherited, yet spoken by a strong cohesive voice, Fielding wrestles with binaries of mind/matter, flesh/spirit, approved/taboo. . . .*

I closed my eyes. The heavy day pressed against the backs of my eyelids. However I might have wanted to return to the past—and I did, it was no longer possible to divorce that desire—this world would be forever foreign from now on.

Near enough I could not ignore her, a server held up a round tray of pre-poured chilled white wines in plastic cups. She was my age, with rusty hennaed hair and a slight scar and a small silicone nose-piercing plug that she had placed in to keep her decorative options open while hewing to her employer's uniform protocol. In New York we might have been working an event like this right alongside each other. Managing a quarter smile, hoping to draw her out, I took a wine, raised it a little in her direction as if in a toast, shrugged as if to say *how silly all this is, you know it and so do I, but what's to be done.*

The server's face first remained flat and then flickered out fierceness, resistance: *I don't owe you anything,* it said, *we aren't the same.* We were the same, but it wouldn't look that way to her now. I drained the wine quickly as she walked away; I trashed the cup and reopened the brochure to obsess again over the text.

"'Sacred glow,' what in blue hell does that mean," said a plummy over-amused voice near my ear. A scarred finger insinuated itself onto the gloss of the page, traced under the words with a trim nail. I felt a disconcerting warmth of proximity, smelled androgynous vetiver aftershave, before seeing the angular, brown face: Omar, of course.

"Dylan, oh, Dylan." With the words Omar breathed the fragrance of the cinnamon chewing gum he habitually tucked under his tongue. "It's hard, isn't it, to see someone so undeserving receive so much praise? Now don't get me wrong. I love him as much as you do. We all love him. I just don't know why we love him. Yes, he's skilled. Yes, he's got vision. But just between you and me—and this is something I was hoping I would *not* have to say, someday, when he finally bloomed or whatever—it's not great skill or great vision. I'm not surprised a bunch of professors are all excited about him. They hardly ever see a thing outside the ivory tower, and when they chance on some half-assed talent it's all *Ooohs* and *Ahhs.* But this? All these socialites, all this fawning? They don't see it. It's a case of the emperor's clothes. You know as well as I do that this exhibit is Dylan's confession. And what's there to confess? Emptiness. He's a fraud—a technically brilliant, deliciously handsome, unregenerate fraud."

"I'm not sure I'd go that far. Should *you*? Aren't you his assistant still?" I tried to make it clear I was teasing, but I meant it, too.

"You can see it yourself if you look." Omar's liquid eyes gleamed with the white of the track lights. "He's tried to redeem his failure by latching onto an age distant enough that it makes his work exotic. Five hundred years ago, stuck in a time that's gone forever. He tries to hide it behind building facades and café umbrellas and folds of drapery, not to say bedsheets. He says he loves the Renaissance, so somehow this makes it okay to be circular and coy and referential and unoriginal. That's why the work is selling so well: because he is *copying*. He has not got the guts to expose himself as he really is. You see it; I see it. And don't we both know, haven't we always believed, that an artist without self-exposure is a fraud?"

As he spoke Omar brushed, with his fingers, his collarbone in the unbuttoned split of his shirt, the hollow below the Adam's apple, using the beauty of his body as its own form of authority, the way some women do: a way Beatrice, for instance, had mastered.

"Now look at me," he persisted, sharp as hell. "I don't pretend to be the next Michelangelo. I cobble together shit from other shit. I expose my own flaws. That's frankness, okay. Honesty. I admit to the world I'm screwed up. But, you know, at least I try to pull the wreckage together, make it worth looking at. Then again, I know other artists who use their work to point out other people's flaws. I think that's cowardly, but it's still a certain kind of honest cowardice. It says: we're all screwed up together, and I acknowledge my complicity in this, and I'm going to show you to yourself so we can laugh about it and try to pull ourselves out of it. It says: it takes one to know one. But to paint with no irony, as though you had no flaws? To paint as though you thought you *were* the next Michelangelo? No one, no one anywhere, is that good. It's an arrogant cheat. I can't forgive him. And yet I sometimes think it's because maybe, not that I'm saying he has really done it, but he's persuaded everyone to believe that he's done it. And maybe, just maybe. It's because he's going to keep on getting away with it."

I wasn't sure whether I agreed, but to say the other side would make Omar argue with abandon, and I felt too tired for agonism just then. I made noncommittal noises, some of them mutations of actual words: enough to keep Omar talking, stop him from walking away.

Omar's hands fluttered like wings between us. "Artists can't protect themselves like this," he kept saying. I half expected Dylan—who seemed to be nowhere—to peek out from behind a painting, to slash his way in with a counterargument.

I shook my head: I didn't then, I still don't think artists can, in the end, protect ourselves in quite the ways we want to: I started to say so, but Omar steamrolled along:

"If he's going to dodge and weave this way, he might as well throw it in and go join you at GryphoLux. Not that I don't think your work has artistic value, love," he hastened to say, in a sweet tone and with a squeeze of my arm that told me he was making up tales, "but for you it's different. No one expects anything other than technical skill only, I mean that is the whole point. Not self-expression. All the expression communicates what other people want said, not whatever you might want to say, if you had the chance. You're selling your abilities, not yourself. The art world makes you sell your *self*. Dylan wants to avoid that. But in the end, I don't think he will be able to. He can't. It's in him to do it. He must. The work is going to make him do it, it's going to force him onward. He can't help himself. I know him too well, you know. Reckless to say the least. One of these days he's really going to let himself loose. And then we'll see what we see.

"But I really don't think you need to feel bad, love," and Omar placed a warm hand on my forearm again, raising his thick eyebrows until they brushed the overhang of his lush hair.

"Who said I felt bad?"

He chose to ignore this. "Art can be a cabaret of human flaws.

You chose early on to guard yourself from that. Some would say—but isn't everyone a critic—you can't separate talent and self, and they would say that what you're doing for work now is a kind of prostitution. But I think that's backwards. I think you should look around at your life and be glad you've been spared. No one will ever come to collect on the requirement of self-exposure." (I cleared my throat at this bit of irony. When he missed my meaning I nodded to the nude lit up above us: but Omar, oblivious, thought I was smiling at his winsome wisdom.) "True, you've not done exactly what you once thought you would do with your life"—the squeeze of my arm again, the thumb feeling the small curve of my bicep—"but you've also avoided the kind of failure Dylan's made of himself."

What failure? Words lay so thick in my mind, like leaves clogging a gutter drain, that they trapped the flow of speech. Another thing: Omar might not have thought, or—this was *Omar*—would not care, that it might be less than best practice to run down your employer to the employer's former flame: even if, especially if, you too are a former flame. He may have thought he would ingratiate himself with me by devaluing Dylan, but since seeing the portrait again I was experiencing too much turbulence even to join in the roast in self-defense. Unless Omar was on the verge of quitting his day job—which, to be fair, he threatened to do once a week on average for the entire time I knew him in New York—it might have been about time for him to check himself. Before I found words for this, Omar dodged the issue.

"And yet you love him." My failure to answer told Omar he was right. "You love him, and so do I. Like I said, I can't for the life of me figure out why." His laugh, at nothing, was hearty but hardly long enough to stop the gallop of his words. "Why, Angele? Why do we love him? I think for me it's even more inexplicable than for you. There was that one time I was with him like that after you two broke up . . . " He saw the blush rising up my neck; with a pathetic scratch of an imaginary itch I tried to hide it—"but no, that wasn't even serious. That wasn't love, that was an experiment, a technical exercise in the art of love. That was me trying to throw off my inhibitions; that was him trying to assert his independence from—whatever it was, whoever it was. Doesn't matter now. So it's not *love* love, not that kind of love. Which, now that I think about it, holds another possibility: the man may simply be so busy scattering his love, or his not-love, around the city that he's squandering the energy that could spark a real breakthrough. . . .

"But you, you could still be *in* love with him, couldn't you? *Are* you? Tell me you are, Angele. It'll make me feel better. But don't lie, tell me really."

"Really? No." The sly curve of his smile told me Omar could still spot my bullshit, as ever. We both knew, and with relief I noted that Omar didn't remind me, who Dylan had been "asserting his independence" from, in their flicker of a hookup. We both knew Dylan did not know what he wanted then from anyone, other than someone to hold him close—for a moment, no more: for a time, to feel contained rather than diffused, distributed, spent. Dylan had never, as long as I had then known him, much cared whether such a moment held any meaning beyond itself. And I—I need things to continue being true once they start.

For sure, Omar wanted to know whether I would acknowledge how much of this I knew. Lived for little titillations like this, "little honesties," he called them. "All we have," he used to be fond of saying. In Omar's personal campaigns to break free of his strict, structured, polite, indirect upbringing in a frightened and frightening religious family in a sequestered corner of California, he had picked up this way of delivering blunt force trauma to any topic at hand. Harmless as we make it seem, inevitable as we want it to be, the shedding of a culture is a war with endless fronts and countless casualties.

So Omar nudged the conversation toward work; I brushed it off with commonplaces. He rolled his eyes, nodded. He rotated one wrist so that the fingers of that hand described a wheel spinning forward. *Say more*, said the motion.

I tried to, but the stock topics that made up those days for me were the stuff of office sitcoms, of unfunny corporate cartoons. They conveyed nothing, contained nothing—at least not here, in this air-conditioned vacuole, where we tried to pretend the Midwestern summer did not weigh us down with more than heat and humidity.

I didn't know how to tell Omar—and, if I had known, I still wouldn't have wanted to say it—about the misery of waking on the couch, forty-three minutes into snooze-alarm territory, to the jangling pink music of a DVD menu I'd fallen asleep to the night before, in the knowledge that I had had no purpose in my actions the previous night, or the previous day at work for that matter: that I woke without reason to want to go to work again today, no reason to want to do anything: that the only defensible motive any more seemed to be money, or what we like to call "necessity:" keeping the rent paid to stay stuck in the same flat near the same office that I had to continually cheerlead, poke, bully, prod, and torment myself into caring about.

Today had begun like other days: Yesterday's clothes still twined around me, eyelids sticky with yesterday's liner, I had peeled myself off the couch, bribed myself into showering—if it takes less than five minutes I'll buy you an iced latte, I bargained, as though coaching a teenager—and with tepid water sluiced off the adhesive July heat, only to be drenched in it again promptly upon descending four flights of stairs to the pavement. Instantly a cloud of evaporated lake water clung to my hair and skin. Every nerve in my body felt like a tooth set down wrong against other teeth.

Late, late, no time for coffee, not capable of keeping a promise, not even to myself, I ran, in heels, in a furor of shame, straight into the woman with the shopping cart who wore two skirts and three sweaters in all weather, who had fled her country in search of opportunity and who now haunted the portico of our office building, having escaped one decline only to fall into another.

"Oh God, sorry, sorry." I picked up her dropped flip phone and handed it back to her before reaching into my bag to disentangle keys and fare card from any loose coins I could swiftly lift out: "Here you go, sorry."

We encountered each other every morning and we never knew each other's names. Once I asked her where she was from. That day she had nodded and smiled and said only, "Thank you," asking me for nothing, although her eyes were asking for something, although it wasn't my coins.

So the rest of today had been lost: the first meeting and then the second one, good time thrown after bad; then Dylan's call, the shock of seeing the portrait; then scrabbling back to the office in inner disarray only to be roped into a third meeting, a " jam session" as Dani called them, which turned out to revolve around an ad campaign for an anti-poverty fundraising drive.

And then what nightmares. I set the scene for Omar: the task of the meeting was to complete a mockup of the poster; the central image, an empty dinghy floating on a grey lake. *We're all in the same boat*, ran the text, in admonitory serifs. Ten minutes of tense crosstalk made it all too performatively evident that we were not all in the same boat. People sat around debating whose figures they could put into the boat without making anyone too angry: which genders, which colors, which forms of status or lack thereof merited pity. Couldn't the boat just be empty? Does it have to be a boat—what about a raft? No, too inflammatory. Can we change the text? Shouldn't the boat be sinking? Isn't the boat already sinking, really, aren't we all flailing and floundering about in the water beside it, now that our 401(k)s are down and we might not take a vacation this summer? Should we put someone *in* the water?

"Maybe we should put *you* in the water," said a sharp voice to the person who suggested this, and no one knew if it was a joke or not. The moment for friendly laughter passed; the moment for hostile laughter passed too, and then the room lay soundless, flush with afternoon sun, stifling.

On the white board beside the mockup, in red dry-erase marker, Dani the creative director had sketched and then wiped out a series of little stick figures. She stood beside the mockup in her pencil skirt and blouse and gleaming gold helmet of hair, holding the marker the way a blasé thirties starlet might have held a cigarette, looking uncharacteristically cross.

Dani, usually an enthusiast—the kind of woman who entered triathlons, baked bread from scratch, taught herself new languages— had had the idea of putting lots of people in the boat together, refugees and farmers and housecleaners, with one midforties man seated toward the front, this man representing a toppled executive, sad-faced in a sober business suit. Earlier in the meeting Dani's idea had been chucked as patronizing. Thinking of our portico, I had raised the possibility of placing a woman without a home on the poster, only to find the woman chucked out of the boat, wiped off the whiteboard, too.

Now everyone else had been erased, and the toppled executive was back in the boat, alone. Dani had asked us once again to suggest ways to make him sympathetic but not tragic, to create urgency without distressing anyone too severely, and the meeting had gone ominously quiet. Earlier I had slid a print of Van Gogh's *The Potato Eaters* into my notebook, and now I suggested to the whole meeting, my voice sounding unrecognizably thin and high, that we all take a look at this example of one approach to the visual treatment of dignified poverty.

The print passed around the table from hand to hand, but no one made a single remark in reply. We all feared the hostility of that silence, its capacity to bloom as easily into hate as into compassion.

"Does anyone have any more *practicable* suggestions?" Dani asked, shaking her marker in the direction of the red stick executive. "I know we'd all rather not hear this, but we need an actionable item before we head home."

"Put some holes in the knees of the suit," Zoe suggested timidly, rubbing her palms against her own bare knees at the hem of her skirt. Dani drew some zizzles across the stick man's knees.

"And give him a little two-day beard," said Annika. Dani made dots on the chin of the round featureless head.

At the end of the table, Arthur, in short sleeves, a stolid, phlegmatic mound of a man, burst forth with one loud guffaw: "Pepperoni on half."

That pathetic crack in the tension was enough. People were snickering into their coffee mugs, putting their heads down, swiveling, hooting.

"Like hyenas," I told Omar.

"Ugh," Omar said. "You should have told her to put the woman back in. And let the woman be a zombie. Let the man be a corpse. Let her be biting his arm off."

I felt sick but laughed because laughter was easier than argument. Laughter released nearly as much as argument would of the heat that had built up in my skull.

"I don't see it," said a voice near my shoulder—not about Omar's wisecrack, which the speaker hadn't heard, but—in a general, broadcast way—about the portrait, to whomever nearby might be listening. "But then I never did. That's all right. I'm not the one he has to convince. He's doing well out of this, I should think."

The speaker's sea-green eyes were Dylan's eyes, identical their heights, frames, profiles, the angles and planes of the face. Age Dylan a generation, introduce no aberrant struggles or sufferings—for thirty more years shelter him in his sandbox, make sure his bills stayed paid—and this was what he would become, at least on the outside.

He introduced himself: "Allen Fielding. Charmed. And you must be the muse. Congratulations."

"Oh, that." I rolled my eyes, laughed, ignored the stinging threat of tears. "Thank you, I guess."

"I can see you don't like the painting? Or is it that you don't like that it's you?"

"Neither," I fibbed; it was both, and more.

"Well, it's lovely. Don't worry."

"I wasn't." I turned away sharply. "Excuse me, I need a drink." Another one. Quickly.

The server stood close by still, her tray empty now, folded beneath her arm between the tie of the black apron and the sleeve of the white uniform. She had stopped in front of my portrait, which she considered in stillness, her only movement a stretching and readjustment of the fingers that rested along the bottom edge of the tray. I could not read what worked behind the softened look on her face.

Omar was already gone, having perspicaciously slipped away into the crowd. In his spot, blocking my way, there now stood a woman in a sparkling beige dress with long sheer sleeves, a Monet waterlily scarf draped around her shoulders. She faced toward the paintings with her arms crossed. One foot in a low-heeled shoe tapped impatiently.

Allen reached a hand to her arm. "Dear. You're in the path."

The woman pivoted. "Pardon—oh well now." Her expression, a scowl, changed as she took in my face. "I suppose I should congratulate you too, as well as my son." She reached out both her hands to shake one of mine: "Elaine. Elaine Fielding."

So these were the monsters Dylan described so often. Like harpies their spirits would pick at his memory, limping away only slowly when fed; I so well remember feeling helpless in the face of his emotional emaciation. Yet they looked polished, lovely, especially his mother. I would have liked to grow old with such distinction, to loop a silk scarf around my neck, to walk all day on delicately veined feet in two-inch heels without showing fatigue, to contrive it so that my hair frosted in only one chosen spot: and how bad could it have been, really, to have married a man like Dylan's father, tall and slender, calm and steady, with Dylan's features and Dylan's rakish smile? That would be success, it flashed on me, although I held the thought at arm's length, uncertain of its worth.

"I know who you are," Elaine said to me. "In the portrait. You're one of Dylan's friends from that first grant project in Rome."

"And from here. We met in school, before the semester abroad. And we were also together in New York," I add. "He and I . . . dated for a while, I guess you'd say."

"I guess you'd say," she echoed, raising an eyebrow. "I'm glad you two can still be friends. He spoke well of you."

"That's good to know."

"And so you live here now?"

"I live here now. I'm a graphic designer."

"You don't have to travel for work a lot? You tend to stay around?"

"This is my home base," I said.

"Good. Let's work on him together, you and I," Mrs. Fielding said. "You know he's *from* here. Chicago is his hometown. He's going to be traveling more in the next few months, he says, but I don't know. You know mothers have a sixth sense, and mine tells me he's not telling us something. He won't say when he'll be staying here longer again, when he'll be seeing *us* more. Anyway, when I went to visit him in New York this past Christmas, Beatrice said to me that you were always the *stable* one in your group. Christ, how my son needs a stable. The animal. I know we've only just met, but I feel so comforted just knowing you're here for Dylan when he's in Chicago. You're someone besides us who he can turn to, if he needs anything."

She leaned toward me, securing my arm in her hand the way a climber might grip rock. Her voice was calculated to make me feel confided in, but her fingers said hunger, ambition. Was this my own perception, or only Dylan's diagnosis of his mother, working on me in default of that drink I wanted so badly?

Elaine clung to me still. I felt frozen, trapped in place. Off to the side, for the first time tonight, there stood Dylan, ensconced in a cluster of gallery patrons who covered him like a copse of trees. He looked intently at a distinguished scarecrow of a man in a herringbone linen blazer, laughed at what the scarecrow said, shook a slim older woman's hand, engaged in conversation with them both at the same time. The cluster listened, rapt.

Then the scarecrow angled into profile and I recognized him: Dr. Linus Hathaway, another of our professors, who first taught us drawing before Signora: perhaps the first man after Dylan himself ever to take me seriously, in student days. He was saying to Dylan *vision, consummation, glory*; he was saying *Titian, da Vinci, Caravaggio.*

Dylan laughed again and said, loudly enough to be heard throughout our half of the room, another line I had heard before:

"Given the technical and conceptual advancements available to us today, in all fairness, there are some things I do better."

"Even the referential canvases aren't copies," Dr. Hathaway said, every bit as loudly. "They're *transfigurations.* Metamorphoses."

Then Dylan's sight line darted in between Dr. Linus' face and Mrs. Hathaway's, slipping past the bodies like a fish through kelp; he spotted us in the alcove beside *Found Analogy* but pretended he hadn't. He nodded enthusiastically at something Mrs. Hathaway said: yes, yes, exactly, his posture said to her, without words.

Then, sharp as the diamond in Mrs. Hathaway's earlobe, Dylan cut his eyes toward me for a second. His whole form shouted *I belong over here where I am, not over there where you are. Stay there, just stay there, and keep my parents busy. Don't let them come over here. Don't let them. Don't let them. Don't–*

But Elaine made her own runway over to him: a barrage of square-heeled stomps, Allen loping alongside. I stepped between them, reached for Allen's arm, guided him toward a Saint Sebastian twined in blackberry brambles—"This one now: the expression on his face"—thinking that if the husband stopped the wife would too. Thinking wrong: Allen stopped, Elaine traipsed on. Her effect on the chatty group was that of a bowling ball hitting pins. They scattered in every direction, and Dylan was left alone in the corner with his mother. Over her shoulder, he glared at me—all accusation.

Awkwardness overcame Allen's graceful form as he smoothed Dylan's shoulder several times without firmness; Elaine moved her husband aside with an elbow and, by way of a hug, critically inspected the individual bones in Dylan's spine: they cannot have been easy to live with. Even now, his visible but silent call for their absence is hard to witness.

After the last patrons trickled out of the exhibit room, disappointed at not getting even their standard three minutes of attention from the star artist whose expansive mood had inexplicably turned to stormy preoccupation and curt paraphrase, the Fieldings too finally left—but first they wrested out of both of us a promise to meet them for dinner the next night.

Then Dylan took my arm in his. We walked out of the gallery together to a bar on Michigan, a glassily gleaming Magnificent Mile place on the waterfront, one I'd never been inside. Standing before mirrored rows of glasses and jewel-toned liqueur bottles he leaned close, spoke near my ear, a shouted whisper audible above the music and yet flushed with a sense of intimacy:

"It's impossible for me to continue doing what everybody wants me to do, expects me to do: it's impossible. What everybody most loves about me is what I most hate about myself," he blurted, and as his hand fell over his eyes and then over the rim of his barely touched martini it betrayed that this was not intoxication talking, that he meant what he said.

What everybody most loves about me is what I most hate about myself: A weighted blade of a phrase, it razed the glass, concrete, and metal from the landscape of my heart, leaving it as it used to be: undeveloped, rural, a meadow between windbreaks of trees. A distant bell sounding over the plain.

If not for this, I wondered—right then and long after—if we would have done what we did. Would we have had that last night together? Would we have reached for each other at the same exact moment; would we have embraced, swaying to the music, our movements married in the mercurial cornflower light, until I could feel the rush of his blood humming through his tense muscles and tendons as though they were my own? Would we have fallen into the taxi, sped away down Lakeshore Drive watching high-rise apartments and amber streetlamps flash past the windows, all the sailboats docked for the night, the treetops clustered around the sails like storm clouds in the charcoal dark?

So easily—with such terrible relief—the choice to stop striving presents itself: to stop wondering and worrying about the lives lived in those high-rises, to stop, for a moment, wanting my life to be one of them, to melt into the past with my back against his chest, his cheek on my hair, his breath on my face.

When that's true, when everybody loves you most at the moment you most hate yourself, he'd repeated in the bar, through my hair and softly into my ear, *it calls everything else into question. Everything but this.*

For a moment we were transported—shaking already with mischievous laughter, with anticipation, into the hotel elevator, down the corridor, into his room, out of time, into abandonment, oblivion. But when I woke again and stare out the window at the lights illuminating the river canal, then, under the shimmer of smugness and buzz I felt just a trace of censoriousness, toward both of us but mostly toward myself: no longer the cheated-on but the cheated-with. For he had already been with Beatrice then, and I knew it: he had reminded me of it himself, told me he didn't care if I didn't, she wouldn't mind what we did, she would never have to know. And I had fallen so far, so far apart, so defenseless by then, had so melted, so completely deliquesced, had so wanted him again just once whatever the cost, that I had agreed.

Without this awareness of having transgressed, I might have been angrier than I was. Instead I lay musing, lost in memory, rage and shame tamed by perspectival shifts.

IV

There was a time when I thought it was an act of freedom, letting Dylan make the portrait—which, although I hated it, I had to admit was splendid. There was a time when I thought it possible to be his colleague, his rival in the best sense, as well as his model, his muse. Still less had I ever wanted to end up a mere envier of him, as anyone with eyes might well become.

Maybe there had never needed to be an opposition. Maybe Beatrice had always been right; maybe I had been completely in the right at no point, completely in the wrong at none either. At the time, the two things I wanted most seemed set so far asunder that I thought I'd have to tear myself in two to reach them both at the same time. Had it been a mistake to see my situation this way? Had it always been possible to resolve the paradox, and I simply hadn't understood how to do it?

This is the core of it, this is what I can't get over: I had thought those gold-and-blue days also brought him all the joy I felt in them. I had thought I was making him as happy as he made me. I had thought it all meant to him something like what it meant to me: and I had been so wrong. All that time I'd had no idea what was going on with him under the skin, no idea what he had been fighting through. I was not the first woman to make such a mistake, but having made it, why would I expect the world to offer it any mercy? History, at least the history I know, isn't rich in examples of such mercy ever having been shown.

*

Dylan, Beatrice, and I had enrolled in the Art Institute as freshmen—same year, same class—but hadn't met until the following fall, when we all took our first intermediate workshop with Signora. Then we were arm in arm, the three of us, almost from that moment, walking from class to Signora's place against the backdrop of the sandy stone buildings with their tidy rows of windows, under the brown painted risers of the train bridge, past the striped awnings. See Dylan in that out-of-date brown leather bomber jacket, Allen's from the 1970s, with its faint evergreen scent of cedar; paint-stained cargo slacks, worn Adidas; see Beatrice's wild curls tied back in a scarf, curves shrugged into thrift-shop skirts, running tights, tank tops and cardigans, any old how. The jacket made his long elegant body look a bit derelict; the skirts skimmed her perfect hips a shade wider than fashion would smile on; I wore three similar outfits in rotation and held my breath in hope no one would notice the repetition. Neither of them ever murmured a mention of it. And before long, their opinions were the only ones that mattered.

There on the terrace of Signora's place, the wind whipping our hair like flags on the harbor, we downed shots of black espresso, we gossiped, we unsteadied the table with our ardor for art. Signora, how we loved her: like us, she did not for one minute believe in Americanized young adulthood, the extension of dependence halfway through the fourth decade of life. We three who were, each for our own reasons, sick already of this breathlessly extended adolescence—in ourselves, in others around us—loved Signora's lack of nonsense. We enrolled in every class she taught. We had no idea how young our enthusiasm for her made us look. Somewhere I still have a sketch of her I made then—that intricately shaded charcoal hair, aquiline nose, Edwardian long dark skirt, and the walking stick that added percussion or punctuation to her speech as often as it lent support to her steps.

She extended welcome to all her students, but like most professors she had her partisans and her detractors. Partisans joined us here and there, slipping in and out of the group smoothly: the three of us were its core, the three of us were never absent. We were the party.

Like goslings imprinted on the mother goose we followed Signora to museums and galleries, drank in her opinions, assimilated them and recited them elsewhere—although to pull it off we had to recast them, remake them, in our own tones. For which of us, really, could ever mimic that voice:

"Those who know how to paint should paint. Those who cannot, only, should take courses in the core skills, or else settle for the work of critique. In the library: this is the place for the writer, not for the maker of the objects of art. Too many times I have seen the darkening of these bright eyes, the grinding up of these quick hands in the gears of this machine, this supposed education. Do not serve the machine! Use your eyes, use your hands. But be careful who and what you use them for. Work, above all work! That is real education. . . .

"I praise very little and I demand very much, yes? We will work. You will be artists and adults. This is what you deserve. And you will treat me and my tradition with respect—this is what I deserve. If you do not like to do this, if you prefer to do something else, you may certainly do that. But not in my class. I praise only the outstanding. And outstanding is *not*—" the rubber cane heel made a *pock* sound on the floor—"slinging paint at a canvas. It is not putting a new coat of red on the barn, yes? It is when you can translate vision into color and form, so that other people, who do not know this thing that we know, this deep dialogue between reality and our inner vistas, can begin to learn its silent language. . . .

"But oh, you American children." *Pock.* "You come to my class believing that, in learning to see, it is only your own eyes that count. But no." *Pock pock.* "First learn to have great love for the vision of another. How can you lead anyone to see what you see, unless you first know what he can see and what he cannot?"

When she said she was leaving to spend a semester staying with family and teaching workshops in her native Rome, we felt devastation followed by wild hope: she had secured a grant, she said, that would allow her to create an ad-hoc senior thesis project and study-abroad program overseas. It would cover everything: were we interested? Oh yes: and so we followed her transatlantic flight.

That semester was heavenly. This may be too tender a line to define a single school term, but I'll say it anyway because it is the exact truth: wherever I go I will carry it with me for the rest of my life.

After graduation, Dylan stayed in Florence on a fellowship secured for him by Giovanni, who was Signora's nephew and a well-connected gallerist with properties in Florence and in Venice. That same year, I went back to Chicago to try to earn, to save up, enough for a move. I lived in a small dangerous walk-up in midtown, had worked at a nonprofit that paid for my Adobe CS2 training, which in a year would lose its shine when CS3 was released, and anyway would be small change with which to trade in a city full of potential interns who could afford to work "for the experience"—which I couldn't. I had applied to graduate programs but had only been offered funding in other cities, not in Chicago or in New York.

A major goal for me then was still to rejoin Dylan and Beatrice. I decided that, if I had to choose between an MFA program and working in their company, seeing by their lights, I valued one of these so far above the other that the choice made itself. So I bought my ticket to New York and found a sublet: I registered for a refresher course, lined up my first temporary gigs, and wrote up a budget: planned right down to the week when to buy new supplies, where and how to start my real work.

By then Dylan and his work had so clearly impressed the right people that, weeks ahead of his planned flight into LaGuardia, two magazines—a glossy art monthly and an iconic culture weekly, both based in the city—had already printed breathless little paragraphs mentioning Dylan's name. As well, Giovanni had managed to sell a few first canvases—one that he had taken all the way to the Biennale—and in this way to place Dylan's name in certain mouths, in certain circles, as a good investment, worth betting on. These were the first snowflakes. Soon, the blizzard.

In this way Dylan and I had arrived in New York one autumn within weeks of each other. We quickly moved in together—both of us were twenty-three—still with the gloss of our ideals not quite worn off: both, I think, expecting to love each other as we had under the influence of Stendhal syndrome, neither of us guessing how thoroughly the world we had known together would be found to have vanished. To have been, always, illusive.

Beatrice had spent that interim year between a place her parents owned in a Manhattan high-rise, which they let her occupy in exchange for performing light landlord duties on other similar properties—this way they never had to leave their own flat in a Greenwich Village condominium, unless they felt like it—and her own hard-to-get studio rental, acquired through strings they pulled for her. At first she worked to refine her own painting and sculpture in line with Signora's ideals. Before long, though, feeling uncomfortably pinned under her well-connected parents' thumbs and lacking close companionship among her cohort, she lost momentum. She diffused her attention first into partying with other young gorgeous artists— "but none of them, none that I met anyway, were one fucking bit serious," she would later complain to me: "they all wanted to be seen, none of them wanted to *see* anything, other than my clothes on their apartment floor."

What she felt as an emptiness drove her, or pulled her, toward what she called "inner work." She had floated, that lonely summer, first into a clinician's office and afterward into a meditation studio. Signs of zeal sprouted up in her rooms: a little jade Buddha, an urn of bamboo. The complete works of Thich Nhat Hanh, along with some poetry and Zen sayings translated by a different monk who used to be a Manhattanite himself, sat bookended by stone elephants on her lacquered japonaiserie shelf. By the time we arrived in the fall, Beatrice felt sick of her own inconclusive attempts at a masterwork and was looking for ways to "change the world."

The moment Beatrice saw Dylan's new paintings, they became her mission. She began doing publicity for him because she liked Dylan and liked the work: sweet-talking journalists and gallerists at workshops and talkbacks; lunches, dinners, coffees, wine tastings; daily and nightly showings; endless, endless parties and after-parties and after-after-parties. This was her mètier already, as the daughter of an artist and a critic. She spoke the language; she shone at convincing others, as she was convinced, of Dylan's genius. Giovanni and his New York liaison Andrew—through whom we'd met Omar, with whom he'd also had a fling, and who now formed part of his loud, gregarious circle—they both, they all, loved Beatrice's savviness, her vivacity. To them she was Dylan's real partner, the one who mattered. They saw me—*when* they saw me—as a low-rent substitute for Beatrice, a work of inferior quality: at most an Echo to Dylan's Narcissus.

Looked at a certain way, it all made sense. Her family's wealth murmured of prior centuries, barons and other dubious heroes of commerce tracing back to the Gilded Age, which had made their own insouciance possible. Money made itself obedient to Beatrice's intentions, and so she had always been able to talk about it with fluency, the topic to her no more or less important than whether to pick up pho or sushi for lunch. She cultivated in herself the ethos of a small, exclusive world, she gave us a gateway into it; she radiated the heat of its starry nights, under the awning in the manicured garden, cooled by mint and lime vodka with ice—and, with no sense of contradicting herself, she mocked it to us the following day over kimchi-topped pork tacos in Hell's Kitchen, "so self-serious, so faux-posh," she would laugh. Still another benefit her affluence afforded her: this easy pretense of contempt. Beatrice could shrug off her own security because she would never have to worry about its reverse.

She introduced the two of us to her parents once, in the Village, on a rare and random Wednesday afternoon during which they had no other commitments. They barely greeted Beatrice—"hi, hon, there you are"—and waved at us without requesting an introduction: "Wine, water, over there, help yourselves," her father said, with a gesture at a small but costly-looking latticed fridge in stainless steel.

Beatrice's red hair evidently came from him, a modestly successful sculptor, and her quattrocento face from her mother, an art critic who wrote for highbrow magazines—hers would before long be another voice raised in Dylan's praise, once she saw the canvases, but her first meeting with him was inauspicious.

Their apartment had nothing of any definite color in it—as if sketched entirely in pencil. On our entrance and throughout our stay, they never once lapsed or changed course in their discussion of de Kooning's paintings of women and their attitude to female embodiment—he arguing to prove the works' misogyny, she, the value of their contrasts:

"Why do you assume that all the sexuality displayed there is of a negative character?—only because it's been so hated and so feared. He hasn't participated in that hate and fear. He has only put the positive and the negative there to be received. What the viewer finds there is no more than what he brings to it."

Or she: "and you're bringing your own positivity to the endeavor, your own sense of inherent worth. You're ignoring the artist's use of distortion, a clearly purposive employment."

"Are you saying that because of the kind of body I'm carrying my brain around in, I have more difficulty being objective than you do? Careful with that unsayable shit."

"Never for a moment would I dare. I'm saying you have a grasp of your inalienable dignity and a tendency to give the benefit of the doubt. Those are personal attributes, not gendered ones. I'm only saying there's more than mere *yin* energy to the depictions in the series, especially in those that resemble women crucified. Their darkness is the darkness of hostility, not of stillness or of rest."

Dylan gathered himself like a runner at the line, shot forward in a false start: "It's a worthwhile challenge, depicting a woman and not having her appearance steal the show. Viewers carry so many preconceptions, about its meaning, about its history, about the interiority it implies. Setting her personality forth without some distortion is next to impossible. And that comes about due to our extremism. Secretly we want the woman to be a goddess—whether of growth or of destruction, we don't always know. Deep down a part of us can't stand the idea that she might be human. That she might not be everything we need—and she might not be a cow standing in shit either. She might be like us. She might prove another self. If only we could stop making her and remaking her in the image of our dreams. Or our nightmares."

Beatrice's mother regarded Dylan with narrowed eyes: "How terribly clever you must feel to have worked all that out for yourself," she said, and turned back to Beatrice's father to draw an analogy between the de Kooning figures and the better-known Ensler play—which work the older man also, with the air of one who plays a trump card, declared anti-woman.

Beatrice apologized afterward, while we walked down Twelfth toward Abingdon Square Park for a smoke. "For all their pretense at refinement they're barbaric in some ways," she said. "Don't worry. When I explain, in detail, to mommy dearest who she just snubbed? She'll be in agonies."

"No, it's okay," Dylan said mildly. "I was raised by successful wolves, too."

Beatrice clapped her hands. "Oooh, wolves. Say more."

Dylan shrugged. "Not a lot *to* say. Psychologist, accountant. Commonplace, distant. They didn't want a child; they wanted a savior. And I hate to break this to you, but I'm no savior," he added, with a wry smirk in the direction of the sidewalk.

That lone visit to Beatrice's parents—we never repeated the error—came to embody my fears about their world. For all their veneer of concern for "those less well off," I was under no illusions about how interchangeable, how disposable, they might be likely to consider someone like me, at least until I proved myself—nor how hard-won must be the opportunities for such proof. And even *if* proof defied doubt, how easily even someone like Dylan could still be done without.

That winter Beatrice sat me down and, over steaming matcha, "leveled with me" that I would never stand a chance to have my art noticed, nor ever become a suitable social partner for Dylan, unless I committed to continuous self-revision (she called it "permanent revolution")—an utter overhaul of my work, my person, my interests—according to some urgently pressing standard of her own.

"Because you're talented too, darling, that's obvious," she said to me (one leg kicking, crossed in tall boots, in cold afternoon light slanting sideways under the tea-shop awning). "So am I, for that matter, but I've come to understand the best of my talent has to do with getting people like you *in*to places you aspire to, making you understand you belong. That one," she said, inclining her head to mean the absent Dylan, "has never in his life known one moment of doubt that he belongs. You, though, coming from where you come from— sorry, love, I know you've told me again and again. My mind's like water—but from wherever backward place, doesn't matter, it makes you think you don't belong. Darling. You, as much as anyone, be*long*. Almost more than he does, and I only say 'almost' because he's so fucking clever that it's obvious, there *is* no doubt; but he knows it. But you're just as clever, and you *don't* know it. You need to know it. You're about to learn it. Come on. Let's see what we make of you."

Beatrice repeatedly laughed off her inability to remember where I was from. This never made sense to me: it wasn't as though I had made any great point of it. In fact, before meeting her and Dylan and abruptly ghosting nearly everyone else I'd ever spent time with, as a running freshman joke of my own I had pretended to a wild diversity of origins. For three weeks I had posed, with transparently intentional falsehood—my dark hair and complexion made my genetics ambiguous, but not this ambiguous—as a Middle Eastern amira who had escaped from a secret compound. Next, the putative reason I would never sing karaoke, not even ironically, was that I was a wildly talented secret daughter of pop stars, trying to lead a normal student life in disguise. I told this story to hide, in plain sight, my desperation to earn attention purely on my merits, my fear of being caught in a mistake—of being seen in any act, mistake or not, by which I could be said to disprove my value.

So Beatrice came to embody, for Dylan and me both, certain things he desired—and also, though for different reasons, feared. Naturally he would accept when, that last New Year's Eve of the decade, she would propose. Naturally she would be the one to propose. And naturally he would feel the demand of filling the role in which her chosen community would cast him—*wunderkind*, young lion. Think of anyone denying Beatrice, backed up as she was by her establishment, her connections, her own selective and self-serving— but on its own terms unassailable—rectitude.

To say Beatrice had a way of forestalling argument is to understate the case. She commanded her reality with such assertion that it would never enter your head to contradict her. Friendly and companionable enough in her streamlined study-abroad life with us, in New York she had changed. Everything about Dylan's professional image fell into her hands, and she became—either a different person, or else the one she had really been all along. She seemed to drop all her personal ambition, to invest it all instead in him.

Even the way she presented herself at this point—all cashmere and leather, black and cream, a work of fiber-based performance art—clashed with the way I remembered her as a student, her delight in disorder. That simpler image was erased from her life first and then, at her hands, erased also from mine. After the remonstrance in the tea shop, I became her sole remaining creative project. Whenever she could pull me away from what I had planned, she hauled me with her to the kinds of boutiques and salons I had only ever seen before on film—often not even in very good films, but Beatrice made me feel that she was pulling me behind the scenes, showing me how things really happened. She made me question my own judgment. She instructed and treated, flattered and admonished; she paid my way, foreclosing every protest; I was her paper doll. And once we both looked right, according to her own standard of "right," she would take me with her to the galleries where she was trying to get Dylan's work seen by the right people—where her standard, in that respect, proved demonstrably impeccable.

My role in all this was not to say or do anything, only to blend in with her so completely as to be accepted as part of her surroundings. Only later, in her studio, would my mind come into play—a sounding board, not to say echo chamber, as she analyzed every word and look, anticipating who was likely to be agreeable to her plans, or where she ought to cut her losses.

This new role called forth in me an edge of contempt and, at the same time, a powerful enthusiasm, both of which I felt I had better try to hide from her. I wanted to resist—I had my own work to do— but to offend her felt unsafe, to contradict her unthinkable. I did want to help Dylan, yes, and making Beatrice angry could have resulted in pointless drama, wasted time, lost opportunities for all three of us. And then again, a part of me sincerely liked her company. Even as I secretly rolled my eyes at her obsession with off-canvas detail, I feared that I might unintentionally drive her away.

Sometimes I think her influence destroyed the artist I could have been: but no, I allowed everything she did to me, encouraged it even, obeyed her behests to study the New York school and the gestural painters, considered seriously her suggestions that what I wanted to do with emotion in my work I might best be able to do by ignoring form and focusing on color alone: in this way I lost the thing I had loved first, the fine detail, the sense of perspective in harmony with precision, that had incited me to begin painting in the first place. Dylan made note of the loss even in my rendering of the Gothic arch I'd slashed on our last night together.

"They were sentimental acts," he said, "both that canvas and your choice to wreck it, but for all that you weren't wrong. I envy your draftsmanship; it's better than mine. You shine at a refinement that wasn't on display there. High modernist style doesn't suit either of us: we're throwbacks to a prior era. We do better to embrace that."

It was, precisely, the question of throwing back to a prior era—what might that mean, what must it imply?—that sparked our arguments over Dylan's portrait of me. Beatrice, who I felt should have understood my hesitations in light of the loyalty women owe to each other, thought I was wasting an opportunity for good publicity. On her terms I had succeeded. On her terms the portrait was my success as well as his.

"But he *apotheosized* you," Beatrice insisted—months afterward, on the divan in her apartment (when I walked through the rooms I divided them into sublets, tallying a means of making work need-less). The portrait had just showed for the first time; Dylan and I had fought and fallen out over it—it isn't worth recounting our fight, its terms and contradictions, because I couldn't then admit to the central problem. I hated the portrait not so much because it reduced me to something I wasn't, but because it revealed me as I was: a competent woman capable of more but settling, as a matter of ease, for the camp disguise of the ingenue—choosing the diminished, regressive role for myself.

Right, wrong, whichever: Beatrice now took it on herself to talk me around, as she had so often before: her favorite task, seated lotus-style, oracular, one hand raised to herald her wisdom. One lamp glowed at the end of a short foyer. Otherwise, the only light in the room was what entered through the window.

"What was the problem?" Beatrice asked. "I wasn't at the showing, but I saw it in his studio. It's not like it's a bad likeness. It's fucking gorgeous. Like you."

"Spare me."

"Why, because it's facile?"

"Because it's meretricious."

She shook her head. "I don't see why."

"Forget it. You're right, I should be able to separate myself from it. I can't, and that's a flaw."

"He gave you a platform, if you'd been willing to use it. An image like that of a painter like you—what a marvelous piece of gossip; you should have brought me on your team; I would have had everybody talking about it."

"Ah, but you know I can't *afford* you on my team. And anyway I don't care. I told him I didn't want that portrait shown. I don't want everybody talking about it."

"Sweetheart, you know I do take pro bono clients. Dylan was one at first."

"We've had that conversation before. I couldn't accept your services on unfair terms."

"It wouldn't be unfair; I've explained that too." She wasn't quite wrong, and I knew it, but I clung to this objection, citing justice. The truth was harder to explain. The force in my bones that resisted her generosity was not justice but instead the most severe allergy to being in anyone's debt, for anything, ever.

"Just like it would be fine if you moved into the spare room here," she went on, with a gesture of her angora-draped arm that wafted an orange-flower wave of scent over us both. "I'm sure I wouldn't ask you to chip in more than you're paying on that tragic place you're insisting on renting, three boroughs away from everything that *matters*. But let's agree to disagree about that. About the portrait, though, I still don't understand. You must have changed your mind. First you let him make the painting and then you don't want him to do what is *done* with paintings. Why? Why reject an . . . an honor like that? It *is* an honor, to be painted by someone with that kind of talent. It was okay with you for him to make the work, but not to share it? Is that what you're saying? Or do you wish he had destroyed it?"

"Is talent a good excuse for being a shit?"

"Well, love, I'm with you there. No one is denying Dylan can be a shit, when he wants to. Although it's usually not that he wants to, he just isn't paying enough attention. Which is, I admit, another way of saying he doesn't want *not* to be a shit, not enough to make any difference. But what made you change your mind?"

"Does it matter? I don't think it matters why I changed my mind. I changed it; I said no. He should have respected that."

"Hmm." Beatrice found this hard to argue with. She could not deny the ascendancy of consent without contradicting herself, but still her discontent showed in the line her mouth made.

"What about the interview in the *Times* where Dylan mentioned you?"

"An embarrassment. It wasn't about anything I *did*."

"And the group show you were in?"

"Forget it. This city hosts hundreds of those every day. Who cares?"

How, she wondered aloud—then and often afterward—could I ask for more? And she was right, up to a point: I truly didn't see how to make capital out of what, in her view, had been given me to work with. Here, I accepted her judgment that I lacked a certain kind of vision.

She thought, too, that it was strange of me not to be quickly capable of "getting over" Dylan—by this time I had moved out of his loft and into my little uptown cell. By this time the two of them were already eyeing one another, though Beatrice swore they hadn't yet done more: "but I'm only holding him off for your sake, to respect the cooling-off window. I mean damn, woman. We are *both* fortunate, you know?"

She spoke as casually as though Dylan's body were no more important than a stash of cocaine from which, if one of us had it, I could offer a line to her or she to me: no less easily shareable, no less disposable.

"He's painted me too, and in the nude," she shared late one other evening, about a month after this. We had just finished unpacking every look and word that had passed at some party: another post-game, another argument. And now this bombshell. "I told you that? I didn't tell you that, I guess, from your face. What a *child* you are. You're so *readable*. Well. It doesn't make me feel like a, what did you say, like a commodity. It makes me feel like a goddess, if you want to know the truth. 'Commodity'?—check your privilege, love; we're sitting yards from a place where human persons used to be bought and sold, body and soul, on a chunk of land that cost the Dutch a pocketful of seashells, a land that they then took and for all natural purposes destroyed. When you look at that, I mean really look at it and don't run away from it, what does it matter what happens to you or to me? Or more to the point, what does it matter what happens to some dried-up pigment and linseed and varnish on a flat surface?—because that's not *you*, no matter what it feels like. If you find yourself identifying with it for some reason, maybe you need to wonder why—I mean, I don't mean to be mean, but really: why? If it feels like someone is somehow going to gain some control over you in the process of giving away money for the ownership of this painting, this *object*, then there may be signs of a lack of agency in that?—something primitive, something unexamined?—and maybe you need to spend some time just sitting with it, just exploring, you know, why it might be that you feel that way?—I'm just suggesting this as a friend, of course; I'm not a professional," although Beatrice in her life had encountered very few problems that hadn't been solved for her by sympathetic people administering therapeutic processes.

Accordingly she found it hard to resist the temptation to evangelize. "*Are* you seeing someone?" she asked me.

"I saw someone," I said, although it had been back in school, on the student health plan, for my own reasons and not for these confused and above all unprofessional impulses. For, again, she had a point: there was a Philistine, pedestrian air about this resistance: the more I knew my attitude to be tacky, unglamorous, *provincial*, the more I doubled down on it.

"Is it a body problem? Because I have to tell you, I hate my body too," she continued, as she put her drink down on a coaster and stretched out on her stomach on the floor. Earlier, she had mixed us whiskey sours in her kitchen, its chrome sink piled with dishes she swore she would get around to washing eventually, if the housekeeper's day didn't roll around first. Now she delicately wiped her wet fingers on her jeans before touching the silk of her loose camisole so that she wouldn't make water spots on the fabric. She pulled the drape of the top up above her abdomen, so that her bare ribs rested on the tatami mat; the fabric skimmed her breasts and then fell to the ground. Even the silk bent to her will, puddling gently on the carpet rather than wrinkling underneath her. She went on talking:

"I mean, I could catalogue for you all the parts of me that look wrong, that *are* wrong, that don't go together with each other, or that mean I could never be part of this profession or that one. Never a dancer, never an actress, never a model, you know?—and in this city, that's discouraging, because this is where you go, where all the world gathers to be one of them. But do you know what? Fuck that noise. It's fatiguing just to talk about it. What's important isn't how the body looks, but how it feels."

Beatrice yawned like a cat, pushed her hands and feet into the ground so that her rear and the backs of her thighs pointed toward the ceiling in an inverted V, and then raised one leg even higher in an arabesque line.

"Ah, that's better. Come on," she said, swinging her leg down toward me, jabbing my knee with her toes, laughing at the expression on my face. "Come on, you too. Don't just sit there. Join me; you'll feel better."

Someone looking into the plate glass window of Beatrice's apartment—as anyone across the way could have done; the floor-to-ceiling blinds lay open, affording a view of the mostly closed curtains of a posh hotel—might have envied our impromptu drunken yoga, our young bodies that had escaped more or less unmarked from the culture of assault. (Though what might Beatrice mean by "unmarked"?)

"But here's the other thing, and this should make you feel better too," she said after a series of stretches (and oh the elegance her attitude gave to her every movement; she made the exercise seem a dance; I could only feign such finesse in a freeze frame). She had disappeared to her bedroom and now returned carrying folded t-shirts to trade for the fluttering silk we had worn to the party. It wasn't really some "other thing" that she wanted to say, but the first thing again, stated in other words, shot from a different angle: "If you're really worrying whether this will compromise your future career, don't. How could it do anything but help you? Even if people do say, 'Oh, but her paintings are secondary to his, her brushwork is this and her composition is that, blah blah,' still the backstory'll hook people's interest? No, don't make that face at me. That *face*. There's no reason for you to quit painting, unless you truly just don't want to pursue it any more. And if you truly don't, then there's no shame in quitting."

I didn't then want to quit; that despondency would only come later. But I didn't bother correcting her. I turned away from the window and changed my shirt and curled up on the cool smooth cushions of her tan leather couch.

Beatrice changed her shirt there too, not bothering to turn, and then lay on the mat, one ankle twined under the opposite knee.

"Oh well, it's your mind: feel as bad as you need for as long as you want: I'm finished trying to cheer you up. But you have to hear one more thing: there's no such thing as pure art, unsullied by the city and all its envious denizens. Drop that tack or you'll kill yourself.

"You can crash, though," she conceded. "If you don't want

to take a cab home, that is. I wouldn't blame you. I hate standing around on sidewalks after about one in the morning."

I slept on the couch that night, as so many nights, as, again, my last night in New York. The afternoon I flew out, Beatrice covered the cab to the airport and joined me; she had a flight that day too, to Los Angeles to close some deal—she spoke vaguely about the details, secretively, said only that the client was a friend of her family—but, she added, this was a good opportunity, her last chance to try to talk better sense into me.

"Although, if you haven't picked up any more hints from watching me and Dylan work by now, I wonder if it'll ever come home to you. Not that you'd be unique in that way. Some just can't take it. Here's the one thing you have to do, here's the trick, and it's so simple: Take on only projects that thrill you," she said. But she had said this already, had said it so often, any time I had complained of the tedious paying jobs I took to make rent. Her pearls proffered nothing new. This didn't stop her:

"Work where you find your energy and passion," she carried on, hands outstretched just shy of a televangelist's or a Broadway belter's gesture. "You need to choose your work, not take what's handed to you. I still don't understand what makes you tick. What's your real problem. Though I have my guesses."

"That's nice to know, at this stage."

"I wonder now if we'll ever cure you of simply taking whatever's handed to you. Or is it that you can't accept what you're really being offered? I would have loved to have you as a roommate. We could have done so much good work together. I can't think why you said no. I have to be honest, it hurts a bit to be turned down."

"You don't know what it's like," I blurted, willing now—at the end—to be blunt for once. "To *have* to accept *whatever* I'm offered. Because I have nothing of my own to give."

"Right there, that. That's it. That's how you and Dylan are alike: you don't see your effect on people. Only he thinks he's too far above others ever to hurt them, and you think you're too low down even to matter. He thinks his talents are all he is. You still haven't figured out yours exist." Beatrice shook her head. "Good Jesus, the things the two of you don't seem to *know*. Who the hell brought you up? They ought to be ashamed of themselves."

It felt good at any rate to disappear in an airport, anonymous, Passenger 26F in coach, no extra charge for the window seat: skies seen through airplane windows had not yet stopped overawing me. As we traced between towers of cumulonimbus I relived that all-night crossing to Italy by way of Switzerland: Dylan's profile traced in ochre light; waking up to find that everything that mattered to me hung suspended in wisps of cirrus, over indigo mountains creased with snow. I wondered now what had happened to the girl who had snored that morning on the other side of Dylan, mouth open like the Bernini St. Theresa's, curls gilded in the sunrise: the girl who had made us stop in front of a duty-free counter in Zurich and, from behind a tall glacier of Toblerone laced with snowdrifts of shredded gold foil, had bought chocolate coins wrapped in a tough yellow plastic net, had cut the net open to pour the coins into our cupped and waiting hands: the girl who had cut class to catch a train to Florence with us, who had run lightly ahead of us up the clay-colored cobblestone streets, out of one gallery and into another, laughing in late afternoon light on the Oltrarno. Why we had been laughing I no longer remember, but we could lark then about anything or nothing, walk for miles without tiring, skim from city block to city block like dragonflies leaping across a stream, and stand in front of paintings for hours, knowing we had, thinking we always would have, all the time we could ever need.

V

"So I won the fellowship spot I applied for," Dylan told me as the last hours of our last semester slid away under the fissure of the oncoming future. He sat trying to look collected across the glass table of the café, under a red-and-white striped awning, the picture of nonchalance. But, as ever, his hands gave him away: he sloshed the espresso around in its cup, studying the ellipses it made; he spun his saucer, traced it with a fingertip, folded the napkin into a hat. "So, yeah. I'm not coming back to Chicago next year."

"You're not going to take the MFA after all? I didn't know we were still following Signora's lead on that. You'd get funding for sure. I still plan to apply."

"Yeah, but this was all Signora's idea. She put me up to it. And then, God help me, I need a break. I've been researching what I'd have to do to apply, and all of the paper just makes me numb. Just thinking about the loans, the side gigs, all that dreck? It's draining. And at a certain point it gets in the way of what it's supposed to be supporting."

I didn't say what, maybe, I should: that I dealt with the loans, the side gigs, all that dreck, and I'd be paying it off until I was at least forty, and yes it took a toll on my time for painting, and that was just adulthood, and not all of us could afford to be art monsters.

"Your parents won't help? What happened there?"

"They can't, they claim. They talk about 'financial difficulties,' about 'assets tied up.' But I never understand what they're talking about when they're talking about money. It's the first time they've ever said anything like that. Before this, any time they haven't wanted to give me something, the story has always been, *We could afford to give you this thing, but we don't think it's good for you to have it handed to you, so if you want it you'll have to work for it.* It was the same story with this trip at first. I think it's the same story now: because they've paid for college, they say they're done. They say they won't support me to become an artist; they assume that means becoming a financial failure. But whatever; screw that. Now, with this grant, I can take a year and apply for next fall if I want to, or not if I don't. And I may be too busy by then. I don't know how I can wait any longer. I've had this series in mind for ages, and now I'll have time just to work on it, all the time that's needed to do what needs doing. That's a gift, and I'm not going to reject it.

"I've already seen the apartment, too. It's little, but bright—most of all it's got this high ceiling and these windows that look south. Proper studio conditions. Did they make you do that same forced march through Dostoyevsky we got sent on in high school?—the man was right about one thing—low ceilings are bad for the soul. So high ones must be good for it. Anyway, the place is furnished, but I'll need to bring all my stuff in. Would you want to come with me on the train ride over? It could be fun. I could use some help setting up."

"I think that could work. I don't fly back right away. I left myself about five days after the last finals to do backpacking and stay in hostels, that kind of thing. No set plans, though."

"Perfect—you can sleep on my couch, which is better because the dorms are closing anyway, we could do all the museums if you want, and then you'll be able to take a train back to catch your flight at the end of the week."

He wanted me with him all week. All week.

"You've really thought this through, it sounds like."

"I wanted you not to have any reason to say no."

So we found ourselves on the train once more, gliding and clicking over the countryside from Rome to Florence. How new the seats felt, crisp and clean, the fresh smell of their gray leather: how new the unruly sky, its endless birthday streamers of tinsel cloud that filled the whole train car, not only the wide windows, with their exhilaration.

At the station we had bought hard bitter licorice in a clear blue plastic cup, and *baci*, chocolate bonbons filled with hazelnuts. The chocolates had strips of thin waxed paper inside their wrappers, like fortune cookies, printed with quotations in German, French, Spanish, Italian, Portuguese, English. We took turns reading them to each other, the whole time laughing about their over-earnestness.

"'It is a strange thing about Americans,'" Dylan said, in a tone suitable for teaching civics to seventh graders, "'that they tend to receive their supernatural mail on foreign soil.' John Updike." Even the name sounded so funny for some reason that Dylan couldn't stay in character; by the end of the line a pompous fake-refined accent had taken over his voice, and we both dissolved in hilarity.

"John Updike in a candy wrapper?" I was falling apart with glee. "I'm sure he'd be appalled."

"I'm sure. But maybe it's the best thing that ever happened to him."

"Have you received any supernatural mail so far?"

Dylan looked arch. "Who knows? Maybe I haven't opened it yet. Your turn."

I cringed at the Italian phrase I had selected with such care—a complete laying of my cards on the table—and then, emboldened by the speed of the train, by the shimmer of the leaves under the silver sky, decided to read it anyway.

"'*Non c'è peggiore nostalgia che rimpiangere quello che non è mai successo.*'"

"The worst kind of nostalgia is regretting something that has never happened," Dylan translated slowly. Then, tracing his eyes across my face, his expression shifted—as fast as the clouds that slid their shadows over it—from amused to contemplative to sly. He had seen through me just then: he knew. He knew then, if he hadn't known before, what I hadn't been able to say, what he would end up drawing out of me word by word: "Ask me," he would say later, would say soon, with his wide warm palms pressed into my back, his lips against my ear, "*ask* me, I want to hear you say it," and then yes I would ask him, then and how often afterward, but not now, not yet, not yet.

"What do you regret because it hasn't happened?" he pressed.

I kept my tone as light as his. "Lots of things."

"Like what?"

"Like not finishing the conversation we started when the whole workshop was out together last weekend. We had this earnest, overly serious, drunken talk which you probably don't even remember."

"I do remember it. And I don't want you thinking it wasn't serious just because we were drunk. I pride myself on being able to have conversations sober that most people can only have when they're toasted."

"Listen to you. Seriously?"

"Seriously." The green of his eyes was the fire of meteors burning through the upper atmosphere. "We talk about things that lots of people won't even think about, or won't admit it if they do. Regrets, art, life, supernatural messages. Why shouldn't I be honest about what I think?"

"We're not talking about those things right now, we're talking near them. Anyway, all you mean is that you're not capable of sustained cynicism. If you could, you would live inside that armor, but—and I'm grateful you can't—you're not able to do it, Dylan."

"Aren't I, though?"

"No, you and I don't really click with people who joke all the time, who'd be fucking joking through their teeth at their best friends' funerals. That's why we go to the museums and they don't bother, for starters. They can't get over their posturing long enough to look outside themselves. But it's just what's maddening about you. I can't tell when you're being ironic and when you're not."

"Trust me, it's a carefully constructed front. I'm just inclined to defend myself even when there's nothing threatening me. Even telling you that is part of the front," Dylan said, producing from a hip pocket a handkerchief he used to wipe the stain of the bitter licorice off his lips. "The fun of it is that, when I want to hide, you're not able to tell which parts of me are front and which parts are real. The hell of it is that sometimes I'm not able to tell, either." He carefully refolded the handkerchief, with the stain now on the inner fabric, and tucked it back into his pocket.

"I'm glad you've finally realized what I noticed right away," I teased. "Anyway, that night you said you thought that the danger in both art and love was that they both got into the blood and drove people to do things that they never would otherwise. That both were dangerous because they made people vulnerable. That you can't really do either well without that vulnerability, which means mistakes that leave marks and so—"

"No, yeah, definitely. Vulnerability is an indispensable danger."

"And a risk *you're* not comfortable with." I made the accusation with a laugh, but I meant it, too.

"No, not true. I'm only too comfortable with risk. But only calculated risk; I like control. I only give what I decide in advance, and I cut my losses when work or relationships start to go bad. Isn't that horrible?"

"Why would that be horrible? It sounds enviable from where I sit." Also I wasn't sure he was quite right about this in himself: I had watched him allowing a slip once or twice, hoped he might be slipping again now, in my favor. But a challenge could return him abruptly to reticence, and I enjoyed this uncommon openness too much to risk that.

"It isn't enviable. No more envy, please. Not here. If you don't already understand why, I hope you never have to. Anyway it's incredibly anxiety-making to be in a state of constant calculation and caution, but I don't know how to stop. I haven't ever let myself be pushed all the way to my limits, so I don't even know where they are. So it's never been real vulnerability at all."

"What is 'real vulnerability'? Is it only real if there's a chance it'll kill you?"

Dylan frowned.

"I would give my life to find out. No lie. How can I exceed my limits if I don't know where they are? How can I take a real risk if I can't let myself try as hard as I can when I might fail anyway?"

We fell silent. He leaned over against my shoulder and, before long, fell asleep to the rhythm of the train's wheels. Though I relished him there, out of consciousness and all control, his heat on top of the afternoon's soothed me to sleep; I remember waking, much too warm, to the sight of grey and ochre buildings stacked on both sides of a golden river, under hills shadowed purple in the late light from a raging orange sunset.

"Look," I said. Dylan woke, too, and saw, and his eyes met mine, and we saw it together, and this was the first moment in which his eyes said, silently, not "I am seeing *this* with you" but instead "I am seeing this with *you*."

We disembarked at Santa Maria Novella. Dylan pulled down his two suitcases, a cardboard box of books, a duffel bag stuffed with linens and dropcloths, and a big red fishing-tackle box full of brushes and tubes, charcoals and erasers, razor blades and rags. I wore my hiking backpack, which held a week's worth of clothes, a sketchbook, a toothbrush, and a half-full pencil wrap. We strapped the boxes to the suitcase handles with bungee cords, and we rolled along, burdened, through the warm blue evening, dragging everything to the second-story room where Dylan would live.

The front room, the studio, had the promised twelve-foot ceiling whose corners were lost in shadow. Through the windows, high above eye level, the blue twilight swelled. Against the opposite wall an easel leaned, tense with the longing to be put to its purpose. There stood a lamp with five or six bulbs on Medusa-like wires, a shelf, the low table, the chair, and the sparse single bed with its white duvet.

The door closed behind us with a snap. The tension had reached the pitch where I thought I might die of not having kissed him. He had held off the possibility until now, fought shy at any moment it could have happened. Then we were there, alone, the door closed, and I felt flattened between the immediacy of the opportunity and the intolerability of its passing without notice. Whatever made him who and what he was, I thirsted for it. I wanted to hear its rhythm under my ribs, between my hips, like a heartbeat, to have the sound of its breath in my flesh as it was in his. It was more than mere desire; it was a whisper away from worship.

"Almost a true studio. Not quite," he said, peering into a closet. "Ladies' and gents' in here." No bathtub, just a showerhead, tap, and lidless commode on black and white tile. "And in here—just empty shelves. Who could wish for better?"—and I heard the wheels of his suitcase hitting the checkerboard floor, the rough plastic of the tackle box being slid onto a shelf. And with that we were free of our burdens. The height of his thin frame in the doorway, his fluid way of crossing the room, the line of his hands and arms as he placed them on the windowsill and lifted the sash: *walk up behind him, put your hands on him, put your mouth on his,* insisted an inner voice. I scarcely knew how to locate this voice within the person I thought I was. But at the same time I wanted it to come from him, wanted to know he wanted it as much as I did, enough to say so first. Not yet. Not yet.

Soon enough—and not soon enough: and afterward a new door opened in my mind, a new room, and in that room I was never not with him: together we lived in time that felt endless, that held itself apart, that remade every other moment in relation to itself. Old news to the old world around us; to me, revolutionary. And yet afterward I continued to follow him as, for months before, I had followed him: sketchbook in hand. We had spent hours upon hours, that spring, in the Uffizi and Accademia, in small modern and contemporary galleries, in the private collections of people Signora knew, and in the chapels of famous churches. Without him, I wonder if I would have worked so hard. Without him, I wonder if I would have discovered that I was—nearly? no, certainly—as talented as he was, that if I could be as reckless and driven, as devout at the altar of the *tabula rasa*, I might even surpass him. No one had encouraged me the way Signora and Giovanni encouraged him, but I knew my work had comparable merit, so I assumed encouragement, or even mere attention, would come in time. And I kept working: even as I stared out that window while he painted me, in my mind I prepared the memory of value, of light and shadow, from which I would later do more work of my own. The three canvases that came from this long stare, I kept for a long time in storage: the same canvases that Giovanni would reject, dismissing them as "journeyman pieces," claiming they resembled arms of the Milky Way more than electric lights up and down the Arno and the autostrada winding alongside it. He had a point: I meant to draw out the resemblance. All he had meant was that he hadn't liked it: that it might be fine to show how nature may be explained by artifice, but taboo to show how artifice may take part in nature. He saw the point I meant to make; he considered it unsophisticated, that was all.

Dylan by contrast had more sophistication than felt entirely fair, and yet with it the disarming humility he showed in his process alone: he preferred learning to being noticed. He knew he could become so excellent that, fashionable tastes aside, one day no one whose opinion mattered could deny his skill and still keep a reputation for good judgment. That gave him a willingness to commit, to put himself under the total tutelage of one dead painter at a time, learning all he possibly could before moving on. He had—no, he gave himself, or he found for the taking, a freedom I had not known life offered: the freedom to choose a project and throw away hours detailing the foreground and perfecting the shadows. He would ponder and adjust for days, and it would look like a waste of time, until he pulled back and what you saw on the canvas was finer, richer, almost more real than reality.

I think again of when Dylan had first said to us that art was from the soul: after our first sight of the galleries of the Accademia, in that falling light struck by beauty, wounded by it. Beauty as those painters and sculptors had thought of it was an obsolete concept, we had been taught. Surely these Victorian stories of people hyperventilating and fainting at sight of the work of the old masters—fabulations, exaggerations. Fairytales. We knew we were blank slates, but even we were not so naïve as that. Nor were we locked into a Eurocentric canon: our professors had revealed the grandeur and power in art from Asia, Africa, South America—but all of it as history, not as a living thing. Yet there in Italy it had lived and breathed, and now I too had lived in proximity to it, had breathed it in and felt so nourished, so nurtured, by such air, I could have lived on it alone.

"Art is from the soul": any other day, Beatrice or I would certainly have challenged Dylan's statement—like him, she then believed in herself above all and, after that, in anything else you liked but only for a moment at a time. I believed at that time in nothing I couldn't taste, smell, see, hear, or touch. Strange to say for a child of the Bible Belt, I had grown up without church or religion. Adults had worked the word *soul* into our pinched dead days mainly as if it meant a common household supply, a commodity people kept around for its use or attraction: *needed a smoke so I banged on that ugly-ass brass door knocker a hers for mustabeen a good fi' minutes but there wadn't a soul inside.* My sisters would whisper "spirit" with wide eyes and surety, telling ghost stories around the fire pit at night. But most of all "God"—always that word, "God." God, as far as I could tell, was someone who damned things, bewilderingly also someone you thanked for it. So at that time, Dylan was probably the only one of us who really believed we had souls. Over drinks we would likely have fought him, loudly, stridently, gleefully: what better way to pass the time?—coy contrarians, as we all were then. But there on the Via Ricasoli, we couldn't deny him this flourish. We couldn't deny, just then, whatever rang joyous, resonant, full: our vision then had all the freshness, the clarity, of daylight.

Alongside this, and on a level with it, Dylan held an awareness, without anxiety, of the sweeping river of art history beyond him, of being carried in that river along with everything else in it—cave paintings, noisy installations, opaque curlicues of blown glass, tribal masks, ink prints, tapestries, bronzes, marbles—but he loved Western Renaissance painting best, and it showed in his work. His conformity to that tradition was itself a nonconformity. Where others would have buried it as a shame, he reveled in it, knowing it set him apart.

I obsessed over the same work, but I fought to hide the influence; I strove for startling postmodern effects and distortions, where his realism took detours into the magical but always in the service of a strict, demanding path toward clarity of light and line. A split had been introduced in my mind, a diversion of the river of my attention, and I couldn't account for the directions in which it now flowed.

Later, in a fit of self-disgust, I would destroy nearly all the canvases I had made while in Italy, under the twin enchantment of the distant past and of heated infatuation—everything except the three Milky Way autostrada-and-river pieces. Once the spell lifted, my churches and courtyards looked jejune, unpresentable. Under the kind of scrutiny Dylan's work was beginning to undergo, they wouldn't favorably compare, although they were the best things I had done all semester—the best work of my life up until then. They aspired to a plane beyond my technical skill; they demanded from me much more than I had learned to do yet with light. The harder I tried to render that vision, the more it crumbled like dry dirt under my hands. Before long all I wanted to do with it was clean it off.

All that time in Florence, meanwhile, Dylan never destroyed a canvas, never one sketch. That year he often painted at fourteen-hour stretches, took a class or two sponsored by Giovanni at a school next to the Accademia in a building that had once been a convent, produced work at an incredible rate. And everything Dylan did, he shipped back to New York pristine, to Giovanni's agent there, a sharp-eyed blond tower of competence named Andrew, a Michelangelo's David in a bespoke suit, who took care of everything. With his own hands Andrew unpacked Dylan's boxes, lined with waterproof layers of bubble wrap, sheets of archival paper tucked in the interstices; Andrew set things in motion, waited on Giovanni's instructions, called the gallerists and the reporters and the likeliest collectors in the order he was told, all the time saying again and again: "I just can't *believe* this kid: you have to look for yourself at what he's done. He's incredible. *Enfant terrible.* Expensive, sure, but my Lord, worth every penny."

When the sales began to speed up—first at art fairs, soon at competitive auctions gambling in favor of a brilliant future—when what happened for a painter no more than once or twice in a generation, if then, happened for Dylan, the only person whose voice registered any surprise—"Who'd have thought it would happen this fast?"—was Dylan himself.

That surprise lands in my ear again and again, whenever I doubt the life I chose, whenever I doubt my decision to discard my own work, doubt the reason for the disappointment in Signora's voice when she looked over my thin portfolio at the end of that spring semester— "What happened?" she demanded. "You do not deliver here on the promise of your earlier work. I know you are a better artist than this."

She pulled out a sketch Dylan had made of the Michelangelo Pietà and one I had done of the same subject, placed them side by side. "Do you see? Do you see? He has the essential form, he will never miss it, but you keep a greater faith with the truth of perspective. Only your work is always too light. He has the advantage only because he assigns value boldly. This is nothing more than maturity of eye. So he happens to have learned it sooner. But he is a perfect colorist not because he sees better than you do but because he shades better. Study the work he studied, don't be ashamed not to be fashionable. You will not lag behind him for long, not unless you mean to. Think of Caravaggio and Artemisia Gentileschi. She was not less capable, she may have been more so: and then consider what radical limitations she had to work against. Consider what she achieved despite them, because of them, because of her need to struggle. Can you justify, to yourself, doing less?"

Then she closed the cover of the broad manila folder, smudged with charcoal fingerprints, and looked me in the eyes.

"Don't tell me that boy *himself* has caused your attention so clearly to wander. Don't tell me he did *this*"—she smacked the folders on the table—"*and also* that"—gesturing wildly at my face, which was nakedly sunrise-smeared with ardor and abashment.

"No ma'am," I said, reverting to childhood habit. "I work harder when I'm with him because I want to be better than I am. I want to reach his level."

"You are at his level," Signora said, pronouncing each word richly. "Or would be if you would only work. If you won't see it, you won't see it. I cannot force you." *Pock* went the cane. "But whether you see or not, you must decide: Will you be a genius, or merely a genius's woman? Not many have both offered them. To choose the lesser honor is a proof you do not deserve the greater."

When I didn't respond, she had read my silence in her own way. She had said then only: "Well, you will choose what you want. I only hope you will want what you have chosen."

Many hours since then—while shivering in my air-conditioned office in the summer, or stripping off my cardigan in the heat there in the winter—while adding angelic swoops and maternal curves to corporate logos commissioned by men taking attitudes too brusque to be borne—while styling words in scrolling green script on leaf-decked posters for polluters—while choosing Pantone airbrush colors to flush models' faces and shimmer their flesh in advertising campaigns designed to deceive, by which I too have been deceived—I have tried whether the words will now ring right on my tongue: *You are a better artist than this.* I have whispered this to myself; have stood up, closed my office door, said Signora's words again, aloud: "You are better than this," hoping they still are, or ever were, true.

I wish I could have proved her right, but I did not then, and do not now, know how to account for my own coldness. Once we had burned, and our own heat and light had been enough. We could talk glowingly about the future without self-consciousness, could be drunk on sunlight: on the tangled strings of gold in Beatrice's copper Raphaelite curls, on the cobblestones glazed yellow, on Dylan's skin melted to bronze, on the burnt-orange tile roofs ablaze.

Struck by vision as though for the first time, we had had no idea how naïve we were—and if we had, it wouldn't have mattered to us. It was a rare golden wine we shared, this short-lived second innocence free-falling toward adulthood.

If the freedom we knew then was not freedom, but mere liberty, then what must real freedom be like?

VI

In the hotel room in Chicago, lit by the pallor of the halide lights ringing the harbor, I grieved the banking of that lost, early fire. The white light through the sheer Chicago hotel curtain liner, a chilling cocktail of LED and halogen, kept me awake much of that last night beside Dylan's sleeping form. Even after I pulled the heavy drapes shut, the glow seeped in around the edges, so that I fell asleep only toward dawn. When we both woke in full morning, when we repeated the caresses of the night before and whispered love to one another in unconsidered words, we did so with a sense of restoration to the living world. For a moment it felt as if no time had elapsed between this and the first morning we awoke entangled together in the Florence studio.

I wanted, in the moment, to believe that what felt so right was right, that we were not breaking any trust that had been placed in us. So badly did I want it to be true that I acted as though it were. Not until long after I found my mistake did I also know that those hours, those errors, were indelible.

I had not gone where I intended to go, had not stayed on the path I started out to follow. Are all lives subject to such bending, such distortion? The effort that, for Dylan, bloomed into creative work I had poured instead into survival: quiet fights to keep my corner seat under the klieg lights of his world. His energy ran along channels that had long since been built for him; I had the work of building the channels still to do.

Not that Dylan ever made me feel this on purpose. Rather he seemed to sense it in me and to avoid it with great delicacy, like a tree whose crown shyness causes it to shrink back from touching another's leaves. He ordered us room-service pastries and coffee; I wasn't hungry, he barely looked at it, the tray sat there dumbly at the foot of the duvet, its stainless service glinting. The surface of the milk in the pitcher trembled in concentric circles as he stepped around the room, gathering up his belt, pacing as he buttoned his shirt.

"Want to do the museums?" he said. He did not add *one last time* but we both knew the likelihood that this lurked under all the brightness. "Not the Institute again, don't worry. The Smart, the Driehaus, the Contemporary."

"Not the Cultural Center, please."

"Right, over-familiar. I hear the Mexican has some good things now."

Stop, stop, turn it back right here, don't let it go any farther. Don't let him have suffered; don't let us have lost this: the plea will not be answered. Or all its answer is contained already in the room with us.

*

That day my body felt like an overstuffed sandbag, as if my skin were strained and frayed burlap that at a touch could tear and cause my contents to spill. I put the feeling down to lack of sleep but I think now, too, I was—however absurdly—grieving. That day brimmed with finality: every act, every step the last of its kind. My mind operated like a camera with an out-of-focus lens. Fitfully I switched back and forth from foreground to distance, from panorama back to detail.

On the train, halfway to the Contemporary, Dylan changed his mind and said he wanted to visit the Adler Planetarium instead. He hadn't been since he was a child; the nostalgia of it would be a treat. "Are you up for that?" I said I was. We stepped off the train at the Eleventh Street stop, under a heartbreakingly blue sky puffed with cumulus clouds, and swung with long steps through Grant Park; as we traversed the Roosevelt Road underpass and then crossed the Ivy Lawn, my mind superimposed on the wide dark green quadrangles the cross-hatched wheaten grass of the meadow beside the green frame house in full view of Interstate 98, in Sepal, Mississippi, where I grew up. Instead of sunstruck smooth greenery well tended and watered, I saw for a moment yellow-leaved banana trees and scruffy unpruned azaleas beside rusted-out car bodies, a skeletal woodshed, stacks of tires half-covered by blue tarpaulins. I smelled, not the halations of decorative kale and coleus in landscaped beds, but instead the odors of that house: burnt cooking oil, motor grease, heating propane, mildew, sour wine, outgassing plastic. I felt suddenly dirty as though the scents must have melted into my sweat, must be rolling off my skin. I veered away from Dylan, loped a few steps to one side of the bright white walk.

"Hey, you okay?"

"Yeah, a little dizzy."

"You maybe shouldn't have skipped breakfast? You look like you saw a ghost."

"I kind of did. It's fine. I'll be better indoors."

We stood in line for tickets under the vast chilled dome. The abrupt absence of heat felt like a weight lifted out of burdened arms; I shivered.

"You're sure you're okay?"

"Fine. Totally. Stop it."

We wandered under the Welcome Gallery tunnel—arched PVC ribs, stretched white fabric through which shone the blended blue and purple glow of hidden bulbs—and into *The Universe: A Walk Through Space and Time*. The walls became multiple backlit screens shaped like rounded trapezoids. Galaxies and nebulae gleamed out at us. The floor glowed electric blue where we stood on a platform like a planet's ring. Dark green space, points of white light, danced on Dylan's face.

Here my vision doubled again. The light of the stars became the light of a white afternoon sky seen through pin oak leaves like polished jade; the light of the sky—one source, many points; one sun, many lights—became again the glossy page of an astronomy textbook I'd seen as a middle schooler, cutting class to hide in the library, to stare at all-absorbing images and to practice in my notebook endless contrast and form exercises out of Ruskin's *The Elements of Drawing*: *It is easy to draw what appears to be a good line with a sweep of the hand, or with what is called freedom; the real difficulty and masterliness is in never letting the hand be free, but keeping it under entire control at every part of the line.* I did Ruskin's exercises obsessively then; I didn't always do them well, at first I often did them badly, but the line on the page felt more real than my own face and hands felt to me, more like my body than my body, and the results taught me true things. I could see what had gone wrong and, sometimes, I could see how to make it right next time. In the best possible way, drawing had always made me disappear, made better things appear in my place.

From here we drifted under *Chicago's Night Sky*; I held a curiosity about the *Community Star* design studio but Dylan took one look and shook his head—"that's a busman's holiday for us," he said—so onward through *Astronomy in Culture* we ended up at a bank of brassy telescopes, with which Dylan confessed to a childish fascination.

"I mean what better thing could you possibly invent, if you happened to be an inventor," he said, gawking into one and then another. "The sheer expansion of vision. Imagine being able to see *that* in your mind's eye, much less to make a thing that can make it happen."

I wanted to enter into his obvious delight but, to my own disgust, felt my entire abdomen cramping. I found a bench and sat down, but didn't find that this helped: what I needed was not a bench but a trash can. The back of my throat stung with acid, my eyes with salt and embarrassment. But Dylan hadn't yet noticed. It was only when I tried to stand up and, instead, slid to the floor that he turned to see what was wrong. When helping me up proved pointless, he hovered there, unsure of what to do with his hands.

"I'm fine," I kept insisting, "I'll be fine."

"No you're not. No you won't. What do you need? What do I do? Let me think."

The security guard who discovered us at this point draped one of my arms over her own shoulder and the other over Dylan's. Like this, she scuttled us off to a back room where she handed me a bottle of water and a granola bar; when I couldn't keep that down, she pulled up the address of an urgent care clinic and wrote it off on a card.

"I strongly suggest you take her here," she said with a sternness to which Dylan, at last, responded with action. "Put her in a cab, young man. Don't you dare try to make her walk it on a day like this. She has a fever. What the hell, son."

Our last afternoon, then, passed not in absorbing culture but in restoring my body to equilibrium. At the clinic a Latina nurse with short licorice-painted fingernails first made me take a pregnancy test—"You never know at our age, we'd better rule it out"—and, satisfied to see the negative result, capably strung an IV line into the inner fold of my elbow. As she worked I read the name tag that dangled from a lanyard across her blue scrubs: *Aminta*, it read.

As the waters dripped into me, returning me to life, Dylan stared alternately out the window and at his phone, enthusiasm deflated. Our gazes floated past each other. Now that my systems had calmed down I found myself oddly homesick—not for my parents, whose lack, whose lapse, whose absence hung heavy on me without the power to absolve: nor for any of my sisters, who had worked as hard in their ways as I had in mine to make themselves absent from Sepal; but for Aunt Rachel, my rescuer, and for Richard, my best friend from the first two years of high school. At a word from Richard, I had decided to be a painter—had made the decision on the spot while driving along another sunstruck road, whirling down 98 in his reno-vated pickup, breathing the scents of the fields, clay and clover and foliage, drinking in the sharp fanged green of the kudzu vines and the red of the blooms that cropped out of the median, thick as fabric, thousands to the yard.

Richard had chosen that moment to ask me the question *What will you become?*, had been the first to believe I could do what I decided to do. *Don't matter how impractical. Dream.* When, drunk on color, I said *A painter* he said *Ahraight, less get you some art books then.* He had driven me to the university library in Hattiesburg, had used his brother's borrowed student ID to get us in and to check things out: *he won't mind, he's always in the lab, he said it's fine, you just can't lose anything 'cos the lost material fee's a hundred bucks.* Richard too had first taught me to read seriously for transformation, not just addictively for pleasure: he had strung a hammock between two pecan trees in the yard beside his ranch-style white house and, there ensconced, we had swung away whole weekends as we lost ourselves in the classics and in his favorites—Gordimer, Morrison, Butler, Le Guin. Good-humoredly in the hundred-degree heat he had, at my timid request, stripped off his shirt and permitted me to practice sketching him, the shades of his brown skin under the leaf-shadows a flawless study in contrasts. His mother, I know, looked out the window of her kitchen at our idyll and hoped I would marry him: but at that time, in that place, Richard was unlikely to marry anyone. We helped each other hide; like children we made a world set apart: it sheltered us, for a little while, just when we most needed shelter. Looking back I see a beauty in the reticence between us, the passionless closeness in which touch meant only comfort and safety, without a whisper of lust. The deep melancholy of our friendship lay not in its never becoming anything else but in our knowledge that we would so quickly outgrow it. We never talked about the place where we found ourselves, only about means of escape from it, an escape to which we promised to help each other even though it would mean losing each other in the end.

Since I was a child Rachel had been sending me and my sisters books and art supplies, for which Amanda and Alexis already considered themselves too old but which, for Anna and me, meant nourishment, nurturance. It was Rachel who had seen the promise in the full sketchbook I had so carefully mailed back to her and, seeing it, had saved me—she had taken me in, had allowed me to stay with her in New Orleans during my junior and senior years of high school, insisted I apply to a dedicated arts program near her university: *You need to see how people really live,* she wrote to me, *and you need to see that you can live this way too.* To my parents she made all explanations and, with their minimal help, all arrangements; to her brother, my father, she began a long impassioned telephone speech during one of his rare furloughs from work and rarer spells of sobriety.

He cut her off, saying only: "Good, she's fixing to find out the world ain't a cake walk, which is a damn sight more than they taught when I was in school."

Rachel, undaunted, sent me materials to prepare me for an on-campus interview in the spring and to help me make my first portfolio, a process that required all kinds of work, some of which I had never attempted before. Arts programs had been cut at my school since long before I entered there.

"I'm lost in all this," I told her on the phone, near tears. "It's beyond me, I don't have the training."

"Give it your best shot. If you don't get in you can just go to the public school," Rachel had told me. "That would be fine too. They have a good program, not like where you are now. But this is special, and you should work toward it. You have talent. You'd do well."

All I could do was try: and as it turned out, for this once my best effort proved enough; I was accepted into the program, and one weekend in August Richard picked me up from the green house at dawn. Within the hour we were on I-10 West and flooring it, the syrupy white-wine light pouring into the rear window as the sun rose behind us.

"Listen," he was saying in the truck, and I breathed in the clean smells of the camel-colored leather seats and the little yellow pineapple Christmas tree oscillating from the rearview and tried hard to focus on his voice, although the noise inside my head was deafening.

"I've changed my mind about becoming a writer," he was saying. "What we need ain't scribes and Pharisees but public servants. Doers, makers. People who can take the things we've understood in books and help make them real in the world. I may not achieve a vision the way Morrison did, a lonely vision that only relies on me to control it. But I can stop the world she described from being the world your children have to experience."

"Only mine? What about yours?" I teased.

"I won't have any. Unless I adopt."

"I won't either," I said. "I wouldn't adopt."

Without him, without her, where would I have been? Richard handed my box of books to Aunt Rachel, handed me my rolling suitcase, kissed me on the forehead, and drove himself back to Sepal, from where he called every Saturday of that school year to see how I was doing although he himself was sinking, that year, under different pressures. Rachel made me coffee while I studied, cleared a table for my projects. She lent me her suit and bought me my plane ticket when the time came for me to fly to Chicago, where I won the scholarship allowing me to study at the Art Institute. In Rachel's apartment, in her front room that was library and study and living area rolled together, I had torn open my award letter and then as violently wedged it into her copy of *The Song of the Lark*, as if otherwise it might spontaneously catch fire or turn into a lizard or a bunch of zinnias in my hand.

What did Dylan know of all this? I had made a point of guaranteeing he would never see it. I had put on an air of confident deserving, secure belonging, in his world: a sleight of hand, a front, my only masterwork. Then I had felt sore with him for not protecting me: why, how, from what? Why should I have wanted to place this burden on him?

Aminta came back in at this stage to check the IV bag, now nearly drained. She took my temperature, which had dropped to its ordinary level, and handed me a juice box and a small foil packet of trail mix.

"You're going to be fine," she said. "If you keep this down for an hour, we can let you go. Just please head home after that and sleep it off, okay? You should be fine in the morning, but if not, call us."

This, coupled with the test, called up another afternoon when Aunt Rachel had taken me to a clinic downtown in New Orleans. There another nurse—I recall, distantly, her bulky body wrapped by magenta scrubs—had handed me a purple leaflet and a round pink packet and a stiff lecture about coming back regularly for more. The message came through, crystal, although the words the nurse used were other: *You aren't ordinary. Your body isn't to be allowed to do what ordinary bodies do. You are special, fragile, so much so that the outcomes of love are likely to destroy you. This chemical is the condition of your freedom.*

By the time we were released from urgent care, it was after five. The restaurant was in midtown; to reach it we would have to take a crosstown cab at rush hour, meaning fifty dollars at least. Dylan argued that, in view of my condition, we should skip the dinner with his parents—"I'll text them, say you're not up for it."

"Then would you go alone?"

He shrugged. "Maybe."

"Oh no. Don't do that. I haven't forgotten." Elaine had never shown much restraint where Dylan was concerned, and Allen looked on powerless to defuse their conflicts.

"Don't worry," he said, "please."

"No, I want to come with you. I genuinely feel fine now. And look, it's hardly even hot out anymore. Feel that breeze off the water." So, as we were, we picked up another taxi—which, over my protests, Dylan also paid for—and met his parents for dinner. I hoped that under the kaleidoscopic light of the Chihuly lamps they would not recognize yesterday's coffee-colored wrap, now stale and creased from its night on the floor, its day on the town. What I could not as easily hide was the shiny striated tape at the crease of my elbow where the IV went in earlier.

At the table with its black cloth I sat watching the man I had given myself to, this morning and last night and years ago, casually ignoring me while methodically shredding the red plastic straw from his gin and tonic. He bent the straw in half until it forms sharp corners in the middle, which then split at the points. Then he teased the splits apart slowly with his fingertips until he had two red half-cylinders, which he finally straightened and then fit one inside the other, painstakingly, as if it mattered, as if the fidget were a necessary precursor to a masterwork. His parents passed the window with exaggerated, tandem waves, about to sit down with us any second.

Our link to one another was nothing we could have walked out of; we'd have had to leave our bodies to escape it. It was not love, not as such, nor lust, nor was it still conflated, as it once was for me, with transcendence. I know no word for what it was. I had better not try to give it one. But I cannot pass it off with a stock phrase, either. I cannot and could not say that "it is what it is." It was not what it was; that was the problem.

"I think I'm done in New York," he was saying. "It's lost its energy for me."

"Lost its energy," I knew, was Beatrice's phrase. The phrase carried her complex fragrance in it, orange flower and amber. And yet this scrap of argot could have fallen from the lips of anyone inhabiting the grid. Complaining about one's geographical privilege was a time-honored local tradition in her city, their city, no longer mine.

So I shrug: "Then why don't you move? It shouldn't be too hard to do; you can work from wherever you want. Travel might even be good for the work at some point."

"I think I would do it, if not for my studio space. Giving up that studio might honestly kill me. It's the cellar where things mature, my country, my home, my whole place in this world, you know? The only place I really feel real."

"You must hate touring, too, then."

"As glad as I am to be here with you . . . I do hate touring. Yeah, I have to admit it. I'd much rather have you with me there—have everyone travel to me instead of having to travel to them."

"Mm. That would suit you."

"I'll try it sometime."

A change in the light caused us to look toward the door. The Fieldings had finally walked in, their faces closed off like windows. They traversed the mirror-bright silver tile, their shadows long in front of them.

"I'm covering the check," Dylan said before either of his parents had a chance to jump at a word.

"I had some doing at the front of the house to convince them you were waiting a table for us," Elaine crossed over him, her voice carrying. Dylan's form followed his father's, but his expressions took more part in hers: their insistence, their intensity. "Why don't you ever answer your phone?" she demanded.

Allen grinned and gripped his son's shoulder without speaking. A look of complicity passed between them: *Don't respond, it only encourages her.* Where Dylan's hands rested at his sides with a shape and strength unattainable other than by constant work, I noticed, Allen's gangled around him: flat, protracted, spidery, undisciplined, like the daddy-longlegs of childhood, the spindly things that liked barn corners and crawl spaces. Harvestmen, we called them: daddies.

"You look tired, son," Allen said. Dylan squinted: close to imperceptible, but I caught it.

Elaine sidled around our table, insinuated herself into a chair next to me. Allen sat down on the other side of her. We ran through the business of fanning out menus, laying napkins across laps, snapping utensils crisply down on to the table. I followed, half a beat behind, still after all this time in their world afraid of missing a cue.

Elaine noticed the crimped tape at my elbow: "What happened, are you well?" When I explained, she didn't respond, only nodded:

"Mm." Went on to say: "Well, this is cozy." To laugh at her own inane remark: a sound as irritating as an itch inside a zippered boot in winter. In spite of her hygienic grin the laugh rang out throttled, hyenic.

More drinks arrived and, soon, platters of tapas. While we handed things around, Dylan explained his plans to his parents in a curt yet rambling way, though as I watched him spin his fork and stir the ice in his tea with the long-handled spoon, I did not feel sure how much of the truth was on offer:

"We'll be gone for months. The usual places, all up and down both coasts. I can't say how long where and when. My agent has all that down. And my new assistant too, Daniel; Omar's just told me he's planning to move on; that's for the best. Best to keep moving, always, I think. Change is inevitable, so cause it, don't let it catch you, you know? Be mover, not moved?

"Which reminds me; we're shaking things up with this tour; we're spending some time in the South—Houston, New Orleans— doing charity events, donating the proceeds to disaster relief. People really don't know how much suffering there still is, after Katrina. So it's important work. I'll be glad to get home, though. We're back in New York for good by the new year."

He said *home*, meaning New York, with force and intention. At the show last night, in a passing remark, a dealer on her way out the door had called New York "home" to them both. Same word, same place, yet Dylan resisted it then. In this conversation he embraced it, declaring his defiance with it. Home isn't where you are, was the implication: it's wherever I choose to call it. What was more, he couldn't be both returning to live in New York and not returning there to live: he was hiding some intention, whether from them or from me—or from himself.

As at the show the previous night, I felt a surge of compassion for his parents. Dylan's sudden switchbacks and reversals compelled me, in that moment, to sympathize with them against their difficult son.

Though I love him I must admit he was wholly impossible: touchy, standoffish, conformist in the very act of making the most cliché choice of all: rebellion. Golden child or no, he was not immune to the pleasure of fulfilling negative expectations. Yet to be fair, he could be so much more than he ever showed himself to be in his parents' presence: and it was this *so much more* that I loved, this *so much more* whose possibility allowed me to believe in a corresponding *much more* in myself.

His parents, too, could prove more than they appeared here. This night, though, everyone looked too tired to feign. In the absence of risk, consequence, or external conflict, with nothing left to gain and nothing against which to unite, Dylan's parents had turned on each other. Allen looked at Elaine with a lift of the mouth that said *What do you expect, dear, you smothered him.* Elaine's face lowered like a hot-air balloon crumpling into a field: *Don't accuse me, I'm the victim of you both.* The sight of their faces lingered behind my eyelids, a photographic negative, during the ensuing conversation about the Fieldings' summer house in Maine, whether they would finally sell it or instead raise the fees for renters. During this I moved my share of the ceviche they had ordered around my plate in its pool of lime juice, watching little translucent flecks detaching themselves and floating in the liquid. I couldn't bring myself to place another piece in my mouth.

After Dylan sent back the check, Elaine produced from her handbag four tickets to a comedy show. "Surprise," she said, with a little smile. *I'm trying*, said the smile, sustained with some effort. *Recognize my goodwill*, her eyebrows asked, double-checking our faces.

Dylan said nothing, only pushed his chair back and walked out ahead of the rest of us.

We all ascended the parking garage and climbed in the Fieldings' car to submit to two and a half hours of forced hilarity, marked at first by a classroom discomfort of mandatory participation that was then, slowly, replaced by a mild glow of martinis and making the best of it. By watching the two or three best performers—and murmuring wry asides to Dylan, out of his parents' earshot, about the whole experience—I found it even possible to enjoy.

Outside, afterward, the sun had nearly finished sinking behind the city. Rose and orange light reached the street in front of the theater, bent down with color like one of Millet's women, gleaning the last benefit that could be wrung from the day.

The Fieldings drove us back to my apartment, speaking scarcely a word.

"We'll just leave you two alone, shall we," said Allen jovially, evoking cringes from both Dylan and me. There would be many more dinners, later, with Elaine and Allen in Chicago, but Dylan would never show up for a single one of these; his absence would fill the dining room of the cavernous house in Glen Ellyn, not the house of his early years but of his adolescence, a place of storms and surges, the first act of the drama. I would listen to the Fieldings reminisce about his idyllic solo childhood of Waldorf schools and watercolor paints, and I would feel that I might as well not be in the room, for all their talk held any relevance for me. I would be no more than a reliquary for their loss.

But there would be no repetition of what happened at the hotel on the river: that was the last time Dylan and I would ever spend together as lovers. Very few lovers, very few friends had ever been inside my Chicago apartment, merely one more fire escape up one more low brown wall—the place, which embarrassed me, was no New York *home*. Not that I had never asked anyone else in, never chased after mere sensation: but at no other time had I known that same tenderness as in the small room in Florence, when almost more thrilling than giving him the freedom of my body was receiving the vision of his form, the exquisite long line of his back a river of ivory, all that I could see of him as he hid his face in the hollow between my collarbone and my shoulder and pressed his lips to my neck. Never again the same totality. Not again, not here, not like this.

We stood on the curb saying our goodbyes. When he left in a taxi for O'Hare, it was the last I would see of him for more than five years. I did not know then that what we had done together had had its own permanence, that its ghost would occupy my body indefinitely. Certain things can't be known until they are lived.

VII

In the garden the cold has deepened. Thomas Augustine shifts uncomfortably on the rock wall. Speech has failed: his breath comes in uneven bursts. His panic frightens me; I hide my distress in the hope of soothing his. But I hide badly.

"Hey. Hey. That's okay. Everything's going to be okay. Don't worry, don't try to say it again right now. Tell me again how you decided to stay here."

That story is easier; he has hinted at it in his letter to me, he must have told it in depth so many times by now. His face changes shape, relaxes into its old assurance: "I painted my way in. People talk about painting themselves into corners. I painted myself out of one. I thought I was only making images until I realized I believed in the power of the images I was making. And I didn't believe that power was coming from me."

"What are you working on now?"

"I'm learning to make frescoes, or canvases that mimic them. I'm spending a lot of time in the library, studying Fra Angelico. It's incredible work. The scope, the size. The sense of completeness. It's so different from the Renaissance. I could sit with it forever."

"Still. Art is one thing. All the rest of this"—I wave my hands: tonsure, habit, guesthouse, high wall, pavilion, cypresses—"doesn't fit with who you were when I knew you."

"I changed slowly. I thought I didn't believe until I realized I did."

"But—everything?"

"Everything, of course, how else?"

"Don't you reject the . . . the attitudes?—do we really have to spell out . . . all the problematic—?"

"It looks like we do."

I try again. "You've adopted a whole system here, one that places you outside the pale in several important ways. Also that places you outside its pale."

"That isn't how I'd put it. Not at all. That's not the truth. The truth is—complicated. And simpler than we make it."

"So you'd say you've been, what, accepted the way you are?"

"More. Loved the way I am. Called, the way I am."

"I'm not sure how it's different."

And here he breaks down.

"This is where I learned that God considers me worthwhile. Worthy of learning to live a vision. A vision—"

And then he tells me what was done to him, and by whom, and I no longer know anything. And I'm not the first to know it either, this nothing, this darkness he has had to face alone. He had had to tell someone, because he had been bleeding. Afterward. He hadn't known even this at first. He had had only a bit of trouble walking, had thought he was fine until he returned to his cell where he had started shaking, trembling, and couldn't stop. Collapsed. Had discovered his wound, had had to find someone to help him: the need to tell had followed from that. Otherwise, he says, he would have kept it to himself.

"Everyone here has been kind," he takes care to say. "It wasn't anyone who lives here who did it."

"Who did—"

I am slow to comprehend what must have been done, for him to be saying these things. When it breaks on me I don't move my body, don't show my shattered face, don't give any hint of what the truth does inside me. I hold my breath. Any word, any motion could prove the wrong one, could stop the emergence of the things he needs to say. I listen, and am too surprised to speak, in discovering how deeply his pain can still hurt me: in finding out, in this way, of all ways, after this long, how much, how completely, I still consider him *mine*. My own grief and his pain fall silently into me together, like plumes of ink that sink down and bloom through clear water.

So I keep my eyes on his face, steady, as he speaks, as he looks not at me but at his own finely wrought hands, which clench and wring the cloth of the habit over his knees. Over and over they let the fabric go, crumple and then clutch again as if for safety. Only after I am sure all the words are out, only after he has stood up as if to walk away and then has changed his mind and sat down again in the mulch, careless now of what happens to the white garment, do I feel it is safe for me to move too. I slide down off the wall to sit beside him, still an arm's length away, in the empty flowerbed.

"I'm so sorry that happened to you."

"It never should have. I know that."

"You still want to stay?"

"Where else would I go?"

"Anywhere. Away. Dylan. Let's leave now. Come on." I clamber up, lift one foot over the garden wall as if to make for the horizon, as if we could escape so simply.

He shakes his head, shuts his eyes. "This is where I want to be."

"I wonder. Is wanting enough here?"

He holds his arms out to either side of himself. "Where would I go to get away from where it happened? My body is where it happened. I could leave the monastery, but I can't leave—this. No—I could, but I won't. It isn't that I haven't thought about it."

"About—"

"Exactly what you think. But I promise you I won't ever do it. It wouldn't be a real means of escape."

"You don't have to promise me. Promise your God instead."

His eyes close on their own as he retreats into some inner room of his mind where I can't follow him. Yet his face in the moonlight radiates honesty without precedent, and humiliation, and self-consciousness, and—can that be pleasure?

"It means more than you know," he says, "that you think I'm capable of keeping a promise."

"I really do. But how could your superiors doubt that, only because this happened to you? Do they think it would make you less able to—keep the vows, to live the life?"

"You're right. You're right. They don't. Shouldn't. It was just my body that was hurt. Only my body. Not my ability to will—not my *integrity*, not that. So I think I could convince them . . . They need to know . . ."

"Slow down. You're okay now."

"I mean you know . . . " He begins to stare at his hands again and then to clench his eyes. He stands up, paces across the flagstones and back, a tight circuit. We are not visible from the main enclosure here, so I must think the tightness is a function of his inner state, not of any risk we might incur. The night wind sweeps freely over us, rustles the branches, shakes their incongruous fragrance about.

"It was terrible. I know."

"I would never. I would never—But they'll think I—"

I hold my hands out to him, but he doesn't take them, doesn't see them.

"It's over now. It's over. You're going to be okay."

He sits back down on the wall too, the same as before, within arm's reach but only just. He brushes at the mulch on the habit. Brown specks of grit cling to the weft of the smooth serge.

"They think that—that the priest who did it—I mean . . . They think that he stole my file. My records. That he used what he found there to. To make his decision. About who to target. Who to pick off. And I don't think that's true but I don't know how to explain. Why I think that."

"What are you saying?"

"The superiors think I was a target because of what I'd already gone through, what I'd done before. Because of all that, he thought I would be an easier. . ." I supply, in my mind, the word *victim*, which Thomas Augustine won't or can't say. A small noise escapes his throat before he goes on. "And I know that isn't true. For one thing, it's not true that the only ones this happens to are like me, with a past like mine. Not by a long shot. Sometimes it's the best who are chosen, who are stolen—only because they're the purest, the brightest, and the Devil hates them for that, hates that light. But that's not why I was. Picked out. Chosen. It was because a long time ago I had been having these . . . I mean you know. Omar. Giovanni. And the ones before, the ones you know about. He knew, too: he already knew about all of it. And . . . he said, if I didn't do what he wanted, that he would tell everyone here. Not only my directors. Everyone. All of it. And I said *but that's not who I am.* And he said *but it's what you were.*"

But *secrets don't keep in the cloister*: how has this escaped notice for so long? Will it be much longer before everyone knows everything we are saying here, now?

"Where did all this happen?"

"He pulled me into one of the parlors."

"Pulled you?"

"By the arm. Whispering *Don't shout.*"

Had closed the door behind them. Had asked for something. Demanded it. Here Dylan, Thomas Augustine, stops telling me, stares at his own beautiful hands again. Clasped in his lap. A statue.

"Asked for . . . ?"

"I can't say what. Even to you. You know everything I've done. But all that's over. I've started fresh. But this was. I can't. I'm sorry."

He starts to tell it again: Someone had pulled him into a parlor. Had shut the door quietly. Had asked for, then had demanded, an act Thomas Augustine had not wanted and wouldn't name.

"And then?"

"Asked again. I was like you are now. Couldn't say anything.

Then I said *no. Of course no.* I said *I came here not to do those things. No matter what.* Especially not—well. No matter what."

Thomas Augustine takes a breath.

"At first he tried to persuade me. Said that . . . it would be an act of love. I said *Not here. Not like that.* And he said *Oh, so you do still believe it was an act of love when you did it out in the world.* I said *Who told you what I did?* He said *That's not important.* I said *Well, it wasn't. It isn't.* He said *Isn't what?* I said *Isn't love.* And then. He . . . started saying other things. Offensive things. I don't want to repeat those either. Then he threatened me. Said that if I didn't agree he would lie to the novice master and say I had anyway. He said he would say that it had been my idea. My initiative. And he'd be believed. Because he was . . . well, he was someone of importance. And I was no one, just some *recovering prima donna,* some *flaming attention whore.* His words. But if I said yes, then he'd cover for me. Lie for us both. By then I thought he was lying about everything anyway. I went for the door but he got my arm behind my back. Twisted it. Pushed me down, pushed. Up against me. Said: *I'm not going to take you. Not now. But I want you to know that I can if I want. And when I want.*"

He inhales raggedly.

"And then he said."

Don't move, don't speak, don't look away.

"He said." The breath is torn apart. "He said *you know what. Yeah. I think I will.* And I kept saying *no. No no no no.* And he kept saying *Yes.* Hushing me: saying *stop it,* saying *shh, just say yes.* And—*The universe doesn't run without our saying yes.*"

And the lie had been inside him, the truth had been torn apart and had littered the floor of the parlor. Falsehood pooled there, spent.

"Then he let me go and stood up. Walked around me, opened the door. Spat in front of me. And left."

I hold him there with my eyes alone, which finally meet his but oh God: what there is in them.

"I'm sorry. I have to ask. You said it wasn't someone who lives here. Who, then?"

Thomas Augustine collects himself as best he can and goes on:

Into one of the early independent shows Giovanni had arranged for Dylan—a show in a tiny gallery, a parquet-floored, jewel-box room walled all along its outer border with plate glass windows, in Chelsea—there had wandered a handsome, sad-eyed priest in a well-tailored clerical suit, not more than halfway through his thirties. Despite the open bar, almost no one else had showed up that night and so the priest and Dylan had sat on a red-leather cushioned bench talking and drinking for two and a half, three hours. It had come out that the priest was, not unlike Beatrice, the child of a wealthy Manhattan family, in his case *nouveaux-riches* financial traders who, in a year or two, would lose almost everything in the market crash. But at the time the young priest had had, besides a modest salary from his diocese, an inheritance from his parents. It was, as he said, "burning a hole in his pocket." The priest had his portfolio index, monthly stipend, charitable donations all set up by brokers, automated, for him. He had no decisions to make, no difficult calculations constantly demanding recalibration between his own needs and those of others. All his life, the priest said, he had had all his wants met, all his doors opened for him. Now he had begun to search for new goals, new glories he could pursue, could attain, in the world.

The priest then confided to Dylan—in a murmur, as if this were the deepest secret of all—that he himself had started to paint, a bit, in a sun porch off the back of the rectory, in a furtive desultory way. He had placed a few pieces in church-basement gallery shows but spoke yearningly of never achieving the level he saw on the walls all around him—"if I had started earlier. Never now." He then spoke movingly to Dylan about the motivations of his art, the things he saw. The beauty, the clean lines of the human form. The interplay of parts, the textures and the colors of the different kinds of skin. "A phenomenology of the body," he'd called it.

The priest's eyes had shone like sea-spray, glazed with the effects of wine. When the handlers came to turn off the lights, the two men had exchanged business cards, but Dylan had never followed up.

After that Dylan had seen the priest over and over at his events and openings but had not exchanged more than ten words with him, had not known what was building between the black-draped shoulderblades, had seen no more than the wistful cleanshaven face staring up at the smooth cheek of a Virgin or the complex musculature of a male nude.

By the time Dylan had taken to reading Thomas Merton in secret he had begun to see the priest's repetitive presence before his canvases as a visible sign, a silent vocable expressing the direction he already so wanted to take. Dylan had not known how to call it what it was. He had not followed the pattern of the purchase manifests as Giovanni had done. Giovanni could have told Dylan what he had seen, if Dylan had wanted to know, if Giovanni had thought it meant anything: which, and how many, of Dylan's own canvases the priest had begun to collect. Figure studies, self-portraits—not devotionals. Dylan had never imagined needing to reach for the journalist's word *stalker*, had had no realistic frame of reference for such a thing. The lines of casual talk that could be unobtrusively followed up after Dylan's disappearance to trace him to Our Lady of the Pines, the stay that could so easily be arranged, the willingness to exploit the monks' rule of hospitality, all spoke of questions Dylan had never thought to ask: some that ought to have been asked and weren't; some that never should have had to be.

*

Before dawn the next morning, the monks, and Thomas Augustine safely back in their company, have begun to pray. Vigils and lauds and then Mass and private devotions. A cutout quarter-sheet schedule on the guestroom desk describes this strenuous intensity to me when I wake.

While it is happening, though, I retreat to my solitary room and throw myself into sleep as heavily as a pregnant woman: as though the confidences of the night before, the words spoken, were taking living root in my body, entwining with my veins blood vessels of their own. An electronic bleat wakes me at length: phone alarm, loathsome cargo. I roll out of bed, dress, and brush my hair in a blurred state of body and mind.

Check the time: 9:17. My meeting with the prior is scheduled to begin in thirteen minutes. The place is like clockwork, Thomas Augustine had said, the way the ocean is clockwork: the hours are tides, the prayers waves. I had better be on time. I pull on yesterday's jeans, sniff the sweater—it won't do—and sort through the suitcase for another garment. What was I thinking when I packed? The place is freezing cold; these knit shirts, thin as paper. I layer two of them, hide my neck in my thick outdoor scarf, and throw on my coat again.

Last night's conversation made this much clear: we no longer share even one assumption about the world as we find it. I thought we had shared those perceptions, once long ago, but now I know we must be seeing different images, hearing different sounds. How he can have suffered so and still believe in any benign providence, I can't credit: unless there is a strain of music, a rhythm, he can pick up on, that is inaudible to me? More likely he has invented music to fill a silence that has become too unbearable. Dylan the fabricator, make-believe maker of glory where none has ever existed.

Even more so now, he will have to invent brighter and brighter lights to contrast the molesting darkness, still more music to counter so much silence. It must all be his own invention: otherwise everyone would see it, would hear it. And, clearly, so few do.

There is not even a moment to prepare for the conversation ahead, a conversation *how can I have*, and I am so far beside myself already that I fear what might come out of my mouth. In my anger I could cause real damage. I am in a mood to slash something, smash something.

A little hand-drawn map, scratched for me yesterday on the back of a brochure by the extern who serves the guests' meals—Brother Michael, he told me to call him—shows the shortcut to the prior's office. The map leads me through an arched foyer and through a pair of doors. These doors open on a smaller hall, lit with fluorescent tubes, carpeted in a mauve industrial rug once woven into tight loops by a machine and now worn down into grey paths by decades of steps in none too clean shoes. The air in this closed-off back route smells stale.

Yet in the offices themselves, although the overhead lights are switched off, the high windows stand open. They let in morning light and a fresh breeze with the grassy haymaking fragrance of late harvest time.

Four metal teacher's desks hunch against the walls, one to each corner of the large room in which I stand. Each desk bears its own burden: Pisa-like stacks of files, magazines, scholarly journals. Behind one of the desks, there perches a monk in a denim habit—another extern. Under a circle of lamplight he sits, studying some sort of document in a comb-bound booklet. His rectangular glasses give him a look of focus, but the oddly cropped and angled disorder of his bristly white hair suggests abstraction. He sits cross-legged in an armless office chair; his bare feet must be hidden somewhere under him, as his empty Birkenstocks peek out from under the desk. A ginger cat is curled on the carpet next to them, flicking its tail.

The monk looks up and smiles in a way that appears impersonal, unfocused, before he really sees me. As he registers my appearance, the monk's smile gains both specificity and reserve. Despite the white hair, his face looks young, his shoulders wide. He nods at me, tilts his head toward a polished glass door painted with gold letters bordered in black that read *Spiritual Direction*. Then he turns his eyes back to his reading.

The glass door, like the doors of certain old-fashioned shops, is rigged with a bell that rings as the door opens: no need to announce myself.

"Welcome," says a voice, lower in timbre than I had expected. Dylan's voice is on the tenor side, with a hint of the shifting upper Midwest in its vowels. This voice, the prior's voice, sounds broad and warm.

"I'm Father Isaiah." His wide hand is heavy with large bones and long muscles: a former athlete's hand. "Nice to meet you."

I receive the handshake. The prior is not as old as I might have expected: forty, forty-five: sandy tonsure, agreeable face, straight white teeth, bright hazel eyes. When Thomas Augustine tells me later that Fr. Isaiah acts happiest in the work shed, breaking rocks with a sledgehammer—the wall we sat on together, Fr. Isaiah had prepared and built himself—this will make sense. He gives a first impression of energy well spent, the freshness in the air after the discharge of lightning.

His desk does not sit between us; he takes a chair in front of a small writing table, flush with the wall, piled high with work. His conference chair was once a luxury, may have been a gift from a benefactor, the web of its high mesh back arched, elegant. Now the black foam armrests are cracked and sealed with fraying duct tape. No computer is in evidence—or, wait, what is that heavy long cord plugged into?—yes, a dated black laptop nearly an inch thick, folded shut and pushed to the side, buried under another stack. In one corner of the desk, also crammed about with papers, there crouches a faded blue landline phone with a rotary dial and spiral cord. Bracketed shelves crammed with books layer the walls above the desk, three or four lines of them, like a professor's office.

I sit down in a green upholstered guest chair, its fabric shiny with age. I expect dust and must to plume up, but smell only furniture polish.

Father Isaiah's wide grin narrows a bit. "So. The visiting artist. You've been friends with Thomas Augustine since college."

"Friends, yes. For a while there was more to it."

"So he told me. So you know him well? I mean as a person: his thinking, his way of being in the world?"

"I used to. It's different now."

"Of course. Five years will change a lot of things."

"Especially these five years." Will Fr. Isaiah take this as an opening? It occurs to me for the first time that I don't know who else knows what happened in the parlor. Nor has Thomas Augustine told me who I may tell and who I should not. I didn't think to ask. It didn't occur to me that I might need to know.

"What have you been up to since the two of you last saw each other? If you don't mind my asking. I wouldn't suppose you did mind, but I don't want to do your supposing for you." His hazel eyes reshape themselves into good-natured crescents. Crow's feet already lurk at the corners; the skin is weather-worn, but in a healthy way, the freckled tan of a pale blond who escapes to the outdoors at every possible opportunity.

"Oh, you know, working, mostly?" I stare at my own hands, which fidget mindlessly with the air, and force myself to still them. "I don't really want to talk about myself." I laugh, although I'm not joking.

Father Isaiah still doesn't speak, although his face softens. He nods his head. Without turning away, he retrieves from among the detritus of his desk a small box of tissues, which he places without looking on a stack of papers near me, in default of anywhere else to rest it.

"You're a good friend to come all this way," he hazards.

"I'm not sure that's true—although maybe I'm not the best person to judge." The word *judge*, as it emerges from my lips, plants itself in front of me, squared off in a fighting stance: spoken last night, accusative; spoken just now, conciliatory. I walk my concession backward: "But then again, I'm not saying anyone has a right to judge me, either."

"I'm not here to judge anyone."

Still, my anger finds an angle, emerges like an asp in sarcasm:

"Right, because your beliefs are so nonjudgmental."

Father Isaiah declines this opening to debate, although a wry look crosses his face. Before he speaks I'm certain he is about to quote the Bible at me or to deliver some kind of sermonic rebuke, jocose or barbed or both, but instead what comes out is a change of subject, a complete redirection.

"Tell me about your family," he says.

"This isn't therapy," I rejoin.

"No, of course . . . if you'd rather not, it's fine. Mind if I ask where you grew up?"

"I thought I was here to tell you about D . . . about Thomas Augustine."

"Yes, he would have told you so. You aren't the first of his old friends he's written to, asking for advice."

"Advice?"

"Yes, he must be desperate for that, to be setting up clandestine appointments in the dark. There wasn't any need for that, by the way. He could have invited you to the parlor, even during his retreat, if he could establish a proportionate reason. The fact that he tried to circumvent the process like this makes me more concerned about him. To be frank, it gives credence to concerns I would rather wish away. If he had simply asked for permission he would probably have been granted it. Now, even if he asks, he may not."

Am I losing my ability to read people, or is Fr. Isaiah on the point of laughing at me? No, but his eyes glimmer: I suspect him of not taking me seriously. A rush of heat floods my ribs. I am sure he is judging us both, all the time, as he swivels in that dilapidated chair. Or—equally possible, and which would explain even more—he is out of his depth in this office. Promoted to the level of his incompetence, surely.

"We haven't really been able to make him understand that the decision on whether he makes permanent vows won't be influenced by others from outside. It's ultimately his own decision. But equally it's the decision of the community, of the group of monks who take the responsibility for leading. The junior director, the novice director, the superior."

These adverbs in his mouth—*ultimately, equally*—fall like blocks dropped on a marble floor. The nouns crash: *director, superior*; thud, thud.

"But we need good information, we need context," he goes on, "in order to make good decisions. We try to take the whole truth about each person into account."

Check your bias, whispers Beatrice in my brain, and I concede her point. I see people like Fr. Isaiah as part of the problem—any problem, every problem. At least some of my shock at having seen Dylan wearing the same drapery, the same disguise, comes from this juxtaposition.

I allow that Fr. Isaiah's *biases*, if that word is generous enough to hold the angles at which we look at things, could be heavier than mine, less consciously examined, less skeptical about their own tilt. Behind that half-smile, the rest of him disappears, leaving only the optimistic line behind. I don't lend the slightest credence to the ideas on which he has staked his whole life—strictures and structures; limitations, prohibitions; prescriptions and perditions; walls, fences, gates. Ascetic practices. Cells. And anyway none of these fortresses, none of these strongholds, has had any success in keeping Thomas Augustine safe. What then are they worth?

"What are these 'concerns' being raised? Do you think he'll become another predator if he stays—because he was raped here? Is that what this is about?"

Fr. Isaiah's face drops open with shock. "That never crossed my mind. Not once. I didn't know anyone outside the monastery knew what had happened to him."

"It's crossed his mind, believe me. He's afraid of it. That he could do to someone what was done to him. I don't think he should be; I don't think you should be: I know him. He's capable of hurtful actions, but not that kind; he's not that kind of person deep down. But his mind has been devastated by this. Can you do something for him? What can you do? I've never seen—"

A tap on the glass, the note of the bell. The doorway reveals the blue habit of the white-haired young extern with the hipster glasses. He holds out a slip of single-folded paper to Fr. Isaiah, who reads it and nods once.

"Could you please go tell them I'll be right there, Joseph?" he says to the extern, and then tips a regretful smile toward me, a full one this time.

"I'm sorry, but I'm needed right away. I'm glad to have met you. I hope we'll have the chance to talk again before you go," Fr. Isaiah says. "It's important, this conversation. I really do want the opportunity to continue it. Please forgive me for leaving so abruptly." His eyes squeeze shut.

"How can we just leave this here?"

"I'm afraid it's unavoidable," Fr. Isaiah says, shaking his head. "I can't say more. I wish I could. Please know we're doing all we can."

And with this, I know he knows what I know. What good can knowing do, when emptiness is the thing known?

The young prior shakes my hand again, no less warmly than before. We walk out together and, as he slips through the enclosure door, I pass instead through the musty outer office, the fluttering curtains, the double glass doors that lead outside.

Over a sere lawn, down a wide white gravel path that leads away from the monastery, a natural dell sinks to the edge of a small pond whose water, in the low light, is the color of slate, slashed with lines of lighter grey.

Beside the pond, on a large cleared oval of mulch, stands a new and overly polished Shaker bench with some donor's name affixed to the back on a brass plate. A yellow gingko, each leaf shaped like a minute umbrella, arches over the bench.

I stand staring across the yard while the late November sun

behind smooth silver cloud cover flickers, gutters, and goes out like a citronella candle in a tin bucket.

VIII

Signora would say to us, so often: *ars longa vita brevis*: life is short, art lasts. She said nothing about the brevity of art, the terrible futility of the beautiful: its helplessness before the teeth that tear it, the slough of entropy that swallows it down.

Layer after layer of pretense lies plastered over both of us. I want to take a palette knife to it all, scrape it down to the threads. Start again, start again. If there is anything I can still do for Thomas Augustine, it may be not so much a matter of what I can build as of what I can break down. Which means I am not who he most needs now.

*

The women's guesthouse, where I will stay this week, has ten individual cells, a small library, and the large garden with its gravel walk and screening hedges where I met Thomas Augustine the previous night. At the front entrance, the house has two wide common rooms sparely furnished with couches and chairs. Most of the furniture is constructed of flat square white cushions on frames of pale lacquered pine. They make me think again of Fr. Isaiah: generously framed but spare, disciplined, innocent of excess.

In the larger of the two rooms, which I enter from the yard through glass double doors, there is a long conference table. Here, at one end, Michael—the extern brother who drew me the map—is setting out dinner in the same sort of large flat aluminum pans I used to fill and serve as a caterer, one among many on my carousel of New York temp jobs. There the pans would have been full of quirky things, amuse-bouches, shrimp canapés, little pastries with cilantro pesto, whimsical curls of carrot: all arranged with such precious finesse that eating seemed a sin. That, surely, was part of the pleasure. Here the earthy, artlessly inviting smell of vegetable lasagna rises from the table.

Is Michael allowed to speak to us right now? I'm not sure, and he doesn't volunteer. He sets down the last pan, smiles, and ducks out a door that communicates with the monastery kitchen.

Two other women were here when I arrived. They both linger in the common room now, wearing the catlike disinterested expressions of people who feel hungry but don't want to ask for what they want. The younger of the two wears an unruly bun with a pencil shoved through it, wire-rimmed glasses, polyvinyl ballet flats scuffed at the toes and crushed at the heels. Her loose marled wool sweater doesn't conceal the line where the elastic of her cheap tiered skirt pinches her soft waist and, in pinching, creates a bulge. A triangular lace scarf twists, knotted, around her neck.

She eyes me sidewise and, giving a lopsided smile that looks insincere, edges away without looking back. Maybe she wasn't doing what I thought she was: taking my measure, appraising my appearance. Maybe I scared her away.

The older woman is also heavy but has a tidy short haircut, a well-stitched tweed blazer, a silk scarf, polyester slacks. She wears bad shoes too, but differently bad ones, trapezoid-heeled boots of a chunky and outdated cut with stretch elastic sides, boots that are meant to be practical but that don't support her feet: obvious bunions bulge out of the boots' angular toe boxes. She gives me a labored smile, more from conscious choice than from a bloom of feeling. And there I am, judging again: I can't know this. I can't know this just from looking. Can I?

We fill plates and sit down at the empty end of the conference table. I know of no way not to feel awkward. The older woman leads a brief prayer that the younger woman knows by heart, in a foreign language. I lower my gaze and place my hands under the table until they finish; I wait to begin eating, as I have seen others do, until the older woman has taken her first bite.

"The monks are good cooks," ventures the younger one, who introduces herself as Marjorie. Her speech drags along, its vowels yawning open: she must be local. She gives a wry smile, a smile fighting against itself, along with a laugh that apologizes for having spoken.

Someone in the kitchen has meant us well: this is a vegetarian feast. Along with the lasagna here are greens cooked in oil and garlic, lentils and goat cheese, a French onion soup with a buttery broth; there are baguettes, gruyère, pears from the orchard.

"You can rely on good food here—not at every monastery you visit, though," the older woman says, without looking up from her place setting. She introduces herself as Mary Russell—she must have already met Marjorie; did they know each other before today, or is that just an illusion fostered by their shared religion?—and monologues to us about the stops on her pilgrimage to Italy and the various meals, more or less disappointing, served to her there—"so surprising, so upsetting, since everyone always says how delicious the food is supposed to be, but everything they gave us in Rome was overdone or undersalted or gluey," Mrs. Russell mopes.

Mary Russell's tone, as she talks almost incessantly throughout the meal, reminds me of the way Dylan's mother, Elaine Fielding, also used to speak about unsatisfactory service in restaurants and hotels and cabs. Elaine, though, instead of grumbling, had had a way of holding up her own privilege by its scruff, like an unruly if well-kempt kitten, and scolding it gently, affectionately, for its dissatisfaction.

Whatever her other faults might have been, Elaine never seemed unaware of or asleep, as does Mary Russell, to the marvels of simply being welcome to sit in a clean room and have a fresh meal; inhabiting wide spaces and having the liberty to move through them with a sense of promise in mind; knowing you can walk down a hallway any time you choose, close a door behind you, and be alone. She may not know what it is to be without any of these, may never have been without them. Elaine never lacked for anything, yet always found something with which to be dissatisfied: yet it was never the surroundings that displeased her, always some disappointing behavior, some failure to follow her narrowly conceived script. Mary Russell seems to be that basest of creatures, a glutton for comfort.

Are we comfortable here? Is this the safe refuge, the haven, I thought it was? The pressure of Thomas Augustine's pain and of his confidence in me packs the room to the walls, seems to seal up the windows and doors. I could choose to be alone here, now, but his pain is the truth I will be alone with. If only I could see him again—out of the question. Even if some comfort from a meeting were possible—I should be the one offering comfort, not asking it. Yet an extreme of empathic passion has left me now drained, simply excoriated.

In my desperation I begin wishing for the awkward dinner to prolong itself, for the women to stay around and be friendly, so I cast about for topics of conversation that might suit them. The easiest route is to start out by asking what they like, but instead I begin grasping inarticulately after things I like that they probably don't: I haven't read the news in nearly thirty hours now; they don't look as if they like edgy theatre or rock bands or clever ribald TV shows; I don't go to church, politics only make everyone sad, since college ended my once lively reading life has been no more than a distant happy dream, and—forget it, what I know now fills every other corner, swamping thought, denying coherence. Even if someone were to bring up Artemisia Gentileschi, I would simply collapse.

So after the meal, in an unsettled quiet, all the conviviality we can muster is to carry the dishes back to a tray for the extern to collect later. When they excuse themselves to the chapel for vespers, I flee to my room.

Not long after the conversation in the garden with Thomas Augustine, my phone battery died. When I looked for my charger, it wasn't in its usual pocket in my messenger bag. I flipped my suitcase upside down on the bed, ejected its whole contents, ran my fingers along every seam and inside every zipper. The threads of the stretchless, stiff faux satin rasped against my skin. Only then, with a clench of my stomach, did I remember where I had left the frayed and many-times-taped white wire: plugged into the station at the airport. Unless I can borrow a charger, I'll have to cultivate self-sufficiency.

The cell holds a bed, narrow, slightly too tall and firm for comfort. A coarse sheet and a gray wool blanket cover it. Under it a blue rug, industrial weight, heavily hemmed at the edges, does not cross the whole tile floor. A pine desk, a lamp, a dorm-room chair, and a nightstand so diminutive it barely holds the two books I've checked out of the guest library, are all else it contains.

On the wall above the desk, three icons hang: a face of Christ, a virgin and infant, a baptism in the Jordan. If not for hours spent in museums with Dylan, I wouldn't have recognized the river scene.

My books are both slim, one a volume of poetry—*God's Silence*, by Franz Wright—the other a treatise called *The Cloud of Unknowing*. The preface of this latter book urgently warns everyone who isn't "advanced in the love of God" that they had better not read it. This of course fills me with curiosity to pry through the pages, but also a sense of dread: these things are simply beyond me. Suppose I were to bring some sort of curse upon myself by opening the book: a childish tremor, magical thinking.

In any case it is a distraction from the pressure of the moment. I don't know how to say what needs to be said to Fr. Isaiah in person: I may do better by writing to him, here in this highly formalized place, where every word from my mouth risks a transgression of some inaccessible etiquette.

Still, I push the books aside and head out for a late walk. The night enfolds the hills. A deep clear cobalt fades through teal to a gold that melts against the crisp black treeline. When my eyes adjust, I can see across the dim lawn into the garden. Mary Russell paces the paving stones between the cypresses. A string of prayer beads jangles between her fingers. She looks quickly up and then down at her feet again when she hears my steps rustling in the dry grass.

I go in without speaking to her. I've avoided nothing, it has remained here to be dealt with, if not now, then later. Pain is patient; it will wait in ambush. I check to see if the door locks: thank God, it does.

IX

Cold gray light enters the window on Thanksgiving morning. As I shower and change into fresh clothes, it occurs to me for the first time to wonder what the two other women in the guesthouse are doing here. Do they too have families they would rather not be near? Maybe they have no one.

Now I feel in the wrong for not trying harder to make conversation last night: rebuked, once again, by the sorts of remarks Signora used to make about the social skills of my generation. She has always been right, after all. I am, we are, self-regarding, self-enclosed. This may be understandable, but that doesn't make it enviable. Or defensible.

And—here it is again, the uncomfortable truth—this sense of emptiness, this armored identity, is a terrible liability to be carrying when I need to form a connection of trust with someone whose cooperation is necessary. I feel called upon to revisit my conversation with Fr. Isaiah, but I do not know how the topic can be touched, let alone what good I could do even by telling him all that I know.

Too distracted to think of eating, I skip breakfast, walk through the common room, and turn down the hall that leads to the chapel, intending to sit in on the monks' morning prayers. Guests are invited, but it still feels transgressive to slip through those double doors and into an empty choir stall.

The chapel's beauty is spare, stern: an aesthetic entirely other than that of the medieval and Renaissance churches Dylan and I once explored together. The intricate details, the heart-pounding colors, have faded, melted, out of this style. Ribs of stripped and polished pine segment the whitewashed walls. The wooden panels remind me of the half-timbering of a Tudor house, only they rise all the way up each side of the room. The ceiling slants to a sharp apex amid rafters. Above the altar, four triangular windows join at their vertices to form the half-inscape of a polyhedron.

At first there is no one else to be seen in the chapel. Then, by twos and threes and finally in long lines, the monks file in to fill the stalls, which line up perpendicularly to the pews on the farther side of the altar screen. There is no difference of height, but a definite distance, between *out here* and *in there*.

A clatter of kneelers, a murmur of pages, and then comes the wholly vocal music. It engulfs the room; it flows like water. It washes over me, carries things into and out of me. I float in it. I hold my breath like a swimmer, pace my inhalations to the rhythm of the waves.

On the ebbing tide I float into the common room. There on the sparse couch, cradling in her hand one of the kitchen's thick ceramic coffee cups, sits Elaine Fielding, who stares at the sunrise as if it owes her some recompense. Her expression, as she sees me, gathers to a point as sharp as an art razor ripping through canvas.

"Oh my God," she says as she recognizes my face. "Oh my God. You're here. Have you seen him? Tell me, what does he look like now? Oh, my God, you'll help me, won't you? I came to get him out of here. Allen's in the other guesthouse, the men's wing. He's allowed to go places in this medieval hellhole we aren't. He'll have to do some of the heavy lifting. But you and I, we'll know what to *say*, won't we. Thank God you're here. We'll get him out."

"It's good to see you too, Elaine."

I am not sure what to say to her, but Elaine does not expect anyone else to speak. She continues to hold forth as I pour coffee from the tall stainless carafe on the breakfast table; I hide my facial riot by slow sipping and blowing away the steam from the top of the mug.

Elaine appears too submerged in her own distress to notice anyone else's:

"Thank God you're here: someone he knows, someone he remembers. Someone he'll listen to: I'm all too aware he might not listen to me. But damn it if I'm not going to try to get through to him, nevertheless.

"You know, Beatrice was beside herself when we found out where he'd gone. You know he absolutely ran off without telling a single soul where he was going or when he was coming back?—not only that, but not even a hint that he was *never* planning to come back! No! We didn't rate a word! None of us: not word one. He didn't tell *you*, did he?" (He hadn't.) "Oh good. I mean, not good, but I mean: friends are one thing, but blood is thicker than water. Not to mention a future spouse—I mean he broke the engagement with her in the rudest way possible, without warning and without reason. What is the phrase you all use now?—he ghosted her. Ghosted his fiancée! I'll be damned if I'll go around letting everyone think that's how I raised him to behave. Not highly likely.

"Of course, it was bad enough when we first found out—at that point I was angry. But I also thought: give him time, let him find out how it is; there's no way he's going to stick it out. I know him, he loves beauty and quality, he loves recognition and praise, and he isn't going to get any of those things in the backwoods. He'll soon have had enough, and then it will be time enough to talk reason, I thought. I *thought*. Well, damn me for a fool, Angele, for thinking. Just last week I get a letter from him, and I find out he's still serious, he's still intending to . . . go through with this. He's planning to take *final* vows. Final! Whatever that means! And at Christmas! Couldn't let us have the holidays in peace. As though, if he really had to do this— which he doesn't—he couldn't wait just a little longer. As though he couldn't be satisfied with ruining his own life, but—"

I start to try to soothe her—she won't be of any help with the real problem until she has calmed down—but Elaine isn't finished:

"His father and I are invited, thank you very much, to the vow ceremony. It's his wedding, we're told. Some *wedding*: I was planning his wedding five years ago. This isn't a wedding, it's a mockery. I feel mocked. Spat on." She actually wipes her cheek as if she felt spittle there; the movement pulls her lips into a sneer. "But that's neither here nor there, is it. The question is really: is this a good choice for Dylan? I know that. It isn't about me, in the end: it never is about the parents: it's about his future. Is this a good choice for *his* future, then? I have to say I don't think it is. It *hasn't* been good for his career. I follow these things as closely as I can, from the arm's-length distance he holds me at. There have been only six painting sales under his name in the five years since he disappeared in this way. Six—in five years—when in the year and a half before he disappeared, he sold twenty-three canvases: *twenty-three. . . .*"

She wrings her hands, which glimmer with gold. "He had done so well, and—look, I'm glad he gave away so much to charity; it's a fine way to use excess; but—did he have to give away *all*? It's completely gone now. No back-up plan; he didn't hedge his bets. If he were to leave the monastery now he wouldn't have a cent, except what his father and I could give him, and I honestly don't know how we would manage for him, everything is so tied up right now.

"All that being the case, I still want to offer him what I can. I want him to come *out* of this place. I don't want him to molder away in here. He's my son. He's my future. He's all I have. You've been his friend now for so long. And you're Beatrice's friend, as well. You must want him out, too, no? No?"

I don't respond. Where to begin?

"Yes, of course," she says: "we all want the best for him, and this place is so obviously *not* the best. I don't understand how there could be two opinions about that."

"Maybe there can," I venture. "I saw him."

"You've seen him? Tell me how he looks."

I stand up, walk to the table again, and pick out a piece of fresh rye bread merely for an excuse to walk behind her chair as I speak, to keep her from observing whatever may cross my face when I think about how he looked, what he said.

"He's . . . very invested in the life here. He wants to make it work. Of course it isn't easy. But nothing is, really, when you come right down to it." I am aware of how far short of the mark this falls. But, to judge from the evidence, Elaine won't be able to hear more of the difficult truth right now—unless she already knows about the assault? She behaves as if she doesn't. Is it my place to tell her?

"Does he talk about Beatrice?" she presses on. "I was so terribly disappointed about their wedding. To say nothing of all the deposits on all the rentals . . . Their personalities adjusted so well to one another. Almost unbelievably so. I mean, God knows whether they could have stuck with it. She told me he had a way of . . . drifting off, so to speak. But a mother has to hope: they were so *compatible*."

I study her face closely: is this remark intended as a cruelty or as a plea for correction? If she knew her son was assaulted here, her words would sound almost unimaginably heartless. If she knew, could she ever again spill over with so much useless grief about such a thing as a broken engagement? *This is so obviously not the best*, she had said: what would she consider "best," what would satisfy her?

She is lost in her own concerns. I came to visit the monastery as Thomas Augustine's friend, wanting, in Elaine's words, the best for him, whatever that might mean. As unmoored as this emotion leaves me now, I still believe I love him. Whether anything good can ever again come from this love, what if anything I can do for him in this crisis, I feel less certain.

"He does talk about her; he did talk to me about Beatrice." This much is safe for me to tell Elaine. "He said that he missed her, but that he didn't want to marry her, or anyone. He said he hoped that, one day, she would be able to understand." I omit *Beatrice was using me for status and image*, omit *If I could have married anyone it would have been you.* Omit *My body is where it happened. Where would I go?*

Elaine doesn't respond with words at first. She only makes a throat-clearing noise and looks out the window, a floor-to-ceiling plate glass inset that affords a view of the hillside where I walked last night. In golden light, loblolly pines crowd the lip of the valley. From the wood's edge, a sere meadow slopes generously toward us, cross-hatched with the wheaten color of dry grass.

"Well." She stands up, strides to the door. "The second they're finished with prayers, I'm going straight to the novice master to indicate a meeting with him and with my son."

I don't move, and she turns to look at me incredulously.

"Are you coming or not?"

*

Elaine is already seated in a pew, facing the altar, when I arrive at the chapel again. Her head tilts down at a thirty-degree angle; she texts so furiously that the silver streak at the front of her hair shivers. She scowls as she pushes the hair behind her ear. Her thumbs punch the screen until the phone in her hand shakes. She must be texting Allen, who lopes in a few minutes later and with a familiar economy of motion takes a seat beside her.

In the pew behind them I close my eyes. I try to empty my mind, as people say you are supposed to do in meditation. (Beatrice again: either perched on one end of her bed, all lotus, directing another of our amateur evening sessions, or dragging me to some class in Tribeca full of coltish, nervous socialites in painted-on colorblock gear.) It doesn't work for me. I lose myself: I relive those hours in the floodlit gallery, the day of the Chicago opening. The hours, dangerously, vertiginously, of that night.

Moments spiral back on one another. They dilate, expand, and contract. They take in all that has come before them and contain it, make it present again. This moment in the chapel, waiting for the service to begin, is surprisingly capacious. It holds, with room to spare, the week in Florence when I posed for the portrait; it holds all the moments in New York that broke my trust in him; then, with a forward leap, it holds the moment of meeting Dylan's parents while standing stunned in front of my own portrait in Chicago, the moment of disclosure in the garden. In holding all these others, this moment's own identity is effaced—the liminal minute of waiting in the chapel pew, behind the Fieldings, for an inaccessible stranger named Thomas Augustine, whom we will see only from a distance and to whom we will not speak, to reappear and disappear like the transit of a planet across the sun. The moment in the chapel becomes merely a vessel for these other moments, for bringing to birth one of the present possibilities that was implicit in all of them.

There is a skill in encountering this kind of time, a skill I haven't mastered yet. How do others push back the past, rule it out in favor of a future that evades its pressure? Do they truly succeed in doing this, or do they only delude themselves, teach the past to play dead?

As the monks file into the chapel in order this time, lined up like elementary schoolers, their backs turned to us, I watch Elaine craning, stretching, trying to see without being seen. She is scanning the lines of men for a glimpse of her son, without finding him, although I have already picked him out by the slope of his shoulder and the set of his neck above his scapular.

Then as the monks take their seats and face the altar, becoming visible in profile, Elaine's eyes widen and roll; her mouth tightens and twists. She murmurs to Allen, and I can read her lips:

His hair. Did you see his hair.

Someone blows a reedy note on a pitch pipe. The monks begin to chant again, an oceanic roll of sound. Elaine's shoulders are shaking. Is she crying? Laughing? Her shriek splits the music, dies away, strikes a second time like thunder after lightning, and I sit fixed in place as she strides back through the chapel toward the exit.

The ocean of chanting engulfs Elaine's cry. The pull of the tide does not change as Allen follows her out, his footsteps soft but clear as drumbeats on the tile. White winter sun thrums steadily through the polyhedral glass—a stray impulse bids me wonder if it is bulletproof—above the altar.

X

In the guesthouse afterward, I find Elaine still in tears, flush and tremulous, seated again on the couch, Allen standing grave behind her shoulder like a Saint John on a crucifixion altarpiece. Elaine sees me before Allen does; she appeals directly to me without preface.

"I don't understand all this about a rule. Rules don't unmake family. Dylan is my son. They have no right to stop me from seeing him."

A look of chagrin flicks across Allen's face. "Dear, Angele has no control over the monastery's visitor policy."

"But she *saw* him. She pulled some sort of string, or it was pulled for her." This is said as if I am not standing here. "If she could go straight to him, why can't I?"

"I wasn't supposed to have done that. I didn't know then," I say. "I'm sorry if I didn't make that clear enough. I've told the prior what happened. I only hope it won't cause more trouble to have it known."

"I hope it does cause trouble, darling. If you must, ask forgiveness, not permission—but don't ask either if you can help it."

Elaine stands up, lightly smacks her cheeks with her fingers, and strides over to the credenza by the door, where there lies a clutter of brochures and photocopied maps of the cloister and grounds. She picks up a map; she hands it to me.

"Here. Point out for me the spot where you saw him."

I try to explain why this isn't a good solution, why we won't find

Thomas Augustine lurking in the guesthouse garden again—I say *Thomas Augustine* with emphasis, hoping to make a point—but Elaine does not understand. She isn't listening. Her mind cycles on to other possibilities, other lines of onslaught.

"All right. We can search the rest of the grounds instead. Let's look at the schedule: when will the community walk or work outdoors?" She flips the paper over. Allen and Elaine argue about whether they can trespass the lines of cloistered ground, which, as the map makes clear, aren't fenced but are supposed to be respected by visitors who haven't been invited into the enclosure. She presses for yes; he leans toward no.

"Fine," she says at last, in a rasp, and with a show of teeth that makes it clear it is not fine. "I still want you to take a walk out there by yourself, Allen, sometime after lunch today. There can't be any harm in that. I'll angle for bigger fish. Angele, come here again, will you please?"

I pretend I don't hear her. I'm not her administrative assistant. During their argument, I have drifted toward the row of bookshelves that calls itself a "guesthouse library," the font more self-effacing than quaint. I act as if I can't hear or am not listening. In fact every word they have spoken has hooked itself into me. I have picked up title after title, trying to find a book I can disappear into; I have opened one that looks more promising than others, have flicked through pages at random.

As they fight on, I read, stubbornly; I block out Allen and Elaine's negotiations with all my attention. Do the two of them have no concept that they will one day die, that one way or another their silent sniping will have to cease? I imagine their bodies, as they sag and decay, turning toward one another in the double grave, lifting skeletal fingers at each other in blame.

"Angele? Come here, please."

When I hear her speak my name again, like a child's being spoken by a teacher with a mind to harshness, I want to lash out at her. I want to shout *do you know what happened? Do you think anything you can do will make it better?*

Instead I say, "Pardon?" Elaine's hand is outstretched over her map, fingers scuttling like a crab with its legs in the air.

"Come here," she repeats, needlessly. "You met with the prior, you said. Show me on this map where his office is."

The map doesn't correspond easily to the sketch that was made for me by the extern, which is back in my room. I don't want to offer to retrieve it. While I am comparing the two, trying to figure out what represents what, Elaine continues to think aloud.

"He'll be starting from nothing. Nothing. That's all right. We'll find a way. He'll need some stability in his life. A foothold. He can stay with us at first. We'll—dear, we'll have to move your office into our bedroom for a bit: your son is coming home. Angele, you're still in Chicago. You could come over for dinner once a week. Tuesdays? Then of course we'll want to set him up in New York again. I wonder if he let go of the lease on the studio. Of course, he would have. He'll need a new space. Maybe we can sell the property by the lake to fund it . . . I wonder if there's any chance of a reconciliation with Beatrice? No, no, of course not. Have you found it yet?"

Why, I am wondering, should I help her? But I point out the corridor where I think the office should be.

"It's outside the cloister," Allen notices over her shoulder: his face looks bored, complaisant. At his temples and jawline there is just a hint that his tan may owe less to outdoor exercise than to UV lamps. "That's good. You can just go there and knock on the door. Can't she, Angele? Was there a receptionist when you went there before?"

I wonder if "receptionist" is the right term for the monk in the reading glasses.

"There was someone at a desk, but it didn't look like a very formal arrangement. You could always try."

Elaine stands up and gathers her handbag. She says, "Allen,

come with me, will you," in a way that is not a question. Without a word he opens the left-hand double door for her; first she, then he, walks out.

Should Elaine be told? She is right, in a way, about her son's needing to leave, without knowing how right she is or what to do about it. She doesn't yet know, though—how could she?—that her son is now exposed to what she would call harm and what I'm starting to conceive of as hell.

*

When they return, I am still there in the common room, reading Augustine's *Confessions*, which Richard once told me was a classic of literature even if you didn't believe a word of it. I didn't get around to the book in my senior year and haven't thought of it since, until now. The other two retreatants have wandered in and are also quietly busy. Marjorie writes in a journal. Mary Russell once more holds a string of crystal beads and paces with it: her heels plod over the white tile and mauve carpet; the beads click, again, through her fingers.

Elaine sweeps over us all with her glance, frowns, and speeds away down the corridor.

Allen sits down near me, looking as out of place as anyone like him—urbane, handsome—can ever look. In an undertone I ask him how it went. He responds as quietly.

"That was disastrous. We weren't expected; we weren't welcome. Elaine said her say, the prior said his, and I stood there without saying anything: feeling foolish."

"And Dylan?"

"Wasn't there, of course. They'll protect him as long as he wants to hide away from reality in here. But he's an adult now, and it's not my business to stop him."

"What do you think he should do?"

"Stay, if that makes him happy. Leave, if that makes him happy.

It seems simple enough to me. I don't grasp the need to create all this conflict. I'm here to keep conflict to a minimum, by keeping the peace with my wife. My son doesn't need me to tell him how to live."

What, I wonder, does it take, what kinds of treaties must be ratified, what surreptitious compromises, to keep the peace with Elaine? This cannot be the first such triangulation among the artless family that cocooned this untrammeled artist: in just such a way they may have hovered at the entrance of an expensive preschool—its classroom walls glowing a womblike pink, its windows filled with clusters of green vines in hanging baskets—arguing in whispers about whether to sign an enrollment contract. Picture the crouching figure of the child Dylan, against the ground of an oatmeal-colored jute rug, desultorily stacking unpainted wooden blocks, not too immersed in the task, already aware on some level of its nature as a performance. "But tell me about the meeting: Elaine demanded that she be allowed to talk to Dylan, and the prior said no, of course? And that was that?"

"That, together with a lot about 'formation' this and 'pastoral decisions' that: all his words, none of which I understand, but as I keep saying, it isn't up to me to understand. Anyway, then Elaine—lost her temper." Allen leaves a breath, his silent signature, between his wife's name and the description of her outburst. This gap provides room to wonder what actions "losing her temper" might have involved. The rotary phone knocked off its credenza; stacks of paper sliding and tumbling to the carpet? No, she wouldn't give ground so gracelessly. Raised voices, sharp words—these were Elaine's countersignature.

Allen is too circumspect to repeat all that was said and done, though. He obfuscates:

"Which was unfortunate, and which didn't get her anywhere, and now we're back where we started, or worse, and it's still Thanksgiving Day. I'm counting the hours until our flight out of Louisville on Sunday."

Allen sits back and rests his ankle on his knee. If he is really so ill at ease, it doesn't show in his posture. He turns the conversation, trying to draw me into talking about myself. By awkward steps I follow, smoothing out as best I can the crumpled story of my halfhearted goal to become creative director at GryphoLux, its inadequate rising action, its anticlimax of having been terminated. I'd lost my job for banal financial reasons in the faltering parent company, but naturally the company had faltered mainly because of factors in the culture: shifting economic demand, the switch from print to digital media, the exposure of Photoshop as a tool of deception, shrinking luxury markets.

Under Allen's gaze, I try to shoehorn the tale into the readily available framework of adversity-and-rising-above, but my face feels dry and heavy as I tell it. The muscles stretch and fold, tighten and slack wrong, don't cooperate. Talking to Allen about this is like interviewing for a new job I really don't want to take. The words push off my tongue like pages off a printer—becoming cheaper, more meaningless, in direct proportion to their quantity. By the end I'm grayscale.

Allen, sensing my discomfort, gently segues into talk of Chicago city life. After my story, he unobtrusively steers away from discussing concerts and theaters, clubs and cafés—expensive places. He talks instead of where in the city to find quiet parks, places to walk, free museums to browse. From the topic of museums, we drift into idly wondering aloud why people don't constantly crowd them: with so much overwhelming richness of visual experience available for free to everyone, out in an exciting world, why people who could do otherwise still prefer to spend money in order to binge-watch shows on screens in rooms alone.

Criticism of others proves uncontroversial and pleasant, and our conversation is comfortably miles away, well out of the monastery, berating people we don't know for choices we haven't made, until Elaine re-enters the room.

"Don't think for a second I'm giving up," she says to Allen. She crosses the room, takes coffee, strides back to us. "If I can just talk to him once, I know I can bring him around." From the depth in her voice, the thickness of emotion, I deduce that the person Elaine plans to bring around is not the prior, but her son.

Elaine turns to me sharply. "What did you do? How did you get in?"

"I didn't do anything. I . . . I found a note. An invitation."

"From him?"

"From him."

"To go into the enclosure?"

"No, not the cloister." I turn, but turn again. "The guesthouse garden."

I have explained this already, but Elaine has forgotten the details. Once more I go over the midnight encounter. "Midnight encounter"—so this is how our innocent conversation appears now, in increasingly lurid colors. I become, uncomfortably, much more aware of the further complications a misunderstanding here could cause. The different registers in which it is possible to say a thing *should never have happened.*

When Elaine hears the story, her eyes light up in a way that alarms me. She thanks me for "being clear" with her; "it isn't much to ask, but it's clearly beyond some people," she says, and then adds with an elaborate roll of her eyes: "I swear to you, Angele, don't ever have children. It's honestly sometimes more trouble than it's worth."

XI

November 2015

"Unbelievable," Elaine is saying some hours later as she sits at the common table, at Thanksgiving dinner, with her napkin in her lap but her plate untouched. "It is quite literally unbelievable: the way they treated us today."

The two devout women guests eye Elaine sidelong. They can be observed mentally adding up the cost of her sequined sweater, her Coach shoes, her wristwatch, her wedding diamonds, and then plugging the total into a function that accounts for unknown variables—upbringing, education, entitlements, privileges, even the numeric value of her body's weight—to solve for x, the proportionate amount of sympathy they will allow her. And I—how easily I weigh the variables also.

"All of that talk about hospitality! And then you can't even schedule a proper meeting. I mean, it isn't as if this is a—what do they call it?—some big high holy day, not for them. Do they do anything the normal way? Father even said that, for *them*, today is just an ordinary Thursday. 'We give thanks every day,' he said. Then he went on to tell me that no, I can't go in to see my son, and no, he can't come out to see me. 'Can we at least talk about why,' I asked, and just like a robot he rapped out that same tired two-sentence script about monastic silence again. Well, they can be silent if they want, but they need to hear me. I don't really understand why I can't be given the most perfunctory time to say it, even if they plan to ignore me completely.

"From what I do understand, we could visit again in two months—in January—but after he's already made his vows. He's meant to be on retreat now, although"—she cuts her eyes across to me, then decides not to say more—"well, it would look as though they change things up when they feel like it and clamp down when it suits them. It's all to do with what they call the 'monasticate,' which is a word that I find hard to say, especially at the table" (she purses her lips) "because it sounds like noisy chewing, but all it means, they said, is the slice of time when he's making the transition from novice to full monk. Which sounds like the title of a Stanley Kubrick movie."

For the first time a gleam of intelligence flits across Marjorie's expression: she understands the pop-culture reference, but she isn't confident drawing it out in the company of Mrs. Russell, who might disapprove. She seems to want to laugh but to be unable to do so. Marjorie eyes Mrs. Russell, who is frowning abstractedly at the gluey green bean casserole on her plate, and then decides to say nothing after all.

With her fork Elaine collects a bite of food, a shred of turkey atop a teaspoon of sauce, homemade cranberry; she tries it and then makes a face.

"Sour," she says.

At this point no one but Elaine has said anything for several minutes. But Allen is accustomed by long habit to his spouse's venting sessions, which fill up time and create a certain pressure, but which in the end go nowhere. He knows how to give Elaine room to expand and then to dissipate her energy, like a balloon blown up and then released. He can deflect her in midflight, so that she stays out of the faces of unsuspecting partygoers. He steps into the breach.

"At least he isn't living in that place on the island in the middle of the river, the one in France, remember? The one we saw out the airplane window on the way back from Paris. It isn't always an island; it's on a peninsula. Then the rains come, and there fills up a natural moat. Actually, I'd go there just to see that happen."

This comment lights up Mrs. Russell's face. She *has* traveled to Mont Saint-Michel, has stayed at an inn inside the walls. Pages of travelogue scroll from her lips. Marjorie makes polite noises, calls Mrs. Russell "Mary," chatters brightly to her and encourages her to say more, as she shepherds her sweet potatoes around her plate with a piece of dinner roll.

Elaine glares significantly at Allen, who has enough manners not to break Mrs. Russell's chain of stories. When it ends, both Allen's and Marjorie's mouths happen to be full, so it falls to Elaine to respond. She fails; she drops to the bottom of the well of silence that develops. From the depths she registers, almost mildly, a complaint that the turkey is dry.

The extern who is clearing our plates hears the complaint. It's not clear whether Elaine meant for him to do so. Either way, he blushes deeply. But he says nothing in reply and, the next minute, brings in a tray of individually prepared dessert ramekins.

"Crème brulée," Mrs. Russell beams.

Elaine pushes her ramekin an almost imperceptible degree away. Until the others have finished she sits, tense as the strings of a badly tuned piano, not speaking or making eye contact.

The phantasm of my mother murmurs in the privacy of my skull: *Come on now, it ain't gon kill you to say somethin nice.* I'm not sure whether the message is for me or for Elaine. At any rate, no pleasant words occur to either of us.

Mrs. Russell eyes Elaine's pristine dish with regret, a gesture implying *what a waste*, wishing mutely just to dip her spoon into it. Instead she chats on about French patisseries. Marjorie encourages her. Their sweets are gone in moments, but they linger over coffee and a discussion of pilgrimage tour group companies, pros and cons, liabilities and perks.

When the devout guests finally clear the room, taking their stiff forays into festivity with them, Elaine releases a groan of exasperation. "Unbelievable," she says again, now meaning the guests' behavior: "unbelievable."

As before, Allen knows his role. "They're barely educated. You didn't expect anything better, I hope."

"No. But the pretension and the dullness: the bovine complacency, the mind-numbing quiescence."

"What do you expect."

"Better, for my son," says Elaine, near tears. "Better."

From the library corner we hear a stifled noise. Marjorie, who we thought was in her room, has been hidden there, listening. She rushes out, wiping her eyes; she barrels up to the garden door, goes out, and lets it slam behind her.

Allen and Elaine exchange a look. Elaine shrugs.

Burying the bitter words that come to mind, I follow Marjorie. I think it would be a kindness to try to comfort her, although she may only glare at me. There may be almost nothing else I can do at this moment. I am putting off rewriting the letter to Fr. Isaiah until I can think of how to say what needs to be said. Mere companionability, at least, feels within reach.

The sun has already crept behind the high ridge, but the garden is still filled with the yellow light of the passing day. Marjorie is seated on the wall at the backmost curve of the flagstone path. Her form is framed by the cypresses, there where Thomas Augustine and I sat next to each other, that night. She is weeping, but not with much conviction. Tears slip down of their own accord, and she lets them. Under the layer of extra weight she carries, a pretty face awaits a sculptor's easy work: her features are pale and small, but smooth and well proportioned.

I murmur how sorry I am that the Fieldings were so rude. She mumbles back, and I can't hear her clearly at first.

"Pardon?" I say.

Marjorie articulates: "It's a crock of shit."

" . . . What is?"

"Their whole—everything, their tone, their clothes, their whole approach to life. *They're* a crock. So much delicate politeness, until you offend their sensibilities, and then nothing they can say or do is too bad for the offender. You spend your life trying not to climb the walls screaming and then they *blame* you for being *calm*. I guess it's possible to offend someone just by existing."

"Wait, 'they' who? The monks?"

"No, the monks are saving my life. I'm talking about the . . . the couple. The man and woman. The young brother's parents. They're just like my parents, and my parents' friends, and my professors in college, and basically almost every adult of that generation I've ever met. They greet you with perfect manners if and as long as you meet their standards. You find total dismissal otherwise. They couldn't even acknowledge I was *there*. They couldn't even try to find a level where we could connect. They assume there isn't one. I've never been good enough for anyone like that, and I'm not sure why I expected it would be different, even here. My spiritual director is the only person of that age who understands me, and even with him, there are things he doesn't get. Not that he has to—I mean, who can get everything? But it's good to have a sister in Christ."

She looks at me expectantly. With less adroitness than I'd like, I explain to her that I'm not a believer, that I'm mainly here for peace and quiet: which, if ironic, is at least somewhat true.

"Well, whatever, but you're still being kind. To me. And kindness matters. It's all we have in this valley of tears."

"Don't worry. It's nothing. And the couple: you shouldn't worry about what they say or do, either. They're like that. I've known them for a long time. The . . . brother who's their son is an old friend of mine, and they aren't happy that he's living here. They want to convince him to leave."

As I say this, I notice that I tend to think of Allen as a nonentity. I ascribe Elaine's words and Elaine's intentions only to the couple as a whole. No one could have said *They're the parents of my old friend, and they don't care if he stays or goes.*

"Hmm. My parents aren't happy I'm here, either. Not that that matters. And I'm nothing, I'm no one, so it's especially kind of you to care. I'm a piece of driftwood washed up from the wreck of culture in the storm of the postmodern era. I'm thoroughly aware you get laughed at for using that kind of language in the world those people are from. Hell, that's the world I'm from. For all I know, you're from that world, too."

"Sort of but not really. Secretly I'm from the depths of redneck country. Mississippi. Left like a bat out of Hades as soon as I could. I don't belong here or there; I don't know where I belong."

Marjorie sighs. She twists her lips. She looks as if there are several things she wants to say, but she isn't sure how I'll receive them, and after beginning on the offensive she is suddenly afraid again of giving offense.

"Me too? I don't know what to do with my life either?" she ventures, at length.

If I speak of myself, maybe this will put her at ease:

"I know what I wish I could have done, but it's probably too late. That's something you aren't supposed to admit, isn't it? Or you're supposed to tell everyone that you struggled, but only after you've succeeded despite all obstacles. I don't know whether I'll ever succeed—"

"—But you're going to try?" she puts in, sounding so much like a child I can't bear to tell her no.

"Sure, but I feel impatient with the fantasy of 'following a dream.' That's sometimes a real thing and sometimes just a cover for creeping immaturity. I followed my dream as far as it would take me, and now I need to figure out how to live in the real world."

Marjorie doesn't respond to this at first. She repeats the twist of her lips. Her next words are surprising.

"There isn't a 'real world' for people like you," she says, with some bitterness. "The 'real world' is for everyone else. You look the way success is supposed to look."

"What is that supposed to mean?"

"Well, look at you." Marjorie shrugs. "And then look at me. I'm not going to spell it out."

In another life we could be friends. Sisters. But in the moment I can't take the compliment. Instead I insist aloud on what I noticed before—her features delicate and smooth and distinctive, like a Van Eyck portrait—until bright pink spreads across them, an intense frown forming like a storm front at sunset. This lavish praise is not soothing her. It is disturbing something that, maybe, should remain untouched. We fall silent.

Very little light is left; the sun is entirely below the tree line, and the field of sky that was lemonade just now has mellowed to a clear jade green.

Marjorie says finally, quietly, when neither of us has spoken for a while, "Look. Some people make themselves and everyone around them miserable by making up their minds to do a thing, based on some idea of the thing, not on reality. They don't understand what it takes and they can't admit they don't understand. They just push onward to save their own pride. And the harder they work, the worse they make everything. . . .

"I'm forced to admit now that I'm one of those people. I'm the thing I most hated. What do you do when that happens? Has anything like that ever happened to you? What did you do about it?"

"That is a good question. I can't say I know the answer. Probably there isn't one answer."

"There has to be *some* answer. There can't be *no* answer."

We go back and forth about it, stepping gently around what we can't really figure out how to discuss: what she believes, what I don't. She won't tell me what she's done, but she wants to insist her mistakes are irreparable. She feels like the absolute worst person in the world. I want to defend her, defend almost everyone, from that charge—not to say there is no such thing as a terrible person. There is *terrible*, there is a *worst*, but just look at the pretty idiot, quivering there: she isn't it. I want to say that mistakes are natural, that hard work is never wasted if it taught you to work hard because persistence is a transferable skill, always of use. She wants to say she has ruined herself, made it impossible for God to work through her. I want to say she is talking nonsense. I don't know what it means for God to work at all, let alone through a human. I think that what we do, we do alone, if we do it at all, if it isn't done to us by circumstance or heredity or social pressure. Or trauma.

"But okay," I say to her, "I'm not saying any of this is the case, or would be. But let's say you have this person you have to trust, this person you have to depend on, who is utterly not dependable. Let's say he suddenly—I don't know, let's say he made a move on you."

Marjorie's face contorts with the attempt to keep her emotion under control: is it fear? I feel a moment of compunction for upsetting her— but even so, fears are better faced: "I mean, would that not throw your theory out the window, here? Would that not make him the worst person in the world? I mean the worst person in the world couldn't still be you then."

A harsh exhale bursts forth from her, not a laugh but an excess of air. "Why else do you think I'm such a shambles? Who says I haven't been—made a move on? Or more than that?"

"Oh no no. Not you too." That is out of my mouth before I can stop it. It is almost as if the agency that has released the words resides in the place, not in my body. But—does Marjorie need Thomas Augustine's story? It might only hurt her more.

Her eyebrows climb her forehead; ripples appear in the skin. "Yes, me. And you?"

"No, not me. Someone—else I've met."

"Someone—who?" She is almost on her feet now, tilted forward with such energy.

"I'm not sure I should—I mean I shouldn't have said that. Really. It isn't mine to tell."

"I'm sorry. I should respect that." She folds her hands.

"No, it's all right. But—if it's okay for me to ask—?"

She nods, gently, knocking her long curtained hair into her face, and I take this as permission:

"It didn't happen to you here?"

"No, in my school. I was, what, nine, ten. But it—kept on happening. I didn't know. What it was. Or that I could say no."

"Oh. Oh."

"Don't, don't. It's okay. They're putting me back together. I promise it is going to be okay."

"Someone should be promising *you* it is going to be okay."

"They are. My director is." She brushes her hair back again, puts it over one shoulder, smooths it with delicacy.

Then she leans forward and clasps my hands unexpectedly: hers are cold, dry. I wrap mine around them, glad of the chance to offer a small comfort.

"Okay. To be honest, I am glad anyone, anywhere, is saying this to you. Even if he's got no idea how he is going to make it okay," I tell her, "even if he is making it all up as he goes along, I still want him to promise you it is going to be okay. I want him to make it true in the future even if it isn't now."

"Same. I mean I want that too. You can't always stop people from doing wrong, though. They can't always stop themselves. That's the mystery of evil."

"And—you believe that—and you can still trust them?"

"Because it isn't them I trust. It's who they're working for."

"Who they say they're working for."

"Yeah, people lie about that sometimes. Or they deceive themselves. But not everyone who says they're working for God is grifting, just because some of them are."

This I can't wrap my mind around. The things we tell ourselves about ourselves are true—aren't they?—because it is our selves who tell them—isn't it? Any other foundation for what we know and how we know it, I don't know how to credit. We must, innately, know the truth about ourselves: we must. Otherwise there is nothing real in us.

We argue this point too, companionably without much insistence, after the electricity of her confession is gone. After a bit too much time has passed I ask her gently if she wants to tell the story and she says she really doesn't, she's told it too often already. Nothing could be more understandable. Eventually, Marjorie goes up to bed and leaves me to think it all over alone.

They deceive themselves. What vertigo if we cannot know what is real in us. Still there has been one time in my life, the only time, when I thought I knew what was real in me. Priceless. Those days in Europe with Dylan, staying in hostels and cheap lofts, skipping meals, hiking trails, hopping trains, serving our sense of superabundance: owning nothing to speak of but sketchbooks and pencils, two changes of clothes, two pairs of shoes, one computer between us, calling cards with limited minutes on them, saved up for emergencies that never emerged—this was before the ubiquity of devices—before the Cloud descended on us. Carried by scholarship and his parents' prodigality, we shot ourselves across the Italian night, effervescent arcs the glow-stick green of shooting stars burning sulphuric in the upper atmosphere, riding such great heights.

The hope of others has its shape and its limits, but to us it felt infinite. How real time feels when you revel in its openness, as if wasting it could make you more eternal, hour after hour of horizon without sphere, fearless. No sight of downturn, of death. An expanse that stretched before us like clean water, inviting us to swim. Its freshness, its splash.

One evening, after Dylan's move to Florence, we were headed back from a day hike in Assisi. We had missed our train, and rather than wait for another, Dylan approached a tour bus driver and in a cobbled-together stream of Italian and English concocted a story about why we needed to travel faster, why we couldn't wait. Euros changed hands, and the driver allowed us one open seat to share.

The man in charge of the tour, not an Italian but a polyglot Austrian on permanent holiday, had with him one and only one CD, a compilation of Beatles songs. "Day Tripper" spun on repeat as the bus sped down the autostrada in the darkness. Still the absurd music served its function, guarding in a public place a private space for talk. We had been working on our portraits—I had been painting him too, catching rare unguarded moments to sketch, from which I made still more canvases I would later destroy—and I had been feeling saturated in Dylan's gaze, overexposed. But in the dark we could only see each other as muted profiles, gleaming pupils. Now and then a flash of streetlight swept over us, then receded.

So much of what we said was forgettable. His tone is what lingers: its conspiratorial hush, its elevation. He delighted in telling me how one of his professors had put him in touch with a prominent Italian gallery owner; he hadn't wanted to hurt my feelings by telling me that the professor was Signora, who was supposed to be equally in both of our corners, who wasn't supposed to show favoritism; I didn't then realize that this gallery owner was Signora's nephew Giovanni, who would repay Dylan's favors of various kinds—I don't believe Signora ever understood exactly what kinds—by promoting his work and fostering, finally, his soft landing in New York. Oh, if Signora had known. Not that she could have done anything to stop the transaction already underway. But she would have been so angry, and her very anger would have seemed to give a justification for mine.

I knew nothing of it either for a long time afterward, would only learn the details of his liaison with Giovanni when Dylan confessed them to me much later, when he asked me if I minded, when I lied and told him no. On that tour bus none of this had hurt us yet. That night the world might have been different, the thing might never have happened. So many things might not have happened. I only told Dylan how happy I was for him and meant it. Too naïve to suppose anyone meant anyone else any evil, I saw nothing to fear, only reason for hope.

Then the conversation drew to a standstill; he shifted closer to me. His almost feverish warmth. His lips, inquisitive, at first hesitant with mine. Earlier, in a field the trail cut through, I had gleaned a couple of red poppies and had tucked them behind my ear. When he leaned against me the flowers fell from my hair and were crushed between us. The scent they exhaled was green and dark as cypress branches.

He placed his cheek on mine, whispered through my hair: "You are heavenly." (Much later, I hear in these words an echo of the postmortem Beatrice would later give us: *he apotheosized you.*)

We clambered out of the bus and ran together, hand in hand, along the lamplit walkway to his apartment. At first shivering all over, although the room was still and warm, before long our two bodies were the only constant and the air and everything else around us was expanding, the air pressure dropping, particles flying loose, wild: electrons shooting out of orbit, the pace of time itself slowing, stretching like a Dali clock, melting off the face of the earth. Well before the moment when I cried out with gratitude and delight and shock, my mind was empty of any other moment, any other consideration or reality. The responsible conscientious unified person I had thought I was had undergone a sea change: lost, overwhelmed; erased by waves.

After, we lay staring awake at a ceiling veiled in shadow, a medium in which mysteries swam unbodied as when you zoom into a black and white photograph to reveal the composition of the greys and charcoals, which all the time are secretly dancing with reds and greens and blues.

"I'm starting over with you," he said, not that night but the next, into the multifarious darkness. "I never had a reason, before, not to be self-centered and fickle. This is different. This is . . . I mean, you're my friend. This is worth taking care of."

I echoed the words. "This is worth taking care of."

"Angele, I . . . I think I love you."

I echoed the words again. What else could I do? What else, and tell the truth? Yet even at the time I wasn't convinced it was honest.

Even at the time, I thought: this is a film we're in, a scene from a film. We have cast ourselves in roles and are choosing now to play them, but we could drop the scripts at any moment and be who we are. And how would that work out? Could we ourselves even tell the difference?

The black air above the bed looked grainy as if captured on old brown reels of recording tape, replayed on an unimaginably vintage piece of equipment, some projector screen or cathode-ray tube where at the touch of a switch the picture could compress itself into one flat silver line, then shrink to a still bright point in the screen's exact center, then become nothing but prickles of rhinestone static, still visible in the cavernous hollow behind the glass where the tubes hunch, hot and frangible.

I'm simply saying lines, I admitted silently to myself, I'm only appearing in the supporting role. Let's be clear. This has all happened before, for him. He's the first for me but I'm not the first for him I'm not the first not at all the first there were others there must have been others and there's no reason there may not be more. Like me. Afterward.

And I remember, too, that I was right from the beginning. I knew from the first, although I desperately wanted not to know, what it was between us and what it wasn't. Later on there was the night in the palmetto-lined courtyard, when he withheld the overtures and false starts but told of the first girl who mattered, for him, the one in high school, when they were fifteen, the youth-group girl everyone thought was a superdevout Lutheran, everyone but Dylan, who knew the flesh behind the front. The girl had lost her parents and was being raised by her aunt and uncle, who then shipped her out to a different aunt and uncle, a still sterner pair who lived in Alaska, when it became unmistakably clear what the girl had been up to: so that by the time I had appeared on the scene with my own projects and plans and had begun to waste away in my self-enclosed prison of desire, a child of Dylan's body was already frolicking in some distant meadow against a backdrop of snowcapped mountains.

Then further confidences spilled out, that night, as if having been previously pressed down, packed tightly in, like clothes rolled into a suitcase that then spring loose in all directions once the clasp is released. There had been the first man, when Dylan was seventeen, a friend of the family, a psychiatrist, the one Elaine had sent him to see informally over his lackluster performance during junior year, academics only part of it—his sense of listlessness, near-total lapse of purpose. Elaine hadn't minded the breach of professionalism involved in the man's inviting Dylan to dinner, but she would have minded, had she known, when he began undoing buckles and buttons, peeling away garments, giving orders—more coach than coaxing, making Dylan feel he had to go along with it, telling him he, Dylan, was already committed to the act, telling Dylan that he, the man, knew what he, Dylan, wanted. Dylan had assumed that the man had been correct, had not then known exactly what he wanted, had, as adolescents sometimes do, merely wanted: hands, any hands, at a certain pitch of desperation it might almost seem not to matter whose, or what else they asked for. He had been young, had not known the law, had not known his recourses, had opted to call what he had given *consent*. He had never told Allen or Elaine. He had wondered at first if Elaine had guessed, had been able to tell: yet as time went on, and nothing came of it, he had set the episode aside in his mind, had learned to call it *an episode*, to tell himself it didn't matter, almost as if it had happened to someone else.

Then, when Dylan left for college, there was a period in which he lived the determined and disillusioned abstinence of the new student establishing a routine. Next a series of hookups, casual girlfriends, casual boyfriends: nothing serious, nothing near lasting.

"Then you came along," he said, "and it didn't dawn on me right away, but when I started to understand what you were to me, who you were to me, I wanted to start fresh. I wanted a clean slate."

Despite Omar, despite Giovanni, when Beatrice showed interest he would want another fresh start, later. "Showed" is right: she was simply there where she hadn't been before, one evening at a party in his loft, her back in a tight black dress turned to me, his arm around her body in a casually possessive gesture, as if it and she had always been in this exact relation.

The night of that party, just as on the later night in the courtyard, I excused myself to the restroom and pressed my forehead to the cool wall tiles (at the Italian resort, an iridescent blue-green with a copperish glaze, small, almost like mosaic materials; at the Williamsburg party, a glassy clear expanse with a flat black background). Both times I pressed my forehead to the walls to feel their coldness, to feel contact with hard truth, and both times I told myself: Cry now, cry now and get it over with, you don't want to be crying alone later tonight, if you cry now you can drown it out by getting sloshed and then you won't have to cry later, when you're alone, but can have already done it and can then be done with it.

So I cried, and was done with it, I believed, until I found myself in the cell in the monastery guesthouse, in the little bathroom without any tiles, with my forehead feeling for a cool that would not come and my eyes aching with what refused to fall, suspended there above the sink and asking myself: why did I agree to come here, why did I allow myself to be drawn back into this man's orbit: why? Why didn't I just stay home? Home. I had none. Nor did he.

XII

November 2015

All night my finished letter to Fr. Isaiah hovers over my head, preventing sleep. It has been delivered— the extern, Michael, took it into the cloister for me, placed it in the mailbox shelf that, he says, is like a college department's interoffice system—but it is still insufficient. Thomas Augustine might not want me to speak the attack back into being, but he didn't tell me not to. And someone must. The unbalance in Elaine's responses makes me fear she is not safe to tell, not here, not like this. And then, such a disclosure between parent and child is not mine to make but her son's, if he chooses.

He told me what happened, and now I take part with those who are working to make him well again. Yet the most urgent responsibility, to keep him close, to protect him, is the monastery's, not mine. I've tried to make this impossible for Fr. Isaiah to ignore. But how can I carry pain that so clearly does not belong to me? I lie awake shivering, and not from the cold.

I wake early on Friday to find that the shower has little water pressure and no hot water. Not at first, when I stand shivering in the scratchy towel. Not after several minutes of standing, shifting from one foot to the other, testing over and over the chill trickle that is all that will come from the showerhead.

I do the best I can, scrubbing hard to remove the soap that won't activate into foam. Its sticky film clings to my skin and to my hair. I comb the long mop and twist it up in a towel and then shake it, doglike, loose. Wrap it again, find the brush. There is an electrical outlet in the room, but it has gone dead. When I plug my dryer in, nothing happens. I push the red and yellow breaker buttons, but this solves nothing.

In a foul humor, then, I dress, wrap my cold hair into a band, pull an extra sweater over my clothes, and lope down the hallway to find Allen seated in the common room with coffee, a cell phone, and a scowl. He wears a pair of rectangular tortoiseshell frames I don't recall seeing on him before, the glasses of someone a generation younger than himself.

"I'm aware of that, I accept that, but at the same time, I said the *soonest possible*," he is saying into the phone, using the crispest and quickest articulation. "I'm a rewards customer, I'm a gold-star member, yet you're telling me it isn't possible to get out of Kentucky before Sunday? I mean, there's no snow, nothing has frozen yet, so what could be the . . . I'm sorry, could I please speak to your supervisor . . . Damn yokel," Allen adds, to me, presumably after the hold music had begun to jingle its calliope into his ear. "Can barely understand an English sentence. Subject, verb, object. *I, need, tickets.* Simple. God. Yes, thank you" (into the phone again). "Thank you, I really do appreciate your attention. We can book a hotel in Louisville, I suppose, but we'd really rather get back to Chicago sooner if we can. We both have meetings on Monday. Yes, we originally booked online. Yes, that would make more sense, and I already tried, but there's no wi-fi and we can't connect through 3G. Yes, I have the confirmation right here . . ."

I gather my coffee and take refuge by the bookshelf. While Allen is still on the phone, Elaine stalks in, her face set. She too collects a cup without speaking and then wanders out again. I glance up from my page and, in doing so, notice the look that passes between them. More than before, the look carries frost in it.

"Thank you," Allen is repeating, "I'd rather be out as early as possible. Are you sure you don't have anything tonight or on Saturday morning? Well, what if we were willing to drive to Nashville? Would you be willing to check what your airline can offer from . . . yes, I'll hold . . . "

What could have happened overnight, I wonder. Elaine paces in and then out again. A call from work, a crisis with a client? Elaine is a psychologist, but I can't remember what Allen does: accounting? Surely nothing could be so urgent about that.

There comes a stifled groan from down the hallway. Allen's frown deepens. Without putting down the phone, he walks briskly through the doors to the guest wing and stays absent. I take my brown bread and butter and my coffee cup out on a plate so that during breakfast I can sit and dry my hair in the thin late autumn sun. The sky today shines flatly, a silver scrim fading to white at the zenith.

When we pass each other again in the common room later, Elaine's hand is bandaged with white tape and smooth non-adhesive pads. Again she and Allen are looking at each other. If I were a child they would be looking at me over my head; I'm not a child, and I don't miss the look. This time the look contains paragraphs, each with its own heading.

"I broke my perfume bottle," Elaine says with a short laugh. "Butterfingers."

This checks out: a strong floral aroma is rising from her skin, although her clothing isn't stained; she must have changed after it happened.

"Packing?"

"You must have overheard. We have to get back to Chicago sooner."

"For work?"

"Well, I do have some catching up to do."

Not really work, then. "Is everything all right? No one's sick?"

"No, nobody."

Changing plane reservations is costly, but Elaine and Allen will never miss what they'll spend, I suppose. They eat quickly and go out to the garden, to see if cell reception is better there.

The other guests: where have they been all morning? It now strikes me as odd that so many were here yesterday, on Thanksgiving, and are gone today, now that the holiday is over. Yesterday I saw them chatting with Brother Michael, complimenting him on what Mrs. Russell called *the cuisine*, thanking him for his work. When he comes in to clear the dishes, I ask him if he knows where they are.

"Mrs. Russell's gone to Lexington," Michael says cheerfully, "to spend the day with her daughter, the one she's on good terms with. Marjorie said she was planning to stay through the weekend. I brought in the first round of coffee at six, and she was out here then. She came to Mass, but I haven't seen her since. Were you wanting to talk to her?"

"She was acting upset last night. I meant to check whether she was okay now."

"She was all right, the last time I saw her. The Mass often has that effect."

I thank him; he disappears into the kitchen; I almost call after him, almost offer to carry a tray, even to scrub mugs and pans, just for someone sane to talk to.

Allen and Elaine sweep past, arguing: "He has to acknowledge," I hear Elaine murmur, although it isn't clear who has to acknowledge what. They depart through the doors that lead toward the offices and are gone.

Michael comes back, wheeling a filled coffee urn on a cart with fresh cups.

"It's the Fieldings I'm not sure about," he says to me, unprompted, clearly unaware that the Fieldings just passed through. "They apologized, after last night. They even offered to help clean up. But it was in the cloister, and she'd already . . ."

The confusion on my face alerts Michael that I don't know what he's talking about, that he shouldn't have assumed I would.

"I'm sorry, forget I said anything," he continues, turning a crepe-myrtle pink above his patchy three-day beard. For the first time I realize he is younger than I am.

I don't want Michael to feel pressured, so I don't ask for details. I don't, at this point, particularly wish to know any. What I have seen and heard already is almost more than I can carry.

Feeling the need to calm down, I slump on the couch with a book that calls itself *Mystics and Meditators* and, with embarrassing speed, fall asleep.

An hour later, the Fieldings wake me with their voices: they are still arguing when they return to the common room.

"If you just could've restrained yourself," Allen is saying.

"Well, if there had been any other option open to us," Elaine retorts.

"Option! What do you mean by options, I wonder. What you did wasn't an 'option;' it was probably a felony. You'll be lucky if the monks don't press charges."

"What about turning the other cheek and all that. I doubt we'll have legal trouble with them. They might have legal trouble with us."

"Elaine. You're not seriously considering—"

"If they're holding our son against his will—"

"It's not against his will. It's against yours." Allen's brow is a scrawl of anger. "You're not his guardian anymore. He's been a legal adult for ten years. Stop talking nonsense."

"And it's legal to imprison someone who's of age?"

"Retreats aren't prisons. He wants to be here. I can't get you to understand that: he *wants* to be here. He doesn't want to leave."

"You're so sure of that. I'm not going to trust anything I haven't heard directly from him, himself. You're always reading about these cover-ups, these scandals. Who knows what could be going on?"

"He wrote to us. He told us himself; he keeps telling us. You don't want to accept it. Dear."

"Damned right I don't. *Dear.* I won't believe he didn't write us that letter under some kind of psychological pressure. Hypnotism, obsession. Or merely irrational belief. Thinking Hell is real, that he's going there if he leaves this place. That is the very definition of a cult. Or only—and this would be enough—that the way he was living five years ago was so horribly wrong. That wanting what he wants, *being who he is*, is wrong. I can prove to him otherwise, I can be the voice of reason, if they'll just let me see him. So naturally I'm not surprised that they won't."

"Elaine, he doesn't want to see you. Even if he did want to, he's on retreat, he's supposed to keep silence, it's like a—a meditation thing. The community won't make an exception for you, but you think they should, and so you're angry."

"I notice they make all kinds of allowances for lurking around with sneaky ex-girlfriends. Just not for *mothers*."

"Elaine. You're judging a boundary you don't understand."

"Excuse me, but which of us has the degree in psychology here. Specialist in subconscious phenomena, need I remind you. When I want help examining my motivations, I'll ask for it, thanks all the same."

Does Elaine (I ask myself, still curled catlike and motionless near the bookcase) truly not notice who is in rooms with her? Or does she only not much care who overhears what she has to say? Or does she believe I'm still asleep? I try not to move. There come footsteps, then silence.

When I open my eyes, Allen is pouring himself coffee. The expression on his face when he notices me waking up speaks of a man who, having decided to travel on a road he knows is iced over, intends to drive until he either spins out or reaches the destination. Without needing to be invited, when I sit up, he sits down on the couch next to me and starts to speak.

"You'll hear about it sooner or later, so I may as well tell you now," he says. "Elaine woke up in the middle of the night last night. She didn't wake me or tell me where she was going or what she planned to do. She took it into her head that she was going to find Dylan and talk to him, permission or not. So she went into the restricted area of the monastery and opened up every door she could find, every door that didn't lock. Some rows were locked: probably the monks' cells: she says she thought about banging on all of the doors, trying to find someone who would answer—but decided not to, lost her nerve. . . .

"Then. Well. Now I don't know if she planned it this way or if it was just the impulse of anger after not being able to find him, but entirely on her own initiative, she trashed the cloister. When I say 'trashed' don't picture a hotel room after a metal band's been through. Picture a sorority house raided by frenzied partygoers. Clods of wet toilet paper flung around, more pulled into streamers, rolled down the hallways. She plugged the sink drains, she flooded the bathroom floors, she emptied the soap dispensers and slimed the counters. She wrote rude words in lipstick on the walls, even on the artwork. Knocked the head off a statue or two. That's as far as Elaine's creativity stretched. God. Like a schoolgirl's."

Allen's finger and thumb creep up behind the lenses of the glasses and press gently against his closed eyelids for a moment. "She ran away afterward. This was not even an hour before the monks woke up for midnight prayers. She's lucky they didn't catch her. I don't know if they know yet who did it. But they must suspect. I don't know what to expect.

"I'm a bit sickened by the whole thing. It's puerile. Regressive. As such, it's—" he sighs. "Not a terribly large surprise, I suppose. Elaine keeps that whole part of her personality, that child-self, so tightly under wraps so much of the time. Every so often, it springs out like this. I'm always a bit taken aback. Embarrassed. My apologies. On her behalf, of course. She asked me to tell you. . . .

"I'm sorry, I shouldn't have said so much on my own account, but she did ask me to apologize to you for how she thinks she came across to you. She didn't say anything about the vandalism. She doesn't know I told you about all of this, in fact, so as a favor to me, could you maybe just not mention it to her?

"So but of course . . . I wanted to try to get us out of here sooner than later. We've outstayed our welcome, to say the least. So I think we'll just head to Louisville today. Tickets or no tickets, I'll just have to talk her into it. Get a rideshare. Get an earlier flight or stay in a hotel or what have you. Just . . . be done. I'll be so happy to be done with all of this.

"I should say, though, before I go—Elaine asked me to tell you—that she's grateful, we're grateful, to you, for coming here this weekend, for standing up for . . . for our son." Allen can't decide—or isn't sure whether to use, can't bring himself to pronounce—either name belonging to Thomas Augustine. "It's all a terrible mess, I know, but we think you're very loyal, beyond loyal, really, to show up anyway and try to offer what support you can. We do appreciate it, even if Elaine doesn't agree that staying here is the best choice for Dylan. We both think that you're . . . you're very brave, considering what it must be costing you. I mean, even if he were to leave the monastery now, you're certainly aware that the two of you wouldn't be getting back together? That that ship has sailed? Although I have to be honest, I like you more than I ever did like Beatrice, simply as a companion, a conversationalist. If I were voting for a daughter-in-law . . . but of course that isn't what it's about; I'm afraid you'll have to forgive me, I'm hideously old-fashioned in that way. And I'm talking too much, on top of it all. Do tell me how you're doing with all of this."

I take a breath. I can't tell Allen what was said in the garden. About the attack. Allen is caught up in his own trouble, and it is trouble enough for him. What good would it do to call upon him in in a situation he is helpless to correct?

Who can I tell? Who will be able to help? What can be done that will not make it worse?

I can say this much to Allen: "This isn't about how we're doing with it. At first I would have agreed with Elaine that—Thomas

Augustine—was making a mistake. I'm not sure what changed. I don't think I could do what he wants to do, but I can imagine it now—why someone would want this life—the way it is meant to work. If he can live it the way it's meant to work, I can respect that choice."

Allen nods. He has a look on his face of mellow acceptance, a look that speaks of college years spent having just such conversations: high on substances, dressed in flannel, seated on carpets bordered by wilting couches: affirming narratives, stating truisms, dispensing advice.

Like the painter I wish I still were, I can't help but contrast this image with the way Allen looked and behaved in those months in Chicago, in the aftermath of my relationship with Dylan—crisp, sparkling, groomed, eager to please. Even after everything ended between me and their son, the Fieldings still invited me over often to dinner, spotted me at openings and said hello. They seemed to feel apologetic, to want to make amends. They invited me much more often than I went, which I did out of a sense of obligation as much as for some remnant of connection to their son. The few times I did show, they inevitably served something excessive, standing rib roasts or wide slabs of salmon; Elaine poured the wine, laughed wry laughs at tired jokes, smoothed her hair, looked out the window.

Those evenings, Allen would always have on a fresh white shirt, would always smile, angled toward me in a way that—this thought causes a lurch like the start of an elevator ride—carried a meaning, signaled a desire. Or did it? My recollection of Elaine's posture, by contrast—angled away from us, avoiding, detaching—jolts into sharp relief.

As soon as the idea occurs to me, I want to jar the image it conjures loose from my mind. I almost have to put my hands up, hold my face, to stop myself from visibly shaking my head.

"You might be right. It might be better," I say out loud, "if you drove out today. It sounds like Elaine needs some breathing room, and it sounds like you're ready to go." I clear my throat. "It was good seeing you"—it is hard to get the final word out—"both."

"Yes. You too. Well." Allen clasps his hands together the way someone might when declaring the ending of a business meeting. "Let's be in touch."

"Yes." No. I want to be as far away from Allen as possible. Him and the woman he helped Elaine become. He cannot help me or his son or—God help him—anyone. Help will have to come from elsewhere. *We don't, mostly. People. Stop.*

"I should let you finish packing. Do give me a call sometime"— why did I say that? "Tell Elaine I . . . I hope she feels better."

"I will." Smiles, smiles. I back out the double door and then, once out of sight, run all the way to the bench and the yellow gingko tree. Those leaves not dangling by fibers are falling by handfuls in the fresh breeze: they loose a shower of gold on the slatted seat.

The book I've brought with me, on inspection, is not *Mystics and Meditators* but *Story of a Soul*, which I had picked up off the shelf and then—I thought—put back. These two books must have had similar covers. Oh well, I think, flipping pages. A line jumps out, hooks me: *I wanted to become a prisoner. Though I knew I still had to struggle and suffer before I saw the gates of my blessed prison open to let me in, I lost none of my confidence.* I sit down to read.

At first the rest of the text resists me, or I resist it, or both. Not much longer. Saturday. Sunday. Flight out of Louisville, 2:09 p.m. Back through Atlanta, its wide white and grey hallways crisp with their smells of carpet and fresh paint, sharp as spray fixative; air chemically frigid with thousands of pounds of Freon: its outsize backlit signage—Kriehl's, Sunglass Icon, TouchTable, Bijoux Terner, Brighton, Coach, Blue Moon Brewhouse, Spirit, ATLNEXT—a litany of the patron saints of the New South, commerce and efficiency and new money, enshrined in a domed and skylit concourse in the round that is itself a pantheon of sorts. Back, on Sunday, to what is—for me, for all purposes—the Old World: Chicago O'Hare, with nothing to look forward to but below-zero temperatures and winds as violent as the hooks of coat hangers.

This Thérèse, though: she is real. She knows poverty, knows pain. Barely more than a toddler, staring at her dead mother; barely a teenager, separated from the sister who raised her; opposed by her father, opposed by her bishop, stating her case before the Pope: she is intense. I squirm at the heat of her fervor; I don't quite dare to inquire what fuels it. She offers her own explanation, but to take her at her word would mark me with the same naïvete she so readily, shamelessly reveals.

The book is soon over, too soon. Oh God, what do people *do* here? What is there to be done? Can you do the things that Thérèse says she does; how do you do them? How would you even begin?

What does Thomas Augustine do here all day? He can paint only an hour or two most days, he said. This must torment him, whatever effort he may make to put a good face on it. I remember him, in college and afterward, haunting the studio endlessly: demanding and receiving his own key to the school's space, then that first month in New York quickly spending all his savings to rent his own, living on credit cards and on borrowed cash from friends, yet all the while arguing with his parents on the phone about how he was going to manage: *No, don't send a check. No. I'll tear it up. Fine, then you'll be wasting your postage.* Dylan couldn't stand to feel dependent on anyone, least of all Allen and Elaine. When I first moved in with him in a tiny, temporary sublet—before his paintings began to sell so madly and he found his place in Williamsburg—he refused my offers of a loan, pleaded with me to bank my extra income, frowned on me paying even for takeout, consistently scraped together his half of the rent even if this meant (as I later found out it had meant) selling his possessions or his own plasma. Dishonest as he was in other ways, he behaved as if he had taken a private inner vow never to cause anyone close to him a moment's financial anxiety, and with me at least he succeeded in this.

Other kinds of anxiety he caused in abundance: crashes from the work room at two a.m. as he stomped through the canvas of a failed painting, broke the frame, kicked the easel into the wall; jolts and lurches of the heart at parties, when he trailed a touch across the back of someone else's neck or shot someone a glance that left me asking myself if they had been together, what if, yet knowing I could never wonder aloud, never without meeting an almost moralistic disapproval in him: *why Angele, why would you even say that, what difference would it make to you, don't tell me you would mind? I wouldn't mind if you did anything like that: I swear I wouldn't: we're creators, we have to follow our desires where they take us. I thought more of you than that, don't cry, you know I love you most. Are you worried about getting sick, I'll go get tested if you want*, he would jest, leaving the decision up to me: whether to take it as a joke or to press the issue, make it serious.

But to make it serious, to insist on exclusivity, would at that time have been to put myself in the wrong with him. Here, then, is the selfish root of my resistance to his new life: I resent that he changed his mind and his life only after I was out of it, only when a desire to give himself exclusively would no longer mean giving himself to me.

How did the change take place: how did he become so serious? How and when did his comedy become a tragedy? I am so far outside my frame of reference: my words to Allen ring empty; no one else's choices make sense to me, and every action I can think of to do next feels like the wrong one.

The sky is as white as a blank sheet of paper. I start walking the trail out of sheer restlessness. The pond is glassy except where wood ducks ripple a path through it, where lines in the shape of an expanding V shear off their feathered sides and mirror the overhead flight of geese in formation.

Damn yokel. Allen's phrase, directed at the airline worker, settles down, makes itself comfortable, builds a nest in my hair. It is after all what I am. I have tried and tried to peel off my past like a worn garment, to lay it aside, slip into a new one. But it may be that no matter what I choose to wear, it will make no difference. My poverty, my earnestness, my ineradicable naivëte dwell in me on a cellular level: inhabit my flesh, slump my shoulders, cramp my hands: mark me plainly, visible to the naked eye.

The landscape whispers a different story. Forget about all that, it says. Look, here are valleys, crests, ridges. Here are brown and ochre, here is goldenrod, here is olive. Here is a sky the color of a canvas. All right, so you hate yourself: that isn't so much wrong as it is irrelevant. Suppose you go in and find a sketchbook. Suppose you go home and try painting this.

I walk on, framing canvases in my mind, until I come to a stark stone edifice at least eight feet high. There is a door in the wall; a broken gate, propped open, leans to one side of it. All along the wall, ivy thrives. The vines shoot from the top of the stonework like water from a fountain before they spill out over the edge and down to the ground. Right next to the gate is posted a small sign. This reads: *Canonical enclosure. Do not enter on pain of excommunication.*

I have seen the same signs on certain doors inside the monastery halls. Clearly they didn't deter Elaine from making her point, or relieving her feelings. I wonder how she had the nerve to do it. I wasn't raised religious, but each time I have walked past these signs I have felt a sort of childlike dread, the same feeling that the prologue to *The Cloud of Unknowing* gave me, a sensation rarely encountered in waking adult life. Far deeper than *Private Property: Do Not Trespass.* It is the jarring wrongness of a certain type of image in dreams, fitting into a category I might call distorted interstices. It is tentacles where a curtain ought to be, a mouth instead of a door, a daylight-showing hole clear through the chest of a live, breathing person. A sense that traversing this space will lead you into another space where other rules obtain besides those of the observable material world.

I don't believe in such rules, yet I can't bring myself to cross that boundary, any more than I would be able to take unironic part in an altar call or a faith healing. How did Elaine do it?

Here is a better question: How, through what series of events, has Dylan come to accept a chain of logic that begins with an untouchable apple in a garden and ends with an unopenable door in a wall? Elaine's hypothesis sounds less far-fetched to me now, standing alone on a meadow with nothing to shelter me from every breeze of thought or feeling that might pass by. I can only too easily think of the sorts of things that might have been said to him here, the pressures that might have been brought to bear. Phrases float up to the surface of my mind, words from documentaries about cults and backwoods church camps, half-formed notions whose referents I can only picture, not define. Rapture. Revelation. The chosen. How could anyone as intelligent as Thomas Augustine believe such things?

At least I can palpably sense how he could come to believe in eternal loss, perpetual separation, the endless displeasure of an all-sustaining force: the fury and the rejection painted across Elaine's own face. I haven't seen the lipstick drawings she left in the cloister, but my mind recreates them as frowning eyebrows angled down toward the noses of stone saints, sharp teeth scrawled across mild mouths. Whatever has been said to him to frighten him, whatever fear may have come to him now, it may be only an outgrowth of the threat of abandonment that has always haunted him.

Then—out of the distorted interstice, an apparition: Elaine strides through the door in the wall, coming from the direction of the enclosure. Her grimace twists like a gargoyle's. She doesn't notice me at first, but when she does, she locks on to me as if driven by some artificial intelligence.

"I can't find him," she says breathlessly. "I thought they were all supposed to be working now. The schedule is all wrong. I don't know where they are. I can't find him. I can't find anyone."

Without asking, she grabs my wrist and pulls me along behind her, back toward the door.

"Elaine? This isn't—I can't—?"

"Come on," she says, "I don't have long. The cab will be here any minute, and Allen is beside himself."

As in a nightmare, where objections and protestations come out of the mouth in the form of insects or balloons, I cannot make my disagreement understood. I am swept along. We cross through vegetable gardens, vast raised beds, some of them bursting with pumpkins and squash. The green wire rings of the tomato trellises, their diagonally up-reaching rays, still stand evenly spaced and leveled although the remains of the vines now have the texture and color of parchment. I expect to encounter startled laborers, to be chased with rakes and trowels, but the paths are deserted. At some moments we are almost hidden among mesh birdproof nets, behind round wire cold frames draped with linen.

We find and follow a bricked path that runs around the edge of the gardens, passes behind a shed, and then leads up to a side door in the main building. Elaine pushes the door open gingerly, attending to the sound made by the sliding of the panic bar. She then pulls it to again behind us, grasping the bar in an effort to silence the lock's triangular, clicking tongue.

In the shady hallway, she casts her glance around, she trembles. Is she afraid? No—she's laughing.

"A return to the scene of the crime," she whispers, not really to me.

We hear footsteps not our own. Elaine yanks my arm, and before I can breathe we are in a dusty room off the corridor, a room piled with broken tables and chairs. It could once have been a classroom or a conference room, maybe meant for retreats. The top half of the door is paned with frosted glass, through which our silhouettes though not our features could plainly be seen.

I flatten myself against the outermost wall—as best I can, finding the base of my spine pressed against the metal rail of a chalkboard—and motion to Elaine to do the same.

"At least they'll remember me," she says in a low tone, her eyes wide. "They won't be able to say I wasn't here. They'll have to account for me."

"We shouldn't be here," I tell her. "You know we shouldn't."

"'Don't touch. Don't taste. Don't walk through the door.' Rules like these are the refuge of the coward," she says. "My son wants to hide from who he is. His leaders want to hide *him*, obliterate him.

They wish people like him didn't exist. If they help him erase himself, problem solved. No big talent making you feel small anymore. They don't understand it for what it is in him: Death wish. Suicidal impulse. Textbook. They're enabling it. I can't let them," and her voice crescendos, so loud now that I feel like a schoolgirl smoking in a bathroom stall, like expulsion is imminent. "Do you see? This is so clear to me now. Look, I realize this sounds self-important, but that doesn't make it untrue: I'm the only one in his life capable of seeing *exactly what is going on here*. That means I'm the one with the responsibility to put a stop to it. I might not succeed, but I have to try," she hisses, as if she wants to shriek it.

There is no way she knows exactly what is going on, is there? I haven't told her; she hasn't seen Thomas Augustine; certainly the monks wouldn't tell her. She might be of help if she could surmount her own disintegration long enough to think of him. Yet whether or not her son truly hovers at the threshold of some private and inner disaster, Elaine stands not far from one.

Should I tell her? Can I? I'm afraid to speak. I try to choose my words carefully, but what needs to be said will not take shape. It is almost as though the words, not my lips, hold the agency. The question I really want to ask her keeps changing its form as it escapes and, serpentlike, traverses the distance between us.

"Did Dylan ever . . . when he was younger . . . did he try to . . . did he say he wanted . . ."

"To kill himself? Not in so many words. Never in those words. I knew."

I knew. "How did you know?"

"Mothers know these things."

Often they don't, I want to reply. To say nothing of the things those mothers' children do not know.

But: "Listen," says Elaine. We stop talking. Silence in the hallway has crept back into the room, threading its way around the edges of the door like smoke. Above the door hangs a plain crucifix, with a corpus carved from lighter wood than the polished bars on which it suffers decade after decade in the quiet.

"Let's go."

"Let's wait. I don't want to be caught."

"Do you think I do? I'd catch much worse hell than you."

"I think we should go back. You said Allen was waiting for you. The meter on the cab is probably already running." Wrong tack. As if money mattered to her.

"I have to try one more time. I'll feel the trip was wasted unless I can say to myself that I made every effort to see Dylan again. To say what needs to be said."

She roll-steps across the room, heel before toe; she grasps the brass knob and twists it with care. I tense expectantly. The tile underfoot feels dusty, gritty.

"Let's go back. We have no idea where he is."

"All we can do is try."

"I just don't understand—"

"Child, you haven't borne children; how could you be expected to understand?"

Now, now I can tell her what she needs to know. What her son has suffered. "Elaine, when I saw him in the garden, when we—"

"Shh, not now." She tries the door again.

Both of us expect to be caught eventually. Neither of us thinks, when cautiously Elaine swings the door open at last, to see a monk already standing there like a Rodin statue, bronze-still, brown face above white habit. Neither of us expects the bronze to fracture. A shock runs through us at the sound of his abrupt, hearty, wide-mouthed laugh.

The sound cuts through my fear so that I begin to laugh too, anxiously at first and then louder and louder. The monk and I laugh together while Elaine stands looking at us both, for once without speech.

This monk is someone we haven't seen before. He is tall as a tree, broad in all directions, young, bearded, dark. His laugh sounds genuine, not mocking. The absurdity of the moment is not lost on him. His eyes glint as he leads us wordlessly out and down the hallway, back through the cloister toward the common areas that are open to guests, and into another conference room, this one freshly renovated, with pale walls and high windows. Long seminar tables stretch out in rows, each with its complement of cloth-covered chairs. Elaine and I follow the tall monk like mice through a maze.

At his nod, we sit down in fabric-backed chairs, facing a white board between two doors. Traces of the odor of dry-erase marker linger in the air, sharp as cleaning solvent but with a sour note underneath. The monk leaves us alone in the room and steps back out into the hallway. It feels as though we are back in college, about to take a test for which we are unprepared.

Like a student aware of constant scrutiny, constant monitoring, Elaine leans toward me in her chair and speaks in a near-whisper, although we are alone in the room.

"I don't expect you to understand how I feel about what's happening," she says. "I realize it's the bitterest, ugliest side of me that's showing right now. I'd simply ask that you not judge me. You're probably not thinking of becoming a mother at this point in your life. But someday you might. When you do, if you do, think of me. Think of this. Think of that tiny head cradled in your hand, still damp from your body, from your blood. That smell of your newborn, which you'll never forget once you've known it. Think what it would mean to be totally cut off from the only person you ever held like this, the only person who grew inside your body or ever will. Think, in that moment, what it would mean to have that person hate you. To have that person never want to see you. To—"

Her speech is interrupted when the tree-tall young monk opens the right-hand door again. Two more unfamiliar men walk in past him, all wearing the blank habits of the order. The young one shuts the door behind them and takes his place in the line. It surprises me when the monks arrange themselves around another conference table, pick it up, move the chairs out from behind it, and carry it forward until it forms one table with ours.

They sit down facing us across the table and introduce themselves: Father Aidan, novice master, lean, balding, wearing wire rims; Father Matthew, cellarer, with, now that he is seated, the aspect of a former football coach; Father Cyprian, senior council member, mild, greying, diminutive, somehow the scariest of the three.

Father Cyprian starts by introducing himself—he mentions in passing his other titles but places the emphasis, the reason for his presence, on his being Thomas Augustine's personal director—and then apologizing on behalf of Father Isaiah, who again can't be present because some other problem has called him away, who has sent Father Cyprian to represent him.

"I'd ask you to tell me why we're here," he says, "but I think we all already know. Still, for the sake of clarity, ma'am." He looks at Elaine expectantly.

"You won't let me see my son."

"Your son wants to make a life here. He wants to respond to God's will in his life. You're having trouble accepting this."

"You're damned right I have trouble accepting it. For one thing, I think it's a heap of—"

"I don't think that's going to be helpful. Even so, we've been over it all already."

"Have we? Forgive me if I say I don't feel you've really heard me out."

"The prior met with you for more than an hour on Thanksgiving Day. I was there, listening, if you recall. He said very little. He let you speak. Let me say on his behalf that we understand your concerns. You're not the first parent—"

"My son's case is a special one."

"Everybody's case is a special one. Some are only more complicated than others."

Elaine holds up her hands, the outstretched ire of her eyes, as if to keep this idea at a distance. "Let's say his case is complicated, then. If we say that, can we agree to look together at the details of it? Closely, honestly? Forgive me if I say I don't think this has been done so far. At least, if it has, I haven't been aware of it. I think you're overlooking the obvious: I think he's here to hide away from his own personal and professional fears. I think that letting him carry on in that way is the opposite of love. It doesn't serve his best interests."

"As you'll be well aware, love is usually not about serving our own best interests, even if we do often find that our needs are also met along the way."

"Forgive me if this sounds rude or obtuse, but what is there, here, to meet his needs? What is there for him to love?"

Father Cyprian only smiles at this. Slowly, he opens his clasped hands, turning the palms upward. The other two monks are silent, as they have been well trained to be.

Elaine persists: "His relationship with his fiancée had hit a rocky patch. His art sales had begun to decline after an intense period of success. He felt he was going into a creative drought. Then this place turned up as the answer to all his problems. Basically, he fled."

"If we believed this was true, he wouldn't still be here. Men and women who are frightened of loss and suffering generally don't last long in a cloistered community."

"No, I suppose not." It has become impossible to tell whether Elaine is being sarcastic or not: her voice has reached a depth and pitch at which it sounds almost like a man's.

"Well." Father Cyprian leans back and smiles at her, not without kindness. "Naturally, it would sound confusing, to be told two apparently contradictory things at the same time. We're inviting illumination and context from those who have known Brother Thomas Augustine well, and yet we're not inviting his friends and family to be part of the final decision about his vocation. This is difficult for you."

Elaine looks grim and doesn't respond.

"And it's difficult for me to have to tell you," Father Matthew speaks up now, "that when guests have shown a lack of respect for the boundaries of our community, it is my duty to ask them to leave."

When Elaine howls aloud at this—*howls* is no exaggeration; the sound rips forth from her—it causes my throat to tighten in fear and furious abandonment.

"Duty," she spits. Then: "You don't understand," she says, muddily. Then with crisper speech: "You don't understand. But how could you be expected to understand. You haven't given birth. You haven't given life. You haven't lived in a body like this one," and she strikes herself right below the collarbone, so hard I can hear the protest of bone against muscle. She hits with her bandaged hand and the white gauze makes a soft crunch as it flattens against her skin. "He is mine, mine. Whatever else he is, whatever else comes—mine. That can't be taken back. Can't be changed. You can't. And I gave so much. Not just the delivery. Although oh God, that would have been enough. All my dignity gone. And blood everywhere. Naked and drugged on the table and surrounded by strangers and past all ability to care. It wasn't my body anymore then, just a piece of wreckage. Not any part of me. . . .

"What no one tells you is that when you go into labor, you go into labor *for the rest of your life.* That feeling of desperation? Of being ripped in two pieces, slowly, for hours at a time? Not knowing, oh God, how much longer can I do this? How much longer can I stand it? That feeling? *Never goes away.* I lost so much. I lost so much. Not only blood. My mind, my time. My clients. I made other people suffer; I wasn't available to them when they needed me. For a long time I had to drop my practice; he was expelled from preschool three times, and for a long time there was no one else who could manage him. Even then, it was a struggle. Even after he went to school—for years and years, for far too long—I constantly had to be available to him. For him. Managing the situation, smoothing things over."

She rises from the chair, paces between the table and the exit, tapping her fingernails on the narrow ledge of the half-window in the door. Blood is leaking through the gauze now, a rusty splotch of it, but Elaine goes on gesturing with the damaged hand, holding it high. A drop seeps from under a bend in the tape and draws a red line down the side of her arm and into the cuff of her blouse sleeve. Elaine does not notice the line.

"But, of course, you'll say, he's been an adult now for years, he hasn't been depending on you; that's true, but still, he hasn't lost this need for dependence. He has always found someone more competent, more of his own world, to depend on: Beatrice would have been good for him, in that way—but up until then he needed me: he has needed someone, always, to manage his life for him: and now that he's come here, it's no different. Only it's you now, it's you he's going to depend on to manage his life. It's you he's going to exploit and use and destroy from the inside out. So I may as well tell you how. How he's going to do it. There's nothing left of me anymore that hasn't been exploited or used or destroyed. And so I should know. If you're wondering what's best for him, I should know. If you're wondering what's going to happen if he stays here, I should know. Better than anyone. So just let me tell you." And then, almost inaudible—did she actually say it and, if so, did they hear her—"'Upon pain of excommunication.'" No, surely they did not hear her.

Father Aidan shifts his weight, as if to stand up, to move for the door, to call someone. Father Cyprian senses the movement and, keeping the rest of his body very still, places one hand flat on the table, gently, in Father Aidan's direction: a clear, wordless "stop; wait." Without turning, Father Cyprian shakes his head almost imperceptibly; he inclines his ear toward Elaine. She goes on:

"You're so fond of rules. Rules don't mean anything to him. He'll comply as long as it gets him what he wants. He'll break loose as soon as it's possible and convenient. He'll tell you one thing and do another. I've seen it over and over. Private school expulsions, conflicts with tutors, untold drama with publicists and gallerists and assistants, an endless string of best friends and partners dumped one after another—" her eyes cut quickly in my direction—"I should say I've seen it all by now. And the thing is he's hardly ever unpleasant about it. He'll make it all but impossible for you to call him out because he's just so damned pleasant. Until he's not. Then he makes it look like your fault . . . But when it comes to placing blame, isn't it what we all do? I'm doing it right now, aren't I? Right this minute. I've broken your rule and I'm making it my son's fault, and your fault for not understanding—which, I have to be clear, you don't—but at the same time, I feel that I'm out of options here."

She goes over to the door and puts her fingers on the lever of the handle. "I've been stonewalled and cut off and explained to, oh my God the unceasing explanations, and you simply have to understand. You have to understand. You'll be making a terrible mistake if you don't try to understand. He can't stay here. It isn't right for him. It isn't right for this place. *He* isn't right for this place. And you don't recognize my authority to tell you that. But I'm telling you that I have that authority. It's right here." She strikes herself on the chest again. "It's in everything I've suffered. From him, for him. To have a child is to be hurt. To have a child is to have pain. And if pain doesn't give knowledge, I don't know what does. I . . . I thought you would understand that—crucifix and all. More than you'd grasp my clinical credentials."

The monks look at each other. No one speaks for some time. No one here is frightened of silence, except for Elaine. She doesn't know what to do with it. Her words bleed out into it again.

"Listen to me," she says. "That's all I'm asking. You can throw me out on my ear. It won't matter because I'm not staying any longer anyway. The cab is in the driveway. I know when I'm not wanted around. But—listen. Think about what I've said. Let it sink in. Take it into account. I don't insist on anything else. Only this: listen. I know I don't know everything, but I know when I'm right."

She grasps the lever, swings the door open.

"There's a taxi waiting," she repeats. "Could someone tell me the way back to the guesthouse from here, please?"

Father Matthew steps out the door with her, briskly but not urgently. I have a sudden urge to run after them; I have questions for Elaine, and it seems as though she could now, finally, answer. Her face as she turns is like nothing so much as the tragedy mask from a Mardi Gras throw, full of frightful frozen insight, certain knowledge. Only the eyes inside the mask look alive—lit with regret, with a longing for restoration that has come too late.

Father Cyprian turns to me as the door closes.

"So," he says. "We found you in the enclosure as well. There's no real reason for you to have been there. What happened? Is there anything you'd like to say?"

I sit; I stare. I can't speak after Elaine: her words drift and float and settle all over the room like piles of scattered feathers, dampening sound.

"It's all right," says Father Matthew on his return, who up until now has been silent. "That was a lot, just now. Let her have a moment."

Let her have a moment. What, if not a moment, did Elaine just have? Then I understand: he is talking about me.

"She pulled me in with her," I say. "I didn't want to be here."

"What people call love," Father Cyprian says quietly, nodding out the door again. "What we just heard and saw. That's what it looks like, so often."

My own voice startles me. "I wouldn't call that love."

"No?"

"No." Now the confidence of Elaine's anger has bolstered my own sense of perception and I know, as I speak, that I have caught hold of the corner of a truth the way a child catches the hem of her mother's dress, looked down upon with more than patience. For when I say *she* I could as well be saying *I*: "She's looking entirely at herself. At who she is in relation to him. She's not looking at him."

"We did give him the choice whether to meet with her," Father Cyprian tells me. "He declined. That was his right. He's meant to be on retreat. It's a preparation for the final vows. This time belongs to him, to use as he thinks best. No one's will is being forced."

This surprises me, but I don't respond to it; I still haven't made my point.

"I mean she isn't looking at him. Or, no. She is looking at him. But that's all she's doing. She isn't seeing what she's looking at."

Across Father Cyprian's face there spreads a look of understanding. "Yes."

"She doesn't see him the way he is. She never has. Can you love what you don't see?"

Father Cyprian considers this before he answers. He adjusts his wire-rimmed glasses as if he would like to make a remark, but he holds back for an unusually long time.

"You aren't wrong," Father Cyprian says at last. As he speaks, the creases in his face shift, placing their own emphasis on the words. "For love to exist, first there has to be some perception of what is there."

"Even if seeing it upsets you."

"Yes. Especially then."

Father Cyprian has brought one arm across his body and the other hand up to his face; now he lifts both hands, clasps them again on the table. "We can't know what goes on in others' hearts. It hasn't been given to us to know that."

"We can know what we observe. That gives you evidence that can be trusted, if you ask me."

"I would like to ask you." The old priest's sudden smile is a sign, an invitation: his teeth are wildly crooked and coffee-stained, and this makes me less afraid of him rather than more so: the flaw makes him human, even endearing.

"Tell me what you've seen," he says.

"I'm devastated. I don't know how I can tell you. What he and I were to each other then. And now—"

"I think I understand. You gave each other the world, in a way. Your youth, your abilities. You were all of that for each other."

"We were. That's why it's so hard to see him like—"

Father Cyprian seems almost to laugh, but without sound.

"Ah, I was wondering when that was going to come out, that you met again, here. Yes, we all know about the midnight summit."

"Oh. I'm sorry."

"That wasn't your fault. He ought not to have written to you in that way."

"I—knew it. I should have known better."

"Don't be upset. You're both young. By now we've seen everything."

"But exactly. You've seen everything, everything. You know how much worse—"

I have to gather strength to go on. Where it is going to come from I do not know; I feel hollowed out, a husk; or else consumed, the core of a fruit when nothing but its seeds are left. My upturned hands on the table are empty. I find myself longing to hide: first wishing that the hills would rise up to cover me, then simply that I could shield myself in some kind of cloak that would protect me entirely from what has to be said next.

"It's hard to see him suffering the way he is. She doesn't know. He didn't tell her. He told me."

"Told you what?"

"You don't know?"

"I think you'd do better to say it yourself."

"About—what happened to Thomas Augustine. The attack. The—the rape."

Fr. Cyprian's eyes close for a moment. His face reddens—anger, embarrassment, I can't tell.

"So he did tell you the worst of it," he says. "Well. It is hard to see him suffering. It hurts us all. That such a thing should have happened here. That it should have happened anywhere."

"It can't hurt you the way it did him. Otherwise why did you let it *happen*."

"Our trust was betrayed. I'm afraid I can't say more than that." Father Cyprian's eyes close again, longer this time. "'No worst, there is none. Pitched past pitch of grief . . .'"

"That isn't an answer."

"There isn't one answer. Only truth. That's much more difficult."

"How can you be sure the attacker won't come back?"

"A restraining order is in place. We reported the incident to the police. Too few have been willing to do that. But this wasn't the only such charge against the man, and Thomas Augustine wasn't the only victim. I've been asked not to reveal any more—to avoid compromising an ongoing investigation, to say nothing of the privacy of others. I know that doesn't, I know it cannot, put you completely at rest about your friend. What I want you to know is that, in the end, if he and the community agree that he should stay, we intend to see to it that he is safe here from now on. That anyone else who comes here is safe."

"Father, I'm sorry, but it's too late. Even one rape is one rape too many. And what about those others? And still others again? The man is still out there; he could commit another rape right now, and we—what, we stupidly sit here?"

Fr. Cyprian takes off his glasses and smooths his eyelids with his hand before putting the silver frames back on. There is no trace of his earlier good humor now, only earnestness. "Whatever the reputational cost, whatever the consequences, protection is our first task. For us and for all. It could well happen that when the story comes out, we lose vocations, to anger or to fear. But whatever it costs us, the man responsible will not come here again. And I pray for healing, but I also pray for justice. 'There is not any thing secret that shall not be made manifest, nor hidden, that shall not be known and come abroad.' I am not afraid of that day. There are some who must fear it."

*

In the end, Father Cyprian agrees to let me stay until Sunday; I won't have to change my flight. On Saturday I wake up and throw aside the gray blanket, feeling furious with the morning light for its obviousness, its overtness. A hand-thrown, glazed clay mug on the desk holds three pencils, casts a shadow; I want to hurl it at the wall, watch it shatter.

I look at the icon, hand raised with the fingers so individually rendered, their shadows a greenish hue cast against the skin's brownish gold, gently lined up as straight and neat as book spines on a shelf. So placid, so unimpassioned, above all so *still*. Putting a stop to things. Passing judgment. But not quickly enough. Not in time.

I throw at him the corner of the blinding rage that must have driven Elaine to wreck the art in the cloister. *You don't understand*, I tell myself, tell him: *you never will, never, never.*

I pull my hair back, the whole tangled thicket just as it is, and wrap the same wide flat headband around the hairline. All the hell required to induce misery can be found within this circle, the rotunda of my own skull. A blighted embryo, the misery gestates. Left to myself, I will surely bring it to birth.

There is no mirror in the room. So when I begin taking my clothes off, curious whether the remembered image of the portrait painted by Dylan still has a living echo in the present, the polished glass of the window gives the closest approximation. The woman in the glass is the same as the woman in the painting, the same woman in the room in Florence whose name he spoke in the soundless language of bodies: he swore a kind of faith, the same as I did, before we both went back on our word.

I dress in clean clothes, take my room key, and set out walking.

Maybe Elaine is right, after all. It's inhuman, what they're doing here. It induces such anxiety that some rupture, some escape, feels necessary. Why is the liveliest person I have ever known seeking this aboveground burial, where real horrors are possible?

I hike the grounds alone for hours, until the moon, already risen, glows unsettlingly in a violet sky. A few nights ago it was just fading from full. Now a scant last quarter hangs above my head: an axe blade, a scythe.

In an otherwise empty common room Michael moves in and out among the tables, clearing up a meal of soup and salad, bread and butter. He has taken up the plates but not the tureen and serving bowl, not the spoons and napkins; I count three spent place settings. Elaine is gone; Allen must be gone; Mrs. Russell is gone; Marjorie remains. Who were the other two guests at the meal?

"I'm sorry," Michael says; "here, let me help," and before I can speak he has taken a clean bowl from his cart, filled it, set a fresh place, and pulled out my chair.

I apologize to him, needlessly, absurdly. But when I push out the chair next to me, Michael smiles shyly and puts down a serving for himself. He sits down and says a quiet prayer to himself, moving his lips but not speaking out loud.

His courtesy poses a challenge. At first he keeps asking me questions about myself, which I'd rather not answer. I brush these off like dry leaves, try to draw him out, ask him questions that might throw light on what I'm still reeling from, start by nudging him toward the topic of what friendships are like in the monastery: don't they develop a hothouse quality, don't they become stifling? I don't quite ask: isn't there a risk of blurred lines, crossed boundaries, doesn't the strictness lead to a lack of freedom and isn't it this lack that causes people to lose their integrity? But he picks up on the concern underlying the words. "Not really. Real friendship has its nature everywhere," he says. "Except more so here." He laughs. "Maybe differently so. We don't talk as much, but we know each other better. If anything we have to respect each other's space more because everything's so closely shared to begin with."

Does he know Thomas Augustine? "Of course, he's your special one, isn't he? Although I'm a little afraid of him," he says with a laugh. "He's so excellent."

This surprises me. The older brothers I've met all speak of Thomas Augustine with some attitude, hardly strong enough to call an emotion, between bemused patience and strained tolerance. They must simply be tired: if not of Thomas Augustine, at least of the disturbance he occasions. Michael's voice, though, quavers with a note I recognize: admiration blended with self-doubt.

A bolt slides open in my brain: at root have we all felt the same response to this man? Have we all been in awe of his gifts, so far beyond the common run, and has this awe only decayed into bitterness and envy when we were too weak to support it? It is so hard to stand the pain he causes. It is still harder to stand the joy.

"But tell me about yourself," I press, and Michael tries to find more to say, tries to be agreeable. Although it is only November, I notice that his lips are already chapped from the wind.

"There isn't too much to it," he counters gently; "I fell in love with this place when I came to visit with a friend years ago. I'm grateful to him for bringing me here, even if we don't stay in touch as well as we could. I wonder sometimes if callings don't very often move on from soul to soul in this way. If they brush past one person only to land on another? Or pass through many hands . . . That's me, then. I don't know much, I don't do much that's out of the ordinary. I love just to be here, to live in this place. To have this chance at a one-to-one encounter with God. I'm willing to pay whatever it costs."

Michael smiles, although it strains the chapped skin of his lips, and at once I can see down into a depth of generosity and sweetness in him. I feel a twinge of regret: *The world has lost a gift in losing you too.* But who knows—maybe he would be more monstrous, if left to the outside like the rest of us.

"My mother really struggled with it when I came in," he says, tentatively, still surveying for common ground. "I didn't know how to tell her that, to my mind, I wasn't giving much in comparison to what I was gaining. It didn't feel to me like a sacrifice. I wonder if it ever will."

"Naturally, I think that's hard for people to hear," I say, thinking of Elaine. "That you don't value the things they value in the way that they value them."

"True. Or simply that your highest—what you called value—is different from theirs."

"That's what makes this decision so hard for most of us on the outside to understand."

"It's hard for you, too," Michael says gently. It is so hard to bear being *seen* this way. And yet he sees well.

"In a way. I once thought our lives would go differently."

"Did you think you'd marry him?"

The naïvete of this question makes me wince. "I didn't really think about that. Whatever we were to each other was always more a direction than it was an image. An indefinite line, extending to the horizon. And now we're at the end of the line and I don't know how to feel."

"That makes sense. We feel our way forward into things; we don't see where we're going until we're there. Sometimes."

Michael is about to say more when a raw voice barks over us, "He's already gone," from several yards away, rending the fabric of real quietude in which we have sat until now. The sound of heel taps and of rolling suitcase wheels pursues us: the voice belongs to Elaine. I had thought she would have been in the air by now.

"No, I don't think so," she responds loudly to the voice on the other end of her cell phone. "No. I won't go back to the house if Allen's there. I'll stay at my practice. The couch folds out. No. It's been time to start the proceedings for a long time. I've been foolish to put it off. Yes. Yes. If he hadn't been so passive, we could really have done some good here. We could have had our *son* back . . . I told him 'Thanks a lot for a lot of nothing.' He's always been a coward. . . . Yes, and I also feel like writing Dylan a letter to say 'Congratulations, you've ruined Christmas yet again,' but of course I'm not going to do that. . . . Thank you. Thank you. You're kind. It's not easy. . . . No . . . " Elaine once again acts oblivious to our presence as she stands with her back to us at the double door of the guesthouse, one point-shod toe tapping on her suitcase wheel, listening to her confidant whose voice to us is no more than an electronically distorted warble, looking out through glass panes at the quickly falling night.

"Yes, I should be back in time for the party. I wouldn't miss it if I could help. The car should be here any minute. The flight is tonight; it was that or the red-eye tomorrow. You're kind, you're kind. I might take you up on that; I might find the door locked if I went back there now. No, you're so right. Oh, here we are. What a relief. Oh, thank you, dear. Yes, I should make it before midnight."

A vehicle has pulled up into the circular drive. In the gloaming the color of the cab isn't easily distinguished; it might be grey or blue. Elaine swings through the exit, trots down the asphalt, lifts in her own suitcase, and slams the car door behind her. The idling engine groans, and she is driven off down the dim mountain road.

Michael and I share a disbelieving look. He blushes slightly. He actually says, "Look at the time." Quickly he begins to clear up the dishes. I step in to help, half expecting him to wave me off, but without speaking he allows me to work alongside him. I wish the conversation would resume, but it doesn't. Without speaking we load the cart, and in silence Michael wheels it away.

Just then Allen whips around the corner.

"Oh damn," he says, "am I too late? Damn. I'm ravenous. Can I follow him into the kitchen?"

"You can. It's not cloistered. Guests help, he told me. Wish I'd asked sooner."

Allen disappears and, moments later, reappears with a bowl of lentils and bread.

"They let me see him," he says, meaning Thomas Augustine.

"They let you?"

"They let me. *He* let me."

"How is he?"

"About the same as before," Allen says, his mouth still half full. "Better, even. Not as worked up." Allen must not know about the attack either, even now. It doesn't surprise me that Thomas Augustine wouldn't have told him, so close to the moment of departure. So much left untold.

"Does Elaine know?"

"I haven't told her." He tears off a huge bite of bread and chews it silently for a moment. "Can't, now, really," he adds, after a moment, through what is left of the bite. "She's gone. Left a long message on my phone. God. I guess she's gone."

"So I saw."

"I waited the first car for her for an hour and ended up having to pay the driver. Doesn't matter. Booked us on separate flights anyway."

"I'm sorry."

Allen swallows. "Don't be. It was coming for a long time."

"I'm even sorrier, then."

"I'm not. It's freeing."

There is an undertone to the way he says *It's freeing,* a lift of one eyebrow, a slyness, that I do not like. "Were you able to find an earlier flight yourself?" I ask.

"No. I'm here another night. We could share a ride to the airport, if it suits you."

"No, that's okay. I think I'm going to stay for Mass."

"Oh, you're going in for that now too? Funny, I wouldn't have thought it of you." The sly curve of lip fades; instead Allen looks at me as if my hair has blanched white before his eyes.

"What's that supposed to mean?"

"Oh, nothing. Just, you know. You don't look the type."

"I didn't know there was a type."

"Well, you saw the type at Thanksgiving dinner. Disheveled, desperate. Not much better to look forward to."

"Hmm."

"I can think of better things to look forward to," he says. The suggestive look, the leer returns, unmistakable now, a look I have seen enough to know it is worth avoiding. Teeth visible like the bad wolf's, baring ready to consume at the first hint of a *yes*.

"Is that so," I say noncommittally.

And in that instant I see what Marjorie was talking about. *The monks are saving my life.* One beauty of this place is that, as long as I stay here, I don't need an excuse to want to be alone. So without saying another word I walk away, leaving Allen to think whatever he likes about it. I can no longer care.

Back in my room I sort through an armful of books I have borrowed from the library. I scan titles and skim pages, but there is a resistance like the skin of water that stops me from choosing one work and settling into it. I wonder to what degree this is a function of plain somber colors and serif fonts, covers that present themselves as almost aggressively *not for me*, unconcerned with anything but their own internal reference: a judgment on the books, a judgment on myself.

Although I have in theory traveled to support a friend, I have been unable to escape from myself: helpless to free him from the cell he carries with him, too firmly trapped in my own. All this time, neither of us has been able to give the other any permanent gift, so much too concerned with what we lacked: *The measure with which you measure shall be measured out to you.*

As much as my work was never his to give or take, as much as I acknowledge my own agency in relinquishing it, what was lost was still lost on his account, because I did for him what I would not have done for anyone else. I allowed my body to become the source, the means, of his success. I did not allow myself the same. Now I understand Elaine a little better: her life, her body, has been the instrument of her son's success rather than of her own.

And his body: what purpose has its pain served? Tell me this pain has been pointless and I'll believe you, although I do not want to, I do not see that, I do not feel it: but I am holding, now, too many feelings, too many images: I need thoughts, strong frames in which to contain them, arrange them. Accept some, turn others away. So tell me anything that makes sense or can be made to. Even if you don't know, tell me something, make it up. Make a conduit for glory where none exists, and then it will exist, it will be known to have existed only because you stood in the beam to reflect it: the solution he arrived at long ago, the solution that—abject, broken, absent—he still radiates.

XIII

November 2015

A Sunday afternoon flight sets me down in Chicago at dusk. As the plane banks, the street grid resembles bars of a cage—a radiant cage, a star-cloud of streetlamps. Along the shoreline of the lake I can see the Navy Pier with its Ferris wheel spinning. The motion recalls the spin of the old watermill I saw on the drive to the monastery, gunmetal against a clapboard structure whose red paint had been picked and flaked like cooked fish by decades of weather.

Never has any other place, not even New York, made me so acutely aware of my own smallness. When I first arrived here, I thought that I had already succeeded, because success was defined as getting out. Success was to have escaped Sepal with all its miasmic atmospherics, its blockages and dilapidations, and even to have escaped New York with its pressures, envies, rivalries: to have found a different place to live, to have started fresh. Success was presence in the new place, survival after transplantation. Dodging taxicabs, sprinting through crosswalks, decoding public transit: learning the speed and pace and rhythm of the city; having the grit to stand on the level ground of the sidewalk at the doorways of skyscrapers and to feel, in the moment, that I had as good a right to stand there as anyone: I hadn't asked for better then. I wonder why I seem to want more now.

Years ago, I dreamed that I could find another America than the one I was born into, a promised land, a place that could expand and extend itself to a genuine variety of people, a malleable cornucopia ever perfecting and perfected, indifferent to archaic molds, refusing to file souls under hovering categories, refusing to reduce them to type. A place where I could be who I was, not what I was: I am dreaming of that still. I have not found it yet.

The airport shuttle deposits me on the curb beside the bus station; I take the bus to my obscure district—cheapest rent in the city proper; then, alone, with my keys held forward between my first and middle fingers, I stride down the several blocks to the walkup where I live. Suitcase in hand, I pause on the apartment threshold; I breathe like a swimmer entering water. There is no elevator. The four flights of dimly lit poured-concrete stairs, with their glistening black sanded treads, frighten me every time. I have never been assaulted, but that doesn't forbid creeps from waiting in the shade. Three different people, Dylan among them, have at different times taken upon themselves to teach me how to use the flat of my hand to break an attacker's nose and push the jagged, dislodged bone into his brain. The other two were Aunt Rachel and my father.

Paramilitary training is dubious evidence of care, I realize. All the same there is a momentary sting in the knowledge that the only people to have cared enough to make sure I knew how to protect myself are now people I never meet anymore.

Inside the apartment things are much as before. If I left I would only miss the murals on the walls. When I first moved here I had asked the landlord whether she would care if I painted them. She made a rude noise and shrugged, which I took as permission. So the baseboards are now lined with red Italian poppies, the ceiling bordered with white wisteria.

I sleep deeply and, the next morning, walk down to the grocery co-op, where, technically, I am still supposed to report for work twice monthly. I make plans to quit at the end of the month; I ask Janelle, the manager, for any spare boxes she has. She gives a stack of banana cartons to me, heavy yet fragile, their open spaces lined with a crisp brown paper that allows the fruit to breathe while the tough walls protect the delicate skin in transit.

"*Vaya con Dios,*" she says.

I fill the banana boxes with old clothes, old books. I roll bedside lamps in sheets, tuck mugs in the pages of free arts flyers taken from the brightly colored lockboxes that stand outside Metro stations. I think I am packing until one day I look at the pile of boxes and realize it isn't going anywhere with me: it all ends up at a Goodwill drop site on Washington Boulevard.

Things begin to fall away from me quickly: false narratives, needless extras. I no longer fully belong to this place, though it cocooned me for a time, and now Chicago, the entire city, begins to peel back the way the skin of a plantain falls away from the soft, ripe center. The rug becomes my office, Craigslist my work portal. I sell my bed and sleep on the couch; I sell my couch and sleep on the floor. I sell expensive blazers, bamboo screens, pressboard shelves, vases, candles, a wine rack and stoppers, a wire cart, an easel, a folding table, a tree of coathooks: the detritus of an unconnected life, anything that might fetch a price.

On the first of December I let the studio go, forgiving the place its ironic title. *Studio.* Not in the most important sense. The lease had been month-to-month, and I had always been anxious about eviction. Now I find a soaring freedom in having stepped in front of that engine: It has always been a ghost train, incorporeal. It has never had substance. It has hit me, and I am none the worse; on the contrary, better. I have a feeling of the last school bell, the first day of summer, open doors.

I take the *City of New Orleans* down from Union Station the same afternoon. The trip lasts overnight, and I can't sleep; Aunt Rachel is to meet me in the morning and I can't stop imagining how she has aged, whether her dark hair has silvered; can't stop imagining her grieved, angry, scornful, disappointed, frustrated, sad.

I stare out the sleeper window—it slides open and closed with a panel like the ones on airplanes, only wide and silver and horizontal—and through this small portal pours the sheer unfiltered size of the unthwarted night sky, an ocean of dark blue filling my eyes, each star like a grain of salt poured into them. The train shakes and shakes; each jolt of the track shuddering through muscle and bone.

After this rough treatment, this wild unrest, Aunt Rachel's wordless smile and hug at the station simply undo me. I break down, bury my face in her shoulder, try to hide. She holds me, collects my bags—nothing much is left, really, besides a small rolling suitcase and a tackle box of brushes and paints; I wear a small messenger bag across my body, and that is all I carry. She bundles me and my belongings into a cab while I fall apart.

The heat of the morning here is gentle but real, even in what purports to be winter. The subtropical sun pulses through the window's darkened glass with all the persistence of a heartbeat. As we drive, the bearded oaks loom over the car; their leaves gleam a deep glossy evergreen, almost black, against a silver sky. In summer they will again show up against surreal blue as violent beryls, so saturated with sun as to make them more themselves than themselves.

The colors of the tent settlement under the grey overpass now look as if selected in Photoshop by a thoughtful designer. Bright quilts and double mattresses laid out in a neat row, partially sheltered by a second row of tents in green and blue and orange and red. The heap of duffel bags piled nearby almost undoes me again, as I realize how easily my suitcase could have been thrown upon it. If not for Aunt Rachel, then—supposing it takes me longer to find work than to live my way through my savings—where else would I go? I don't know if I have it in me, the way others do, to depend on friends during a rough patch—after so long away, I no longer know anyone besides Rachel in New Orleans whom I trust enough, this much. I would have to live among strangers wherever the rent is lowest, or to find some illegal squat, or some temporary shelter, or what then? If I once begin to "fall through the cracks" I feel, I fear, I would fall still farther, until

I found the ground floor, the basement, past which there is no more falling. The final circle.

Then again, we rarely know with any accuracy what we do have in ourselves, until we are asked to produce proof of it.

By the time we arrive at Rachel's place—the same as I remembered, my home, my haven, that last year of high school—I have calmed down enough to ask how she is doing.

"About the same," she says; "the department's under financial strain, of course, and the students are lazier every semester, but every semester there are still one or two who show up, who have a spark, who aren't jaded yet. They make me want to stay. They make it worth my while."

She makes me a cup of jasmine tea. She sends me into her room to lie down alone until dinnertime. Then, having returned from a walk to the market, she loads the tiny table down with round plastic containers of chicken salad and olives and hummus, with fresh croissants and white wine, then calls me to come in to dinner.

Yellow tulips on the sideboard. White curtains blowing in at the open window. The tent city recurs to my mind. That, not this, is where I feel I really belong. I have earned nothing; I deserve nothing. Why instead this welcome, this generosity, this unearned abundance?

"What are your plans?" she asks me, and I have to admit that I don't have any yet, beyond using my dwindling savings to help me hang on while I look for new work. I offer to pay rent to her; I'll take odd jobs until I find regular work, "hopefully within a year," I add, in the hope that a timeline will make the idea more acceptable to her. Just in case she is peeved, I add: "Or a few months."

Aunt Rachel somehow makes her face shrug. "Please, you didn't pay me rent when you were seventeen. If you're as conscientious now as you were then, I doubt you'll be here long enough for it to make much difference."

"I'm not really sure what I'm going to do, though. I don't want to spend any more of my life feeling trapped in a corporate culture.

I don't really want to do design for salary and benefits, although I will if I have to. I don't want to end up in debt. I've had my chance at enjoying life, and I've tried to be conscientious, but there's more to life than just fun and duty. If I want to keep making art, I need to get—this is going to sound insane to you, Aunt Rachel, but hear me out—I need to get less serious about it, not more so. I need to start fresh. I need to figure out how to build a life—one that makes sense from day to day—a life that lets me respect myself, sure, but also to really—without meaning this in too weighty a way—contribute to the world, and not leave too much of a mess behind me at the end."

Rachel leaps in: "What a thought, just imagine you dying—or rather don't! Don't think about any such thing. You're still in your first bloom." (But my mind calls up, as if in resistance, a line of chant I remember from Thomas Augustine's chapel: *Wretched, close to death from my youth, I have borne your trials; I am numb.*)

To please her, I drop the topic; I agree to another sandwich, a movie, another bottle of wine; I listen to a summary of her research on microeconomics, to long stories of students' and administrators' antics; I fall asleep on her couch with too few questions resolved and wake again to the white-skied, glossy-leaved world of my last year of childhood, as if nothing had changed.

XIV

January 2016 – September 2017

The old year ticks over into the new. Weeks pass into months. I apply and interview for jobs and don't hear back; I send out more applications, schedule more interviews. I find part-time work at Rue De La Course—a coffee shop near the university, in what used to be a bank building—and in another funky little grocery co-op, a health food store where the air always smells of alfalfa sprouts and lavender oil. I spend hours, days, packing espresso pucks, discarding crates of unsold lemons dusty with blue mold, pushing mops across terracotta-colored tile floors that gleam aggressively in angled light through glass doors. I start to put away savings again, begin dreaming of renting a studio space. I am still, as fifteen years ago, borrowing Aunt Rachel's clothes. She keeps me afloat.

We hang with her friends now and again, but the age and culture gaps always make this slightly awkward. Her friends are almost all professors used to airing their research ideas to each other and complaining about local political corruption and professional rivalries over takeout pizza and medium-shelf boxed wine. They get lost in abstractions, squabble over points of fact, disappear down conversational rabbit holes. They mis-hear phrases, misunderstand each other's meanings, sometimes on purpose, for the comedy of it. In their enthusiasm for what fills their heads they forget where their bodies are, forget they have bodies. Some speak several decibels too loudly; others are barely audible. One time we go to a salsa club and find, to our great amusement, that not one of them, other than the film professor Dr. June Johnson, has even a fragment of rhythm. At the same time, they're often clever and funny, fair-minded, patient, tolerant, gentle; they have their own quirky charm. In its way, their circle becomes an oasis. Or a mirage, but it keeps me walking forward, either way.

The azaleas bloom and then fade; the magnolias whiten and then brown. The heat swells, thick, oppressive, tinged with car exhaust uptown, with sulfuric paper-mill smells at the outskirts, with salt down by the waterfront.

And it all happens over again. We spiral around the sun. This time, early autumn arrives far too hot and lingers far too long. The weather has to break. When the inevitable hurricane comes up the coast, we evacuate. We go to some English professor's family's country house all the way up in the Delta, far from where the streets have become canals, rivulets for boats and rafts that people pilot toward safety.

The house is an unvarnished pine cabin with a tin roof, a time machine made of tongue-in-groove boards. Here, we huddle on the wooden floor around a coffee table aglow with candles, drinking bottled water and bad merlot. I play seven-card stud poker by candlelight with a couple of graduate students while Aunt Rachel listens in the kitchen to June, who for all her kindness before I left for college is still Dr. Johnson to me. She lost family in the last major storm eleven years ago and is understandably in a state over what this new storm could do to the survivors. I am trying not to overhear their conversation but can't help picking up fragments that drift in across the bar stools.

"They did everything they were supposed to do, and it wasn't enough. That's the pattern. That's the way. What's worst, though, is that they should have been safe. I offered to have them to stay. They won't have anything to do with me, though. They think I'm the spawn of Satan because I teach *A Clockwork Orange* in class.... It's not that my place isn't safe right now. They would have been safe there. But I couldn't be home, I couldn't be alone. So I gave Monique the keys to my place. She's got a few people with her there. I offered to my family again, but they said no thank you, we're fine, although you know, Rachel, and I know, that they're *not* fine. . . . They'd literally rather die than depend on the tender mercies of the governor or on the generosity of what they consider to be a wicked woman" (gesturing toward herself, vehemently, the movement a protest against her family's failure to see what she sees; the tendons stand out in her wrists).

"And look, this society *owes* us, it was built on our backs and on the sweat of our brows, but things are so badly managed as they are that I can almost, almost, understand that feeling that my family have. It's like they think they're better off without whatever it is that's being offered to them. It's pride and it's foolish pride, sure. Easy to say. But it's also a certain stance of dignity, right, even if taking up that stance results in dignity and life itself being swept away in the end. It's just so hard, because it's going to be swept away one way or the other, it's so hard that we can't do anything about it, and, well, what the hell. Now I sound like a kid, clamoring about 'it doesn't seem fair,' but you know what, I agree with that kid right about now, Rachel: you know it, I don't have to tell you, you know and I know it isn't fair."

It isn't fair. Days pass. The floodwaters ebb. Things are bad, but nowhere near as bad as before, they tell me. The worst of the damage has fallen on Houston after all. We caravan an hour and a half back to the city, buy bread and milk and bottled water and beer, treat ourselves to lattes and beignets because we can.

On the first day classes resume, Aunt Rachel takes coffee and pastries to Dr. Johnson's office; it turns out that her family are all fine, but their home was flooded, damage done far beyond what they can afford to repair. Rachel asks what she can do for them.

"Pray," she later tells me, was all June said. I'm not sure if Rachel is serious or kidding. I'm not sure what direction June took the word in, what it meant to her. But when Rachel retells it—how the family again refused their daughter the professor's help, how they told her they were better off without the help of someone like her; Rachel won't repeat the names they called June, the things they said—I think despite myself of Our Lady of the Pines, and I decide a letter can't hurt: I write to ask for prayers. I put Thomas Augustine's name on the salutation line.

In return—about a month later, when the live oaks are dropping acorns—I come home from a run in the park to find a short letter in the mail.

Dear Ms. Solomon,

How good it is to hear from you again. Thank you for reaching out and for sharing the sad news with us about the struggles of your aunt's friend in caring for her relatives after the storm. We certainly will keep the family in our prayers.

From your letter, I surmise that you have not heard that your friend Dylan (formerly Br. Thomas Augustine) is no longer living here. Toward the end of Advent in 2015— a few weeks after your visit to us, just before his planned profession—he made the decision, in mutual agreement with the community, that it would be best for him and for everyone if he were to return to the world. I believe he is now living in Chicago with his father; at least that was his plan when he left us.

Although it has been more than a year since his departure, I thought you might like to know, since you hadn't yet heard. But by the time this reaches you, you may already have crossed paths.

With gratitude for your continued friendship,
In Christ,
Fr. Isaiah Bowman

I roll my eyes. I almost fold this into a paper airplane and fly it off the balcony. *Struggles, mutual agreement, return to the world. Continued friendship. In Christ.* Forget it. I have to shower, I have to get dressed, I have to go to work; I'm on in the café until closing time tonight, one a.m.: the Saturday night shift, serving fried and sugared dough to drunken tourists.

Tonight I will earn enough to buy a small blank canvas. Tomorrow I will sleep in, go to brunch with Aunt Rachel—her treat—and then walk with her in the square for a while. We'll bring a couple of blankets and the *New York Times* and sit companionably on the grass, trading sections as long as the sun lingers. I have no time for the past. I know it will fill every spare or empty corner of my mind if I allow it, so I work hard to leave no corner unfilled, even if all I am doing is cluttering up the places that house the darkest night.

I style my hair carefully, make up my eyes, choose peacock-feather earrings as if it mattered. So few other choices are left to me. I brace myself to be on my feet in heels for hours, since selling my appearance is still the game I am forced into playing. Tomorrow I will wear flats: this is the size down to which my agency has been trimmed, three and a half inches, give or take a little. Tomorrow I will pretend, for a few hours, that I am free.

*

The spring semester begins. Aunt Rachel comes home with a surprise one day: a key to the art studios down on campus.

"Technically it's against policy," she says, "but I talked to the department chair, and she says that as long as you clean up after yourself and don't disturb anyone, you shouldn't run into any problems. It's flagrantly underused."

On my first visit to the building in mid-January the afternoon is unseasonably warm and surreally quiet. No one is around in the sawdust-smelling, high-windowed room besides one or two eager undergraduates who are getting themselves used to the space, setting up, inventorying supplies: not the kind who dwell in the hive-mind of the dormitory, but self-starters. Familiar souls.

This kind of solitude, this kind of silence, has not been available to me for a long time. I climb the stairs and look out the long row of windows that wraps around the building. From here it will be possible to watch both when, in a chromatic haze, the sun rises over East New Orleans, and when it sets downtown in tantrums of orange and purple.

There is now a reason to get up in the mornings. First I make coffee, and then I take the trolley to the student shuttle and the shuttle down to the studio, where I paint. I take the bus to my first shift and then back to the apartment to shower, change, and eat before my second shift. On days off, I'm back in the studio as fast as public transit can move me there.

And my portfolio grows. Besides the canvases of Appalachian hills and autumn countryside that I started with, there is soon a series of bayou wildlife, another series of cityscapes: riverside skylines, sidewalk scenes, parks full of oaks crawling with Spanish moss. The angles and colors of the sun's rays at given places and times are everything in these. Beatrice, if she saw them, would scold me for how literal, how representative they are. "Figurative drawing," she would growl. She would say she didn't know me any more. You're right, friend, I tell her in my mind: you don't. I squeeze her hand and leave her there, walk with Ruskin instead.

At first I had thought that after a few months I would move out of Aunt Rachel's, find my own place. Then one day last year she said, out of the blue, that I should stay as long as I wanted, that she liked my company.

"You're good people," she said. I can't recall when I've received a compliment that's pleased me more, especially since I'm unsure if it's true.

I get my mail in the lobby of her apartment building; the cold brass key is pleasant and light in my hand, the way it suits itself to the frosty metal bank of mailbox doors recessed into the wall. They are not beautiful in themselves—neither is the lobby, with its rubber-edged red-and-black marled rug, its half-century-old linoleum, its warped plaster walls the blue-gray of decaying bread—but they have come to mean a security of sorts, a predictability that has a beauty of its own.

I sort out Rachel's mail for her; I bring everything upstairs and usually open mine at the bar counter before sorting things into folders, one for pay stubs, one for painting sales—contracts and invoices—and one for the odd note or card I want to keep.

There aren't many notes or cards lately, so a folded letter in a short, thick ivory envelope, the address handwritten in fountain pen ink, stops me right in the foyer, under the guttering fluorescent tube. The postmark, dot-matrix printed with a Chicago zip. The sheet is handwritten too; the handwriting is familiar. It chills me.

I run upstairs, drop the letter on the kitchen counter, fly to my room, change into running clothes and shoes. Circle Audubon Park three times: it does me no good whatever. Home, I shower and dress again and pick up my studio key, but my body won't cooperate, won't move past the counter, the letter. In the end I put everything away and decide to skip a day of painting: to delay facing that silence of the canvas, the memory that waits between me and it.

XV

All the way to the café, on the exhaust-redolent bus ride, I'm setting the scene. The photographic moment when Dylan and I will face each other presents itself to mind, immune to brushstrokes or digital alteration, and I worry it over again and again.

The words we might speak to each other under such circumstances take part in convention, in self-interest. I write myself a script ahead of time.

"Hey, you."

"Hey."

The side-armed hug, the step backward, the forced cold reading of the other's expression: how can it be that this is the same person with whom, for whom, I have gone through so much?—and yet here he is, or is going to be soon. We will exchange absurd pleasantries, choose a table.

I will light a cigarette for him and then one for myself. We will breathe the warm air slowly, nonchalantly. We will sit outside, under a covered veranda with fans, framed against a tangerine-colored wall. Ferns will curl in hanging baskets, screening our view of the street; banana fronds will sway beneath the awning. We will feel the security of being near to signs of other human life, of prosperity, of the flourishing of others even if we don't share in that flourishing. We will feel all the relief distraction can afford us.

Dylan will build on the news from his letter, his mouth full of language of the early days. He describes his *energy*, talks of *manifestations*. He is passing through the South for another touring show, another benefit for charity: Austin, New Orleans, Atlanta, Nashville. This time the show is a retrospective, although new work too already stands stacked in the warehouse, ready for revelation when the moment is judged right. Giovanni has ignored, after all, Dylan's instructions to liquidate everything. After Dylan entered the cloister, Giovanni had held on to a core of temporarily not-for-sale work, hedging bets in favor of the future he always assumed was coming. On top of that, there were the fresco-influenced canvases made in the monastery: a fresh interest hook for a brand-new series of exhibitions. Financially at least, Dylan will be fine, will never have been for a moment at any real risk of being otherwise. Which is worth less, finally, than I first thought.

Dylan will describe to me the new life he has found for himself in Chicago. He has been sleeping in the spare room of Allen's small apartment near Lincoln Park, in a building called The Patricians, and he is renting a temporary work studio not far from our old college: but he plans an eastward expansion before long, intends to move back to a space in New York, even his old space if it opens up again.

If I know him, he is likely to repeat the text of the letter almost as if he had not written it: "I need to have a retreat," he'll say, "a place where I feel grounded, and Chicago provides that, ever since Elaine moved to Philly. One metropolitan area has always been too small to hold both of my parents at once, but Dad and I get along fine as long as we're left to ourselves. It's a bit of a boomer cave, sometimes excruciatingly so, but he means well at heart. I need to work steadily for a couple of years, no parties, just production. With his support I can do that."

What about his abandoned plan of life; does he ever miss anything about the monastery, I'll ask? "Sometimes, of course," he'll say. "It's been a terrible blow to realize that I could have been so mistaken in my sense of purpose. Then again, I didn't give myself enough time to think before jumping in. It's like—it was like a long engagement. Like when people get married too soon or to the wrong person. The ties of religious life, once they're final, are hard to undo. That's why people usually wait longer than I waited, after conversion, before trying to enter a community like that. Our Lady of the Pines made an exception for me and then came to feel as if that had been a mistake. What can I say, I corroborate their concern. I wanted that life, but no matter how much I wanted it, I wasn't being called."

What I most want to know, I don't know how to ask him: whether he is healing, and if so how. I cannot square this man—glib talker, blithe glider through the world—with the frightened child behind the screen of cypresses.

Think again of the way he sounded, flung down in that flowerbed as the windbreak of evergreens sheltered us. All that he said then— the person seems to have vanished who could have spoken this way, who really said such gentle things to me, at last sufficiently unburdened of his ego to feel them; such terrible things about himself, none of them true.

Who are you really, I want to ask him; I want to shake him by the shoulders, to shout *What do you really want?* Futile impulse. I do not know if he himself really knows.

But has he, then, really somehow kept the same beliefs? "You still accept those people the way they are? Hate, fear, superiority complexes, and all?"

(Here I begin to lose sight of the unreality of this framed, feigned new moment of meeting, of the self-manufactured nature of my friend's responses. As if I know what he will say. As if my own tongue will not betray me. What his letter suggests he might be thinking is this—)

"In the end, they wanted the best for me. They wanted me to thrive and didn't think I would ever really put down roots. Beautiful as the monastery is, there are people who can be happy there and people who can't. I couldn't."

"You were pretty clear on it when I saw you. It seemed like no time for you to be making major decisions. You were vulnerable."

"I had it all wrong. I was still making assumptions based on the things I'd been told on the outside, no matter how hard I tried not to. But my inability to get those preconceptions out of my head, to stop thinking in terms of power dynamics—to stop judging others without really knowing their hearts, to stop judging myself without really understanding my own motives, to stop imputing a motivation to every action—it was all part of the larger reasons why I couldn't find my way into the life. Couldn't find myself at peace."

I imagine a silence falling between us for a moment, only because I can't sketch a way of asking him to recur again to what happened. To what he told me in the garden. That conversation will have to originate with him.

Then again he may ask about my work, and I hope he will: it seems to have found its own footing at last, as if this were a thing it had done on its own, independent of my effort.

"You should let me take a look at your canvases sometime. I could interest an agent," he might say.

I will smile and say no thank you, that's all right. I will describe the New Orleans gallery where my paintings have found a home— even those first Florence paintings, the freeways-as-galaxies, have now sold. The place is small, almost unfindable without a guidebook. Yet people do find it. The atmosphere is that of a hidden garden. Green light, *viriditas*, floods it, filtered through a screen of leaves. The polished pine floors whisper underfoot. For me it is a fulfillment of ambition: a safe place, a cloister: where my work is welcome, where it can be itself.

For in the end I do not really want to live as Dylan does, to deal with that kind of publicity. I would rather paint as a localist, working according to my own lights in obscurity, than in an international spotlight acquired at secondhand. If success on my terms is failure on his, I will take my terms over his every time. And—even so—there are collectors interested in my work, interested in its fine details. Interested, finally, in seeing what I can see, in finding out what I can do with it.

We'll make a gesture at hugging, an affected air kiss—cheek brushing cheek—and some courteous sounds, before walking out together into the glare of a late autumn as hot as midsummer. He will turn one way, I the other. What will it matter?

*

None of my imaginings occur in life, none of the scripted words are said. The filmic, shadowless light of projection disappears as soon as my foot touches concrete below the step of the bus.

Dylan is already waiting at the stop for me, having guessed where I would disembark. It was never the kind of thing he would have done before. His smile has deepened since I last saw him.

His arms are open and then closing around me; just as quickly, I'm wrapping mine around him; a breath of cooler air in the wake of the departing bus flashes by us, floods my lungs. The blood speeds through my veins. My eyes sting. Be still be still.

"Hey, you," he murmurs into my hair.

"Hey."

We both burst into laughter for no reason I can name. I can't see him clearly anymore.

We never make it as far as the café where we had planned to meet, a bright blue house called the Corner Muse. Several yards from the bus stop, but still within its sight line, we sit down on a wooden slatted bench that has green painted wrought-iron arms. Between us on the seat lies the book he was reading while he waited for me. He had left it there when we embraced, and now the cover has curled up in the breeze and the glare: only the flyleaf is visible.

We fall deep into conversation. Not a single preliminary. The walls I had put up in my mind, the painted scenarios have all been struck, a temporary exhibit, never any more than scaffolding.

"I've been seeing a counselor," he is telling me. "Someone to help with all that there still is to process. I'm starting to understand some things more clearly about the trauma I went through—what it was and what it wasn't. Most of all, I'm no longer blaming myself for what happened."

"It wasn't the attack that made you leave the monastery?"

"It was everything: it was the vows, not just one of them but all three, and not so much the vows even as my own constant anxiety. I couldn't look at the future with peace. I wanted to, and I wasn't discontented. And I wasn't afraid of the . . . of anything happening again. I knew it wouldn't. Couldn't. I just became . . . convinced, deep down, that I was walking the wrong path. Not a wrong path for everyone, God no, I saw some really bright souls there, you know? But the wrong path for me. And where the brothers had been saying before, 'Stick it out, forget yourself, try to think less about what you want,' they started to say, 'You're overcorrecting.' They started to say, 'You don't have to disappear. It's okay for you to take up space in the room. Look for ways to love, to give yourself, to grow.' And I couldn't fulfill that without leaving. They could see it; I could see it. So they let me go."

"It wasn't—you really weren't worried about—?"

"No. Fr. Isaiah told me about the restraining order. I trusted him. Trust him. But sure, I'll always wonder if having to relive it again every time I walked that hallway is part of why I couldn't stay. I don't want to minimize what happened, but I've survived and I've been able to work through at least some of it. Some aren't so lucky."

I am not so sure that luck has any traction here, where they left him: alone, unsupported. I can't get my mind around the consequences, or lack of them.

Out loud I only say, "I'm sorry. I don't mean to press you. You must know better than I do how hard the pieces are to put together. But Fr. Cyprian said there was an ongoing investigation against your attacker. Will you ever have to testify?"

"I don't know. It's in the past now. This may sound strange but I want to leave it there as long as I can," Dylan says softly. "Fr. Isaiah tried to make that possible for me. He set up an opportunity to make a statement. I have to grant that that was kind in intention," he adds.

"To make it possible to. . . ?"

"Not testify in court. If there is a trial. That is, there won't be a canonical one. He's leaving the priesthood to duck it. The civil charges may or may not still be dropped."

"I can't imagine what that must have been like. Must still be."

"I can try to tell you, if you really want to know."

"Don't do it for my sake. Only if it would help you."

*

The conference room again. Thomas Augustine sees everything. Eyes shut or open, it doesn't matter. The three listeners, the two priests and the lawyer, lined up like a dissertation committee, hover there in front of him. The table so smooth, not real wood but pressed particle board; the walls so clean, white plaster and gloss: the air so cold, not climate controlled but allowed to breathe, through open windows, the freshness of frost. Besides this, the whole room smells of new carpet, dry-erase marker, cleaning ammonia.

The space feels as if it is floating on water: as if the meadow, the valley around them, might be an open sea. Thomas Augustine watches the watchers, watches himself, as if his seat of consciousness were perched inside the little fish-eye camera mounted on the upper right wall beside the door with its mottled glass panels.

If only the listeners were here to review him on his merits. Of his merits, he is confident. Of the truth, not as much. Then again he fears his merits may be at fault here, for drawing attention to himself, for pulling him into this—situation. Contretemps. Challenge. Setback.

(Do not think *disaster*, he tells himself: not the loss of the stars, a third of them hurled to earth. A part of him still believes, even now, that thinking so makes a thing so. That if he does not think *disaster* it will not have been one. And so, in some unlit back corner of his soul, he harbors a fear, wish, hope?—that what happened really is explainable, explainable because it is somehow his own fault, his own fault because he thought of it, because he allowed thoughts of it to have a place in his consciousness even before it happened. Now that it is over he still relives and relives it. Not enough time has passed. Or not enough space. If he allows it to be his own fault—if he clings to that, calls it an event he could have controlled, prevented—he thinks that then he will be able to control what happens from now on, that then he will be able to stop.)

Maybe I am a saint now, he thinks. Maybe I am unbeknownst to myself being immersed into the vision of God. Because I suffered, I did suffer. That much I remember. Maybe I died and this is purgatory: that would explain why I go on and on and on even when I wish I didn't. But no, if I were part of God now I would love and I don't love, I don't: not true, sometimes I love, sometimes not. Sometimes I hate, I hate: him, myself, everyone, especially—

"We'll begin with a prayer," says a voice as mild as pear's flesh, rising from a body draped in white like Thomas Augustine's own. The blond, tall priest, Fr. Isaiah, even though he is prior, still feels most at home when at work: digging in the garden, planting cabbages, marigolds, snap peas; chopping firewood, hauling loads of it to the shed behind the refectory. Building fences, driving in the nails with a mallet. At home, too, he passes calmly in Thomas Augustine's mind's eye behind the cool white marble altar in the chapel, two long strides from the epistle side to the Gospel. Here in a black fabric chair too short for his long limbs, Fr. Isaiah looks awkward as he leads the three men and the one woman in the sign of the cross. Here in the conference room, no one is at home.

Through the rote words that follow Thomas Augustine's mind keeps revving, backing up and starting over, making three-point turns. He is looking for a better angle from which to ask what happened and what must be done next. If only he hadn't looked up from his breviary during vespers when the visitor was here, supposedly on retreat. If only he hadn't met the visitor's eyes, hadn't acknowledged the man as familiar, as someone he had met in that New York life. Maybe he had—had he?—seemed to look with longing? If only they never had met, never spoken. Or spoken more often, Thomas Augustine thinks—maybe then a less violent appeasement of such fury and need and abandonment, maybe these would not now take up space in Thomas Augustine's own body. This is not blaming myself: so he says to himself. Of course it is blaming himself; he knows better. All the same he cannot stop.

The body should have never been part of the equation. Should never—oh God, help, oh no. Stop, stop, clear everything away. Look at the Cross. But even on the Cross, the body, the corpus. A block of rough carved stone: a stumbling block. *Every time it starts to happen,* Fr. Cyprian had said, *stop. Don't see what your memory contains. Only see what is in front of your eyes. Notice five details in the room around you. Give your mind time to walk out of the room where trauma lives. Close that door.*

The windowpane is whitely streaked with dust and cleaner from where a novice has imperfectly wiped it. The hills outside, the land of the farms beyond the lip of the valley lie bare, straw-colored (close the door, close the door). The white serge he wears is not warm. The tiled rug, laid in cross-grained squares, contains strands of paler gray and red and is stained across one joining with a single circular brown drop of some spilled liquid. The black sock inside his sandal has a thin patch across the toe, where the untrimmed nail inside catches on each individual thread.

"Amen."

Thomas Augustine works the word out in chorus, through dry lips. He hears Fr. Isaiah's mellow voice supporting his thinner one and carrying it along. Hears, again, the mellow voice in memory: *It wasn't your fault, what happened. You have to understand that. Please, you must accept it.*

What if I can't? he demands of himself. Should I have hurt him worse than I did, could I—? Tendon and ligament were ready to separate but still—He blames himself, though he knows he must not, for not having been able to escape even though his hands, wrists, were pinned behind his back: he left a bruise on the other's cheekbone, knocked his wind out before the man trapped him, but still—

Whenever Fr. Isaiah is tired he pushes his pale hair around on his tonsure line above his temples, as though scrubbing soap through the narrow stripe. He does this now as he says, "Brother, forgive me for putting you through this one more time. You had the courage to tell the story to me already. I hope this will be the last time you'll have to tell it. If we can obtain a good statement today, my hope is that the law firm can take matters from there. You won't need to be disturbed again."

Thomas Augustine, by now, has nurtured a knack for repeating words learned by heart. "I was raped," he says without preface. "By a priest. But he doesn't live here."

The woman, the lawyer, speaks through petal-painted lips. "Remind me, then, what he was doing here."

"He claimed to be making a retreat. We had met before."

"Had you had any relationship before, then?"

"Only conversation. Acquaintance."

"But no physical contact?"

"A handshake. Not more."

"Nothing that could have been—misconstrued?"

"I'm not sure what you mean."

"He hadn't made advances?"

"Not that I picked up on. It wouldn't have occurred to me. Any such thing."

"And you hadn't?"

"Hadn't what?"

"Made advances. Suggestions. Not that I'm saying you—"

She doesn't look evil, this lawyer who drove down from Louisville earlier today, from the district attorney's office: only prim, professional. Outside this room, among people she finds more sympathetic, she might be kind. Here, now, in her lapis lazuli blazer, she looks afraid, therefore dangerous. She clutches her fountain pen as if it were a knife whose balance she tests: a weapon of self-defense. The plane of her cheeks below her eyes lies flat, hostile, cold as porcelain. She is speaking with her eyes fixed on her notes, as if she finds him too distasteful to look at. He reminds himself: She is not intentionally cutting into him. She is not trying to lance the feeling of guilt he bears over all the times he has used others' affection to advance his own wishes. And yet.

"Absolutely not. He had developed this—obsession. First with my paintings. Then, I guess . . . "

"Let's move on, then. You think this—obsession—is the reason why you were assaulted?"

"At first he talked and talked. He—he wanted me to—to consent. I wouldn't. And so I thought it would all be resolved without a problem, I mean, I thought it would be only talk. Then he—grabbed me. Fought me. I—it—"

It wouldn't go in sequence. Thomas Augustine kept forgetting how it had started, how it had gone on. Only one thing was beyond forgetting—the shove that had torn flesh. Shock sent him falling, fetal, later, on his side in his cell. He stayed that way until hands lifted him, still until the car slowed its awful speed, at the urgent care clinic seventeen miles down the road. The stitches had been put in—dissolvable, black thread—with a wicked needle curved like a hoop earring.

"There was no way in which I invited this." Having to say it, having to defend himself, sends a hot twinge through his veins, like the stab of anaesthetic before it stops hurting.

"And—I press this one last time not because I don't believe you, but because the record needs total clarity. You don't remember having said or done anything that could have been misunderstood as—welcoming?"

Now he wants to shout: *hear me, you witch, have your ears fucking died and left the rest of you living?* He must press his palms tightly together in order to speak in a near-whisper—the way a doctor puts pressure on a wound to slow bleeding.

"It was because he had my arms pinned. My hands."

Again and again after this Thomas Augustine had told himself that he would have accepted even the loss of the muscle memory that lived in those delicate tendons and joints. Yet he had not in fact ripped away his hands and arms in a way that would have broken bones. He could not stop asking himself: could he have fought harder? If he had fought harder, could he have won? If he had not died resisting the attack—as he had heard, once in the first perfervid days of his falling in love with God, an elderly priest talking about a girl-saint who did die in just this way—*she gave up her life for her purity*—did this mean that he himself bore responsibility? That gentle old priest, perched above the pews in his pulpit, had spoken his sentence with implausible simplicity. Had spoken as if everyone were given this option.

Thomas Augustine had fought. He had fought. He had stopped trying to free his hands—at least he thought he had; the memory lay scattered like broken glass around the floor of his mind—but he had not stopped fighting, he had only changed tactics: he had kicked out, he had arched and flailed in an attempt to hit the priest's nose, with his elbow, his shoulder, the back of his skull. But Thomas Augustine could not prove that he had done this, other than by saying so. He had not wrenched his hands away; the grip of those other hands had been strong enough to break the tarsal bones and he had not felt sure, if he had allowed them to be broken, that they would ever heal the same. Would he ever heal the same? Had he somehow been at fault? He knew he had been at fault otherwise, much earlier, with others. He still felt not wholly sure he might not fall into fault again. He had fought but had not won the fight and so he could not prove that he had tried his best to win it.

He thought he had wanted to kill his attacker. Whatever he wanted to do he was accustomed to accomplishing. Yet he had not accomplished this. The attacker had lived, had vaunted over him like some monster of antiquity, some perverse Zeus. Yes. Only by freezing it into marble, classicizing it, can he deal with the image. So had Thomas Augustine in some dim corner of himself not really wanted to kill him? Had he, Thomas Augustine asked himself in the tones of Allen's own voice, had he really tried his best? If he had tried harder, would this make him a murderer in his heart? If he hadn't tried hard enough, would this make him complicit in what had been done to him?

Reason said of course not. Yet what had happened to him had brought him beyond reason, to an empty place where he only knew that the more effort he applied, the more miserable he felt. He had never been anywhere like this before.

"What was because he had your arms and hands pinned?" the lawyer asks now.

"It was because of that that he was—able to—to complete the assault." Thomas Augustine doesn't want, in front of her, to put it bluntly as it must be put. But the lawyer insists:

"To rape you."

"Yes. God why do we have to keep saying it."

"Forgive me," says the lawyer. "Just a few more questions."

Fr. Cyprian, silver-haired, silver-spectacled, has sat silent between Fr. Isaiah and the lawyer all this time. He speaks now to say: "Remember, we're doing this so that you won't have to appear in court to answer more questions. At least, we hope not. There's always the possibility of a full trial. But a plea bargain looks much more likely at this stage. This priest was a favorite of his bishop until the stories started to come out. He had a plum job. The chancery will try to shield him from the worst of the storm."

The worst of the storm. As if pressure currents and shifts in electrical charge had called up thunder and lightning; as if the man were mere air. Oh stop talking will you please stop: has Thomas Augustine not already borne the worst of the storm? No, worse is having to tell about it, to open the wound again. Please, he wants not to do this. He wants to be *I want to be left alone. Alone alone alone please God with my God leave me alone.*

The collar of the lawyer's white oxford moves lightly against her throat as she leans a few degrees forward. She places her palms flat on the folder of case notes she is taking. If she wants him to feel better because she is not writing now, well, he does not feel better. Her trimmed nails have been painted a cloudy, bridal opal.

"Can you describe your injuries?" asks the lawyer in a voice of ice.

"He does not want to," Fr. Cyprian says, standing and stepping closer to Dylan—as if in defense.

Yes, Father. He does not want to. The question he wants to ask is *How do you heal after this happens, how are you whole again?* And maybe she does not want to ask, maybe she merely must. But if it must be done, Thomas Augustine can describe his injuries. The rip in the ring of muscle. The pain that revisited daily so badly that at times he bit his arm to keep from crying out. The bleeding that trailed on for weeks. He watches the orchid skin under the lawyer's eyes contract as he piles details on details. Good, he thinks. He knows it is her job to make what was done to him as bad as it is, as bad as the jury should find it, but he feels obscurely that she should be made to pay for this. That someone should.

The priests, like unshockable police, have heard it all before. He is no longer sure it hurts them, but he knows it hurts her. She looks younger than he is, much younger than he feels. He has to fight off a flash of hatred: how dare she sit there so untarnished. How dare she show her pain on her face. The orchid skin deepens with a hint of the blue veins beneath it. As he finishes speaking and she begins writing again, a silence falls, and in it Thomas Augustine has plenty of time to see the tautening and blanching of Fr. Cyprian's face. The old priest's lips twist in disgust.

And this twist breaks Thomas Augustine in two. He knows the twist is meant for the abuser and not for himself and yet there is not enough space in his own mind to keep them apart. He could begin sobbing but doesn't. Instead he sits quite still, feels the flow of the future subtly rearrange itself around him, and knows he will not stay here. He has been at war with himself and now the war is over, there has come peace, but not the kind he had hoped for. He can forgive the old priest's disgust but he cannot continue to live with it, to consume soup across the table from it. He knows too, knows well, that Fr. Cyprian is at war now, that it has cost him a battle not to shout his rage and vengeance at the word *penetrated*. He knows what Fr. Cyprian's calm presence has meant to him until now: safety, solidity, a show of strength his own father never displayed, and now that strength has broken and Thomas Augustine must look for it elsewhere. That show of strength is now revealed as what it always, maybe, was: an illusion. As empty as his own sense of having been called to a way of life, Thomas Augustine thinks now, tasting bitterness with the thought. "Thomas Augustine." Who is he kidding: Dylan. Dylan Fielding. *Prima donna, flaming attention whore*: it is not who he is, but it is, he feels sure, how he is seen.

Dylan feels tempted to start telling lies now, to endorse the claim the guilty priest had made to Fr. Isaiah's face: *Nothing happened between us*, the priest had said, *that wasn't entirely called for*. What would it be like to see Fr. Cyprian's face wrung out like a rag, the way it would fold in on itself if he believed Dylan believed that? Even now Dylan cannot quite bring himself to commit this cruelty. He believes he would allow any harm to himself now to prevent it. If it would help anyone, he would accept a version of reality that would obliterate every good thought they had ever had about him. Instead he holds to the story of what really happened, as much as he can remember of it, because he still would prefer that Fr. Cyprian not suffer any more than he must. Things are broken enough as they are.

The lawyer's face greys a shade as she finishes taking down her account. She collects her papers, adjusts her cuffs: smooths, to soothe herself, the silver links in the apertures of her French cuffs.

"I think I have all that I need here," the lawyer says. "I'll draw up a draft for your approval. With your signatures, we can move forward."

There is a scattering. Dylan will never remember afterward how he makes his way from the conference room to the chapel after this. He will only recall lying there on the floor, hot face to cold stone, eyelids squeezed tight, forehead and nasal bone pressed to the hexagon-crossed sandal-prints left by other men in the terracotta tile, in the posture he would have taken for the ordination which will not now take place.

For a long time to come he will live, inside himself, not on the ground in that garden but grounded, here, in front of this altar. His soul will lie face down on the floor, under the shadow of the purple cloth draped from the lectern, in the quivering draft looping through the rose ribbons trailing off the candlelit wreath, smelling remnants of iron oxide in the red clay stains under his face, breaths of frankincense wafted from an altar he will never again serve. When it is time for the vigil Mass they will find him here: two of them will have to hold him under the elbows and around the shoulders to walk him to his place in the choir. Until then he will stay, face down in the knowledge that the next day will be Sunday, only twelve days before they place the cold ceramic child in the dusty yellow straw of the crèche. Until the child is born, he thinks, he will lie here on this floor, he will wait, he will not move until there arrives a purity of heart that will be new every morning, that will be strong enough to scour away the pain, to purge the horror.

The oak boughs nod above us. The lights and shadows shift across his face.

"Are you still angry?" I ask him.

"Oh yes. All the time. But at last it's with the abuser, not with myself. That may be the best I can expect to do for a while. One day I may be able to pity him. Given sufficient distance."

"And now what's next?"

He breathes deeply. "I don't know," he repeats. We sit in silence for a moment.

"I don't know," he says again. "I've thought of some possibilities. One of them depends on you. Only if you think—we could start fresh one more time. For good, this time. And—forgive me—I don't know if I can, really can, give you all I wish I could. But—I would—I would give my life to find out. No lie."

I note my first reaction, my second; I hold them in check, examine them. He sits saturating my profile in the green of hope. He is no longer afraid of the silence. I wish I could say the same.

"I can't," I tell him at last, on a long breath out. "I'd love to see my way clear, more than anything on earth." In a way it would be—so easy. "But I can't."

"I'm not asking quite what you think I am. Not at first, not right away."

So he says, but look at him: the upturned palms plead what the words don't. Every cell singing aloud, asking. *I want to hear you say it.* No use arguing the point.

"I know what you're asking—finally. It's more than I can give in return now. And even if I could—still less than you deserve."

With the care his hands might pour into preparing a brush, he lights a cigarette and shoves it between his own lips. How I could wish myself otherwise. There is nothing in him I could not accept, could not embrace. How easily, now, I could lay claim to him, with the same ease with which he offers himself. But when I take his free hand in both of mine it is a moment's comfort, nothing more, that is intended or that passes. Before long we both feel it and separate.

"Where will you go?" I ask him.

"Back to New York, in the end. There's social capital there for me; there's opportunity, and I'm fresher than I was before the break. It shouldn't take me long to find my way. I had hoped I wouldn't have to find it alone."

"You're not likely to be alone for long."

"I know. That's exactly what concerns me. I don't think my faith is likely to last long, if I ever come to feel as if I have to choose between faith and—well, not being alone. But as much as you don't share my faith, I feel you could have helped me hold on to it. You could have kept me honest. We might have built a new world together."

"There aren't new worlds to build. There's only this one to do with what we can."

"Don't leave out what's beyond it. We have to meet that sometime."

"Maybe. Whatever that might be."

There is no such thing as wasted time, but you can pass the trail-head at which you could have begun. Such is the place where we have now found ourselves.

We sit together quietly for a while and watch the traffic on the sidewalk opposite, awnings, gleaming storefronts, men in khakis, girls in jeans. Streetcars clang along the line. A bus, too, comes lumbering through the stop, but the backlit placard shows that it isn't on my route.

On the sidewalk opposite us, blocking a shop window, there gathers a cluster of young women in pencil skirts, debating the merits of a white dress on display. Their shrieks of laughter cross the street to reach us.

"I can't," I say again, surprising both of us. "I couldn't."

"It's okay. I know. Can I. Can I just ask you why?"

"I know I'm—not. I wouldn't be. Ready."

"How long? A year, five years? I'd wait."

"It's not how long. It's—if. Ever."

"I think I can understand that." He stops then and, more fully, takes in what I am saying: "No, of course. Of course I understand."

My bus pulls up to the stop. When I stand, Dylan stands too. He embraces me again, quickly this time, then opens his arms to release me. He presses the book that was resting on the bench between us into my hands.

"Keep it," he says. "It's for you. And—don't be a stranger."

His eyes fill now with other, unsaid words, but the bus door is open, and the current of stale air and disembarking passengers flows out. I run the short distance down to the stop, step up and in without turning back. He follows me a few steps down the walk and then pauses, staring not at the bus but instead down along the avenue of live oaks. Over him the sky hangs heavy with heat, blinding with white sun.

The book in my lap is *The Cloud of Unknowing*: paperback, wrapped in the greyscale image of a thunderstorm, with Dylan's number inscribed on the flyleaf. *Dear Angele*, he has written, and a fragment from a poem by Dunstan Thompson:

> As for water, we have our own wells here.
>
> This ordered life is not for everyone.
>
> Never, to their surprise, for those who run
>
> Away from love.

*

That moment, although I didn't know it then, held within it the seed of everything my life has become since. How else would I have come through the waters? How else would I have come to be telling you, Mother, all that I've seen? How else would I have learned to want what I want now? I want peace, I want clarity. I want certainty, I want permanence: to stop shedding, like a snake, superfluous skins that reveal no new growth underneath.

And I want to ask these questions—since a postulant is one who asks: Who am I, when what I am is stripped away like a garment and set aside? Can I be who I am, can I do what I do, without being destroyed by what I am, drowned in the ways I can be put to use?

Not every seed that falls is able to die and produce much fruit. Some are dried in drought, others washed away by floods.

If I allow myself to fall into the earth, will I be allowed to die, to break open, to release life? Can the force of my shattering underground suffice to push that leaf into the air, to lift the thirsty tongue of the cotyledon, to be the strength that anchors the green fuse until life can thrive alone?

Is there any way on earth to be free from all this *I want, I want*? Is there no way into that glory than through this death? And above all: where is the new growth to be planted?

This is the center, the crux; this is where I find myself lost, this is where I need to be found. Look for me here, Mother, if I am anywhere that is not an illusion, if it means anything to say that my self exists. If it is possible to say that I live now, not I, but Christ in me.

*

For I had never known love at all, until that night under the monastery cypresses, when he asked:

"Forgive me, please. I need the freedom that your forgiveness would give me. And I—no, but if I can finish. I know you'll say you do forgive me, and it'll be easy words. They'll fall out of your mouth like a piece of spent gum. You'll throw them at me like you'd throw a piece of gum into the trash can at the entrance to the subway.

"I don't—please don't be angry—I don't mean that as harshly as it sounds. I say it only because I know that's how I forgive. I shrug things off without looking at them. If I looked, I'd be furious. You've looked. You've had to look to survive. You've had to be furious. I want you to know that I know that. It's all the more reason I want this apology not to cost you anything. For once I want it to cost me instead. I want to—I want you to know that I know how bad it was. What I did to you. Not in itself, maybe. But for you. In your eyes. I know how much I'm asking.

"I know I've bound myself to you and you to me. That's what we're doing when we harm someone: and then in trying to get free from them, we tie ourselves all the tighter. I want you to know how much I admire what you've done with your life and how little sense I can make out of what I've done with mine.

"For all the liberty I've had, I've never been free before. Not really free, not free to do the best things I was capable of. It was never that I was forced to do anything. Never that I couldn't have chosen otherwise. I didn't have to do any of this. I found myself left to myself. Capable of making art. Capable of pleasure. But when I started to try to limit myself, try to place others first—I didn't find myself free to do it. I couldn't limit myself in that way because I had already limited myself in another. I had made myself into a person who was unable to do it. No matter how hard I threw myself against that wall, I bounced every time. The wall never came down. I threw myself and I threw myself. Nothing but bruises. And blood.

"I still don't know. Am I supposed to stay here my whole life, throwing myself and throwing myself? Is the wall ever going to come down? Is that what faith is, throwing yourself at a wall for years, decades, a lifetime, believing that it won't be solid forever, that next time it won't throw you back, next time it will crumble? I don't know. I don't know whether I'm supposed to know. It could be that not knowing is a gift. But I'm desperately tired of not knowing. Desperately tired. I want to know something. I almost don't care what the *something* is that I know. I just want to know it and to know that I know it.

"Once I thought it was you that I knew, when we were young. Of course I didn't know you, and what I did know of you I betrayed the moment it was any advantage to me to do so. I knew your work was as good as mine; I knew that all along, but I was afraid of it. Of you. And of myself. I was afraid I'd stop being able to do work as good as yours, that you'd outgrow me, surpass me, and I'd be left behind you. So by making the portrait, I did what I could to stop you from ever getting started. I did it, not exactly knowing that was what I was doing, but knowing I would know if I stopped to let myself think about it. If I'd thought about it, I must have known it would hurt you. On some level maybe I wanted it to hurt you. So I made myself not think about what I was doing. I didn't stop. We don't, mostly. People. Stop. Even here. I was so disappointed about that. It was so bitter. Not as bitter as realizing that I don't know how to stop, either. And now I don't know where I can go to learn.

"That's another thing. I don't know how to be silent and I don't know where I can learn how. I thought I could learn here, and I haven't. Inside there's always noise. And fear. Noise and darkness and fear. In the city I was drowning in my fear of all the things that could happen to stop me—not so much to belongings but to bodies— not only my body but the bodies of my canvases—bombs, germs, falling airplanes, falling buildings. Shatterings. Collapses. I thought the cloister would be a safe harbor from all those familiar terrors. It hasn't been. Not for me.

"Here, especially after what happened, I'm always afraid of—it isn't too much to call it annihilation. I'm afraid that what can happen to me can wipe me out as if I'd never existed. I'm afraid of no longer being what I think I am, of no longer being who I think I am: I don't know how to separate those two things, and you always have known, I think, and that's what I envy you. You seem to know who you are underneath what you are. You always seemed to.

"And I used to think that if I knew—if I knew who I was, it would save me from always being what someone else wanted me to be. Now I know that in the end you are always what someone else wants you to be. No matter how authentically you live, someone else will turn you into their version of you, and that is who you will be for that person. . . .

"The only person I've ever met who saw me completely, completely the way I am, who didn't try to turn me into their own version of me, was you. And in exchange for this, in exchange, I turned you into my own version of you, and I used that version of you to serve my own wishes. And I'm sorry. I'm sorry. It took someone doing it to me for me to know that I had done it to you. After—after the attack, I looked at—at him, and I saw myself. I saw myself."

"Oh no. No no, you aren't—"

"I am. I am. I am."

"No. No. You mustn't think that. Maybe I don't understand. Maybe I can't. But I don't know how you can be so unjust to yourself. Art is proportion. So is justice. Dylan. Don't. But listen. I forgive you. I do. But can you forgive me?"

"What on earth for?"

I reached across the space for his hand, and my palm flicked out pale against the cypresses, looking like the wing of a bird. He allowed it to approach, to remain. Then he took it; he moved right to my side, closer. Eyes closed, he dropped the bridge of his nose against the outside of my shoulder.

The tears that had stayed on his face, that he had not yet wiped away, soaked into the cloth of my coat. I leaned my cheek toward the top of his head until I could see, growing back within the ring of the tonsure, his crown's dark roots.

*

For now my new name is no more than *aspirant*: one who breathes. I inhale, exhale, this need for freedom; it lives under my ribs, between my hips, in every cell. You call me in with a bell and I follow; you send me out with another and I move into the open evening air, sit beside the pond, where now again the oak leaves have bronzed and dessicated, where they scatter across the grass, click, shuffle, come to rest. The sun falls. The pines whisper secrets. At the edges of the clearing, seedlings tremble in the wind.

There I rest, motionless, till the chime rings: exile from paradise, waiting for day.

AUTHOR'S NOTE

The scenarios and characters in this novel are the product of imagination, not of observation. This commonplace truth about fiction demands more urgently to be repeated here because situations of scandal have caused a radical loss of trust. No place, person, or situation I depict here has any conscious or intentional real-life analogue, and none should be presumed or imputed.

All the more because I have had the chance to live among Catholic believers in fidelity and peace, my heart breaks for those who have known betrayal at the hands of those who should have been trustworthy. My hope for this novel is that it may help to lift burdens rather than to impose them: to ease communication of truth, not to block it: to heal rather than to harm. If I fail anywhere in this with you, dear reader, I ask your forgiveness.

The task of art is to represent, at some depth, reality as we find it and as it might be. This includes the front line of the battle between good and evil as Solzhenitsyn writes about it, a line that—too true—runs through every human heart without exception. On this line, at the moment of dramatic choice, the art of fiction must work, if it is to work anywhere. On this line only will we be able, if we really wish it, to find ourselves.

Houston, Texas
January 2, 2021

ACKNOWLEDGMENTS

A novel so long in the making gathers a lot of supporters in its wake. My thanks first of all to Joshua Hren, editor in chief of Wiseblood Books, not only for much-needed time and space but for solidarity, friendship, and camaraderie. Without his patient and generous editorial and spiritual encouragement, and without the Wiseblood writer-in-residence program under his direction, all this work may never have borne fruit; Joshua, I can't say it enough: thank you. To the entire Wiseblood team, and to Belmont Abbey College, which was willing to host me although in the end the vicissitudes of 2020 prevented my visit in person, I am also grateful. To Roberta Ahmanson of Fieldstead and Company, and to Kathleen Madrid, for their generous support of the Wiseblood residency, deeply felt thanks for making resources available to nurture this work and to make a "room of one's own" possible just when it was most needed.

Bernardo Aparicio Garcia, founder and publisher of *Dappled Things* magazine, has stood in my corner from the very beginning and cheered me on even when the path seemed impossible. For this and for every vote of confidence, without which I would not have traveled this far: Berni, dear friend, thank you. Other early readers, too, have made this a much better book than it would have been without their input. Don Clemmer, Matthew Lickona, Andrew McNabb, Eleanor Nicholson, Colin O'Brien, Victoria Seed (proofreader *extraordinaire*), Mary Zito Smith: warmly, thank you. Thanks to Thomas V. Mirus and Anthony Santella, whose descriptions of scene and milieu helped me render a more realistic New York than I'd otherwise have been able to do. Louis Maltese, thank you for the beautiful cover design.

Many years ago Dr. Fred Arroyo read and helped me revise the short story that served as a first character study for Angele and Dylan: Dr. Arroyo, thank you for treating an absurd undergraduate with the seriousness I wanted to deserve, and for teaching that a writing life is a real life. John Chambers, thank you for never failing to ask how the work was going, even when "It isn't" was the honest answer. Alex Gamble, we'll always have Belgium.

A non-exhaustive list of books I've relied on for research, nourishment, and inspiration includes (in no particular order) *The Art of Rivalry* by Sebastian Smee, *Seven Days in the Art World* by Sarah Thornton, *The Painted Word* by Tom Wolfe, *Art: A New History* by Paul Johnson, *Lost Illusions* by Honore de Balzac, *The Good Soldier* by Ford Madox Ford, *The Masterpiece* by Émile Zola, *Roderick Hudson* by Henry James, *What Happened to Sophie Wilder* by Christopher Beha, *Burning Down the House* and *The Art of Subtext* by Charles Baxter, *The Art of Time in Fiction* by Joan Silber, *The Body Keeps the Score* by Bessel van der Kolk, *The Rule of St. Benedict*, and various works by Thomas Merton, including *Mystics and Zen Masters*, *No Man Is an Island*, and *The Seven Storey Mountain*.

A portion of Chapter 7 has appeared, in slightly different form, in *Windhover* 25.2 under the title "Perspective."

My apologies to Tulane University for fictionally endowing it with a multi-story arts building that affords a view of the river. As far as I'm aware, no such building exists in reality on such a beautiful campus.

To my parents, who have supported me to fly as far as I needed to go: thank you for being first to believe.

Joan Carl, thank you for so much, so many times over, but especially at this moment for making it possible for me to participate in the Wiseblood Books residency intensive sessions. Invisible work should be made visible.

Brian Carl: thank you for being there. My home is wherever you are, always.

Made in the USA
Las Vegas, NV
06 December 2024

13499068R00128